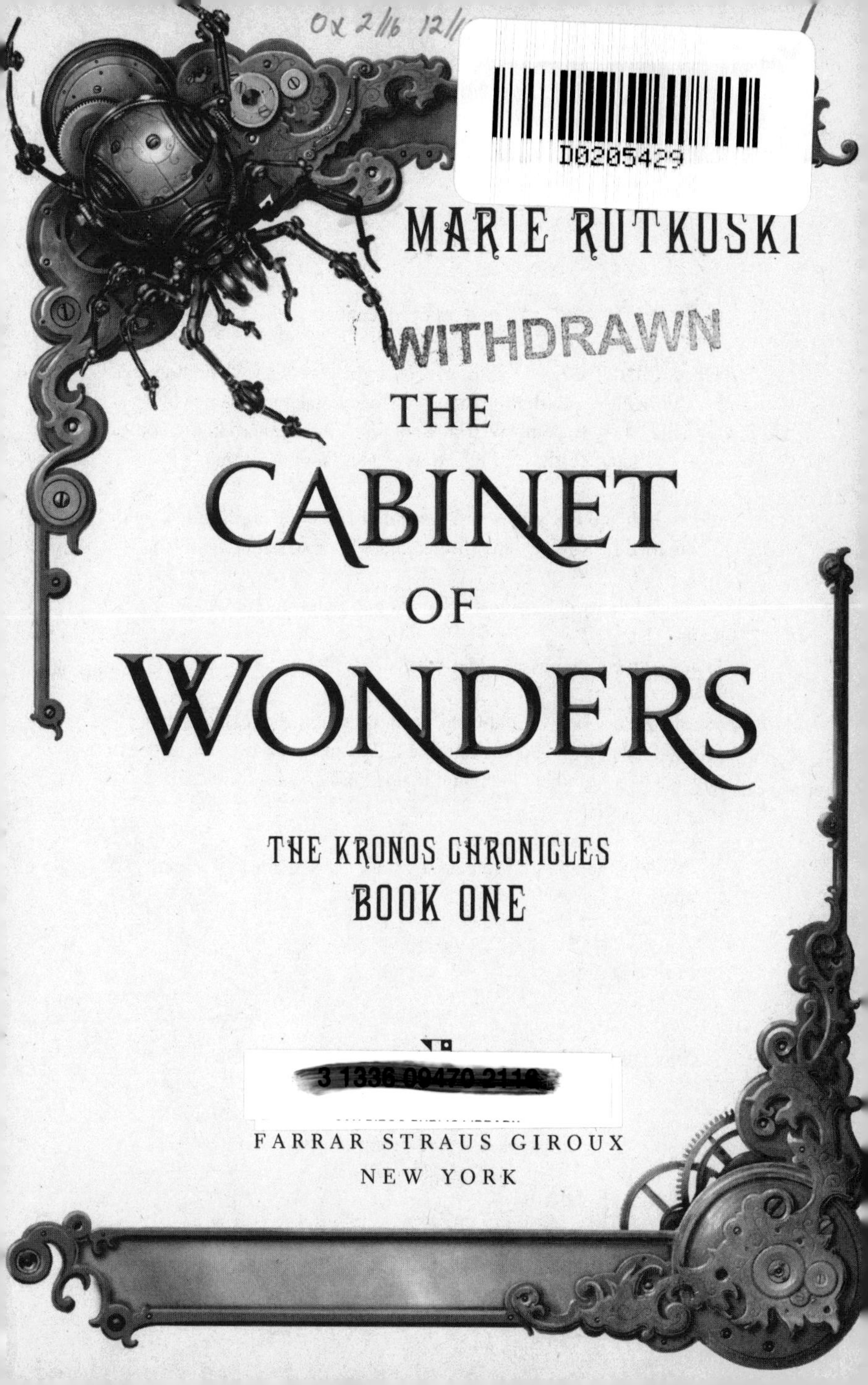

MARIE RUTKOSKI

THE CABINET OF WONDERS

THE KRONOS CHRONICLES
BOOK ONE

FARRAR STRAUS GIROUX
NEW YORK

This book is dedicated to my parents, Robert and Marilyn Rutkoski, and my husband, Thomas Philippon

SQUARE FISH

An Imprint of Macmillan

 Printed in the United States of America by R. R. Donnelley & Sons Company, Harrisonburg, Virginia. For information, address Square Fish, 175 Fifth Avenue, New York, NY 10010.

Library of Congress Cataloging-in-Publication Data

Rutkoski, Marie.

The Cabinet of Wonders / Marie Rutkoski.

p. cm.

Summary: Twelve-year-old Petra, accompanied by her magical tin spider, goes to Prague hoping to retrieve the enchanted eyes the prince of Bohemia took from her father, and is aided in her quest by a Roma boy and his sister.

ISBN 978-1-250-01804-5

[1. Magic—Fiction. 2. Princes—Fiction. 3. Romanies—Fiction. 4. Fantasy.] I. Title.

PZ7.R935Cab 2008

[Fic]—dc22

2007037702

Originally published in the United States by Farrar Straus Giroux

This Square Fish Edition: January 2013

Square Fish logo designed by Filomena Tuosto

Book designed by Jay Colvin

mackids.com

2 4 6 8 10 9 7 5 3

AR: 4.9 / F&P: X / LEXILE: 720L

Contents

Prologue

THE YELLOW HILLS rose and fell in sunny tops and valleys. The Bohemian countryside on this August morning looked almost like a golden ocean with huge, swelling waves.

A rickety cart was wending its way through a valley. Two men were perched atop the riding seat, watching the sturdy horse as it pulled them along. There was a bundle wrapped in cloth that took up most of the space in the open cart bed behind the men.

One of them, Jarek, held the reins. He coughed. "I should be paid extra for this," he said. "What a stench."

"What do you mean?" said Martin, Jarek's companion. He turned around to look at the bundle.

Jarek saw him do it. "No, not that. Those blasted brassica flowers. They stink fouler than a five-hundred-year-old outhouse."

"Oh, that," Martin replied. "They smell sweet to me."

The yellowness of the hills was caused by thousands of flowers, clustered and thick.

Jarek gagged. "I wouldn't like to be one of you hill people, working the flower fields. My clothes are going to smell rotten by the time we get back to Prague."

Too lazy to get offended, Martin leaned back in the cracked

leather seat. "Many folks enjoy the smell of brassica. It's just one of those things you love or hate. Like eating asparagus."

"Raised with the stink as you were, I'm sure you're used to it."

"And remember"—Martin wagged a finger at him, pretending he had not heard Jarek's last comment—"Bohemia needs those flowers. Bet it'll be a good harvest this year. Soon the farmers will be out in the fields to collect the seeds and press them into oil. You can grumble like a goat about the scent, but that brassica's used for all sorts of things."

The horse took a turn in the dirt road and one of the cart wheels dipped into a large hole, jolting the cart.

The bundle in the back groaned.

"Here now!" Martin craned his neck to scowl at the dark shape. "None of that! You'll give us a bit of quiet." He made an impatient sound at the back of his throat. He took off his hat and fanned the sweat on his face. "It's very hot," he said, and sighed.

"Yeah," Jarek drawled, staring ahead.

"Good money, though, this trip."

"Hmm." Jarek flapped the reins. "We're almost there, anyway. Should take us about half an hour."

"What, have you been here before? I thought you never left Prague. How do you know this area?"

"I don't." Jarek shifted in the seat. "But the horse does."

Martin gave him an odd look. "And she told you how long we've got left, did she?"

Jarek laughed, possibly for the first time during the whole trip. "Nah, course not! I was only joking."

But it seemed like a strange sort of joke.

"Do you know what he did?" Jarek said, jerking his chin toward the bundle, whose breathing had gotten louder and ragged.

Martin was still looking at Jarek suspiciously. "No. Didn't ask, and that's the honest truth."

Jarek nodded. "It's best that way."

"The order," Martin said, "came from the prince himself."

This was news to Jarek. Learning this detail made him realize that he had been in a dark mood for the past several hours. Realizing this was like suddenly getting a cramp after sitting too long in one position. And, as a matter of fact, Jarek then thought, he *did* have a cramp in his lower back.

"You didn't tell me the orders came directly from the prince," he said.

"You didn't ask."

Which was true. Jarek did not ask any questions when Martin, who also took care of the prince's horses, proposed they make a delivery to the village of Okno (with some of the profit going to Jarek, of course). And Jarek did not ask any questions when two castle menservants met him and Martin in the stables, carrying a man who seemed barely conscious, and whose face was wrapped in a bloody bandage.

"Ah, there we are," Martin said, pointing his hand at a nest of buildings. The houses and shops began to distinguish themselves, and the dirt path became the main cobblestone road that ran straight through Okno.

The village looked prosperous. There were several stone houses. The wooden ones were in solid condition, often with pretty patterns of different-colored strips of wood decorating the window frames, many of which had real glass set into them. Shop signs advertised goods: leather tack for horses, books, carpentry, glassworks, and cloth. Women walked by in full, unstained skirts. Even a passing stray dog seemed rather fat for an independent creature. The road turned into a small square whose center was marked by a fountain that was well designed, its water bubbling over three tiers of stone.

Martin dug a parchment out of his jerkin pocket and consulted it. "Turn left here."

"It doesn't make any sense," Jarek mused.

"*I* am the one with the map, and *you* should turn left."

"No, I mean *this*"—he tilted his head toward the back of the cart—"doesn't make any sense. What could he have done to deserve that kind of punishment, and get sent home instead of being clapped into the nearest jail cell?"

"Dunno." Martin waved his hand airily, chasing away a fly. "Maybe he killed someone."

"Then he would be in prison or executed or both."

"Maybe he killed the prince's favorite dog."

"Then he would be in prison or executed or both."

Martin laughed.

"All I'm saying is this," Jarek continued, "if you want to get rid of a weed, you don't just clip some of its stems and call it a day." The road they turned down had fewer houses. Ribbons of wind passed between the buildings and through the men's sweaty hair. "The weed'll grow back. There's always the chance for revenge."

"*Him?*" Martin laughed again. "Oh, I'm glad I picked you to drive. You're a funny sort, you are. Weed or no, this fellow's in no shape for action. Hold on now—" Martin looked at the map again and glanced at a tall, skinny stone house set far apart from the others. As they drew closer, they saw that the ground floor was a shop, its windows crowded with bizarre metal objects, clocks, and tin toys bouncing like grasshoppers. Jarek could not read the words painted over the door, but a sign hanging from the corner of the house showed a many-pointed compass. "Stop here," Martin said. "This is it."

Jarek pulled on the reins. His hands settled in his lap, but they still gripped the leather straps. "He may have sons. Angry ones."

Martin thumped Jarek on the shoulder. "No fear, my friend," he said, and pointed toward the door, which had opened. In the doorway stood a girl, tall for her age, which was twelve. Underneath a long tangle of brown hair her face was wary. She was dressed in a nightgown, but stood defiantly, as if to say that she knew that wasn't normal but didn't care. She stared straight at them. Her eyes were narrowed—but perhaps, Jarek thought, this was because of the sun and not because she already hated them.

Martin leaned to whisper in Jarek's ear. "As I said, don't worry. He's only got her."

It seemed to Jarek that his backache had gotten worse.

The mare sighed. Then she spoke silently in his mind the way she did with no other human, for she knew none who had Jarek's gift to understand her. *If you were a horse*, she told him, *you would be used to bearing such unpleasant burdens.*

1

The Sign of the Compass

EARLIER THAT MORNING, Petra Kronos had woken up to the *tick tick tick* of metal. It was not, as you might imagine, a clock. It did not have chiming bells, and it did not have two hands. Yet it did have eight legs and something like a face, a very tiny one punctuated by two eyes, specks of twinkling green. Astrophil, Petra's tin spider, scampered around the nightstand next to her bed, calling, "Wake up! Wake up, you sloth! Cave bat! Ground squirrel!" His shiny body vibrated as he shouted.

Petra rubbed at the grit in the corner of her eye. "Just because you must have stayed up last night reading a book on all the animals that hibernate doesn't mean you have to show it off."

Astrophil folded his front two legs in a good impersonation of a human schoolteacher. "In fact, sloths do not hibernate. They are simply very, very lazy."

"Hmm." Though the morning sun was already making the room warm, Petra snuggled under the thin linen sheet. "I bet they're stupid, too."

"Oh, yes."

"The sort of animals who just can't take a hint," Petra said. She yawned and closed her eyes.

"Well . . ." Astrophil relaxed his legs out of their stiff pose.

"There is *one* rare sloth, the Spotted Angola Sloth, which is known to be quick-witted."

Petra lay still.

"And generous of spirit."

No response came from the bed.

"And easily moved by the persistent pleas of friends," Astrophil added.

Petra rolled over, her back to Astrophil.

"The Spotted Angola Sloth is also prudent, especially when threatened by the prospect of waking up one morning to find sticky, metallic spiderwebs crisscrossing her entire face."

"A dreadful fate," Petra declared. She flung back the sheet and slipped out of bed. The sound of clucking hens floated in through the one tall window. A rooster must have crowed sometime earlier that morning, but it had not broken Petra's steady sleep. She pushed back the tousled hair that she stubbornly refused, against the repeated wishes of her grownup cousin Dita, to braid into something resembling neatness. Petra's eyes were gray—or, to be more precise, they were silvery, like they each had been made with liquid metal anchored in a bright circle by a black center. They looked just like her father's eyes. In general, she resembled him greatly. This usually pleased her.

She turned to a shelf that ran along the white wall between one corner of the room and a rectangular bulge, which was the chimney that began in the kitchen fireplace just below. The rough wooden shelf was littered with bottles, sheets of heavy paper, a few broken goose quills, and a small box the shape and glossy brown color of a horse chestnut. It was wooden and had a hinged lid. Petra took the box and plucked down a bottle.

Astrophil shot a sparkling thread across the room so that it hit the wall next to the shelf. With one swing, he launched himself several feet to perch on the shelf's edge.

Petra uncorked the bottle and opened the chestnut-shaped box to reveal a miniature spoon, into which she poured thick green brassica oil. Astrophil sucked from the spoon with a delighted noise. After he had drained the oil, his eyes deepened in color and glowed.

"Well," Petra said, corking the bottle. "If you're hungry, the others must be, too."

Astrophil quickly crept up her arm and dug his legs into her shoulder, piercing through her thin summer nightgown.

"Ow!"

If she expected Astrophil to apologize, he didn't.

"By the way," he said, "I was not reading a book last night."

"Oh?" Petra shut the bedroom door behind her. She jogged down the stairs with unnecessary force. The spider bounced up and down. They reached the second floor. A whirring, clanking sound began to come from downstairs. "Then why do you suddenly know so much about zoology?"

"I was reading ephemera," he said, referring to the thin booklets stacked in her father's library. "You know I can only turn pages, not those heavy leather book bindings. If books are not already open, I cannot open them myself."

Petra raced across the landing and began to hop down the next flight of steps. Astrophil gripped her more tightly. The whirring sound was getting louder.

Astrophil said, "If someone does not remember to leave out the beautiful, big books for a poor insomniac spider, what is a poor insomniac spider to do but consult the badly written ephemera?"

"Why were you reading about sloths and squirrels anyway?"

Astrophil paused. "I wanted to learn about creatures like me. But there was nothing in the ephemera about spiders."

Petra stopped. She began to walk down the steps at a normal pace. "I'm sorry, Astro," she said. And she really was, for there was no book that could tell him about creatures like himself, even if she took down the zoological guide to arachnids her father had consulted when he made Astrophil. "I'll remember to leave a book out before I go to bed."

She reached the ground floor and opened the door to her father's workshop, which was also the family store. It was here that one could buy metallic objects and machines crafted by Mikal Kronos.

"It is just that I am a very fast reader," Astrophil said.

"Yes, you are," Petra responded with pride.

The workshop looked like you would never find what you were looking for, and sounded like you would never be able to match up a noise with the thing that made it. But it was—or so her father always claimed—arranged in a very logical order. Then again, it was a logic that only he could understand. But in his absence Petra learned to find what she needed (usually), even if it took her twice or three times as long as it would have taken him.

Squeaks came from a very large cage under a table in the corner of the room. The tin pets were hungry and eager to be let out. "What took you so long?" some of them cried. Like Astrophil, all the creatures possessed tiny metal vocal cords. Metal naturally amplifies nearby sounds. Petra's father had designed the animals so that their metal bodies magnified the volume of their voices. Astrophil was a quiet spider, as spiders usually are. He liked to share his opinions on many things, but he liked best to share them secretly with Petra, hidden in her hair and whispering in her ear so that no one else would understand why she giggled. But the tin pets could be loud if they wished. A screeching tin monkey was proving this very point.

Some of the pets ran in circles on the floor of the cage or climbed up the bars. When Petra opened the cage, five fist-sized scarab beetles, three puppies with tin scales instead of fur, a finch, a raven, two lizards that would have to be purchased together or not at all, several mice, and the big-eyed monkey burst across the room like a comet. When they saw her reach for a jug of brassica oil and a large saucer on the table, they rushed back to cluster around her ankles.

"Such behavior!" Astrophil sniffed, as if he had taken a leisurely stroll to have his breakfast.

The pets dipped their beaks in, lapped up, or sucked down the oil. Petra nudged the monkey aside to make room at the saucer's edge for a beetle, which was ramming into the monkey's bottom. When they had drunk their fill of breakfast, they moved about the room more calmly, except for the three puppies, who started to wrestle among themselves. They were the very youngest of the tin pets. They had been completed only six months ago, just before her father left for Prague. They were his latest experiment. Unlike the other pets, the puppies were designed to grow.

It was very boring for the animals to be locked up in a cage at night. They were filled with energy. Years ago, when her father had begun crafting the tin pets, he let them have the run of the house at all hours of the day and night. And what happened? A total disaster. Jars of pickled vegetables were smashed on the kitchen floor, vinegar spilling everywhere. A squirrel got into the linen cabinet and tore several sheets into rags for a nest. A bird cracked a precious mirror by tapping its beak repeatedly at its own reflection. If Dita and her family had lived with them at the time, you can be sure she would have quickly put an end to the pets' freedom. But there was only seven-year-old Petra, who howled with laughter at the toys. Her father barely noticed anything. It wasn't until one poor rabbit went missing, and they discovered her trapped and starving inside the gears of one of the models for farm machinery, that her father decided to keep the pets locked in a cage at night. They could play only in the shop, and only during the day when someone could keep an eye on them.

Astrophil was the exception to the rule. But then, he was the exception to almost every rule. He was well behaved from birth. He took his good manners as a point of pride. He learned Czech quickly, speaking in whole sentences when he was just days old. He was the only pet her father made who learned how to read. Astrophil actively sought out books on everything from poetry to how to make Turkish delight. Petra often teased him that he was filled with useless information. But while he learned many things Petra never would, he never managed to learn how to sleep. Most pets, when they were about two years old, would begin to doze for a few minutes at a time. A year later, they might be able to sleep through the night. But Astrophil, who was six years old, showed no sign of doing more than blinking once in a while.

Petra tidied the shop to make it presentable for business, dusting her father's handiwork: horse bits and plows, intricately engraved silverware, a collection of music boxes, compasses, astrolabes, and clocks that began chiming ten o'clock. It was already late to open the shop. Dita's husband, Josef, would have left hours ago to work in the brassica fields. Soon Petra would unlock the front door facing the street. She hoped that she might sell a few things. Above all, she hoped her friend Tomik would stop by.

Although it was incredible that she would have heard a shuffling of feet over the noise in the workshop, Petra did. She turned around to see David, Dita's son. He was a few years younger than Petra. "Stella!" he called.

The tin raven flew across the room in a shiny blur and settled on the boy's shoulder, gently poking her beak into his curly hair.

"Upstart crow," Astrophil muttered.

"I am a raven!" Stella cawed back, insulted.

It was clear that the raven had no intention of being sold to an Okno villager or a traveling merchant charmed by her glossy feathers. The raven liked her life at the Sign of the Compass just fine, and had grown fond of David, who was stroking her head.

"Mother wanted me to see if you had *finally* woken up," the boy mimicked Dita's exasperated voice. "She wanted to know if you were taking care of your *one* duty in this house."

"Well, I obviously am."

"Well, you obviously can't greet customers in your nightgown."

Petra started to say something rude, but David began singing loudly, looking everywhere around the shop except at her. "*Oh, she's a lovely lass in her nightdress! But her hair's a mess, I must confess!*"

The raven cawed.

"*Oh, she's a—*"

"David, be quiet!"

"*—lovely lass—*"

"Stop!"

He did, for he realized that she was no longer looking at him, but out the window. She had a worried expression on her face. "What is it?" he asked. He saw a cart driven by two men in tattered clothes.

"I'm not sure." As she pushed the door open, Astrophil climbed into her hair and clenched his legs around a snarled lock of it, looking like a flower-shaped hairpin with eight petals. The animals eagerly rushed for the open door, but David darted across the room to stop them. He hustled them back into the cage.

The two men stepped down from the cart, one of them laughing. The other man glanced at Petra, looked up at the sky, and stretched in the sunlight. They turned away from her and walked toward the back of the cart, heaving at some load in the flatbed.

At first Petra could not believe that the long, angular form the two men carried was her father. But then his head flopped back in the fat man's arms and she saw his long gray-black hair, his wide mouth, and the rust-colored bandage crossing his face.

She looked over her shoulder at David, who was waiting in the shop, gazing out the door, his eyes wide in horror.

"Dita," Petra whispered. She had lost her voice.

But David easily found his. "Mother!" He spun around and ran into the dark depths of the house. "*Mother!*"

2

The Making of the Clock

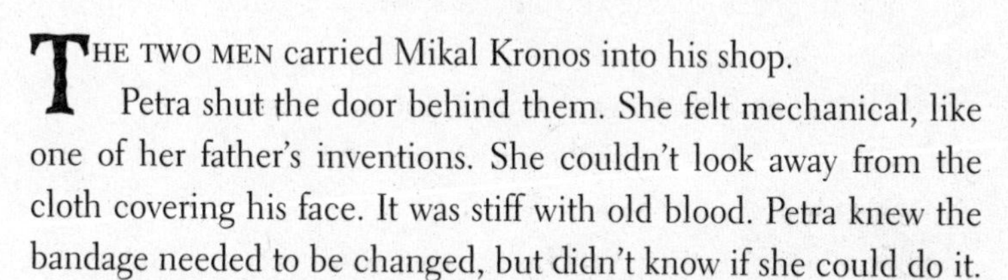

THE TWO MEN carried Mikal Kronos into his shop.

Petra shut the door behind them. She felt mechanical, like one of her father's inventions. She couldn't look away from the cloth covering his face. It was stiff with old blood. Petra knew the bandage needed to be changed, but didn't know if she could do it.

A thousand questions tried to claw their way out of Petra's mouth, but only one escaped: "What happened?" Petra was astonished to hear her own voice. It was small and frightened.

"Your da had an accident," the heavyset man replied.

Dita briskly entered from the hallway. Her back was straight, her hair wrapped in a dark blue scarf, and she was wiping her hands on her starched apron. David followed her, carrying Stella on his shoulder. Dita caught the tall man staring with curiosity at the bird. He glanced away, embarrassed.

"'Lo, missus," his companion said. "My name's Martin. Sorry to be the bearer of bad tidings. Your husband's had a hard journey. Would you show us where we could set him down for a bit of rest?"

"He is my uncle." Dita frowned. "Come this way. His bedroom is here," she said, and showed them to a small room on the ground floor with a square window and a narrow bed.

After the two men had laid their burden onto the bed, Dita took her uncle's hand and bit her lip as she looked at his bandages. "David, get some water."

David ran out of the room. But Stella launched herself from the departing boy's shoulder and flew back, settling on a bedpost. The raven craned her neck to watch as Dita gently peeled away the gauze covering her uncle's face. "How did this happen?" Dita demanded.

The two strangers exchanged a look.

Petra hung back. Her hand was braced on the door frame. Dita's back blocked Petra's view of her father. Petra waited for someone to speak. When no one did, she answered her cousin's question. "They said it was an accident."

"Really." Dita's voice was flat. She pinned the men with a fierce glare. "An accident? You will have an accident, too, if you don't get out of this house right now."

Martin smiled and spread his hands. "Now, you can't blame us for—"

The bird shrieked and sprang from the bedpost, diving at the men with sharp claws and a sharper beak. Startled, they ran from the house, tripping, cursing, and covering their faces with their hands as Stella darted at them like a flying dagger.

When Dita spoke to Petra her voice was both rough and kind. "I want you to leave the room as well."

Petra hesitated. Then she slipped into the hallway. She ran upstairs to her room. Through the window, she could still hear the bird's furious screaming.

After that, no one questioned that Stella belonged to the family.

DITA HAD MOVED into the house with her husband and son years ago, after a long drought that had made the brassica fields dry, crisp, and useless. There was no harvest that year, and the one the year before that had been poor. Farmers across Bohemia grew desperate. The prince's court in Prague felt the pinch of higher prices for reserves of oil used for cooking, lighting lamps in fashionable homes, and making weapons, which relied on the intense heat of fires made with brassica oil. The young prince's response was to raise taxes.

Outraged, the countryside began to plot against the prince. But then key members of the rebellion mysteriously disappeared from their homes. The plot came to nothing. Some men lost their lives that year. Others, like Josef, lost their livelihood.

Josef and Dita came to the house at the Sign of the Compass with not much more than their son, David. Their farm, their home, and almost everything in it had been sold. Though Petra knew why they had come to live with them, she also knew that her father hoped Dita would become a second mother to Petra. Petra resented this. First of all, she had never even known what it was like to have a mother, since hers had died while giving birth to her. Petra felt that there was no need to replace what she didn't feel was missing.

And she loved living alone with her father. He taught her lots more than she had ever learned from the wig-wearing village schoolmaster. He sometimes followed her advice, like when he began working on metal tools that were invisible. Petra always enjoyed watching him work. He didn't use his hands to build anything, but stared at objects with concentration, making gears and drills and nails dance across the room in a shining pattern. He explained to Petra that using his hands was slow and cumbersome. His fingers would block his view of the very thing he was working on. When he said this, Petra suggested that other people would like to see the holes they were drilling. Might not invisible tools be useful? Petra's idea was good in theory but not in practice. Try hitting a nail with an invisible hammer and you will understand why. But at least her father took the idea seriously and produced a few tools that he stored somewhere in the shop. Petra could never find them, though. This wasn't very surprising, since the tools were (after all) invisible.

The very best part of living alone with her father was that Petra was free. She was free to wear what she wanted, sleep when she wanted, eat what she wanted, and say what she wanted. It might have crossed her father's mind that he had no idea how to raise a young girl, but if it did he was quickly distracted by a few days locked in his workshop with a loaf of stale bread and the beginnings of a fresh idea. He was happy and Petra was happy. But when Dita's family lost their farm and he invited his niece to come live with them, he began looking at his daughter in a thoughtful way. He had had the same expression on his face when the tin rabbit was lost, when it suddenly occurred to him that he was responsible for something he couldn't take care of all the time.

And so began a struggle between Petra and her cousin. Petra waged a war of resistance. Dita fought back with persistence. Still, over the years, Petra had come to value many things about her cousin. One of them was the woman's honesty. Dita did what she said she would. And she always said what she thought. Dita was not one to mince words or use them lightly.

So when Dita knocked on Petra's door an hour after the strangers had left, and entered without waiting to be invited, Petra held her tongue, though at any other time she would have shouted about her right to privacy. Nervous dread sang in her stomach.

Dita sat in a chair near Petra's bed and sighed. "The prince stole your father's eyes. He had them removed and preserved."

When Petra first saw the bandaged face, she knew that the gauze hid something terrible. But—her father, blind? He would never be able to work again. "That's impossible. Why would the prince do that? Father is making a magnificent clock for him. Father can't finish it if he can't see."

"He has already finished it, well ahead of schedule. He wanted to return home as soon as possible. He says that on the evening when he put the last gear in place, he was surprised by several soldiers and a surgeon, who was a magician of some sort. Then the prince arrived and thanked him for creating such a beautiful masterpiece. The prince said that no man could, or ever would, build anything like it again. And then"—Dita's mouth twisted—"he ordered the surgeon to take your father's eyes."

"But why? Why would the prince want them?"

"I don't know. Petra, you can speak with your father about what has happened." Petra leaped from the bed. Her cousin held up a hand. "But only for a little while. He is very tired and his wounds are sore. He needs to sleep."

After Dita left the room, Petra changed out of her nightgown. Wearing it all this awful morning had made everything seem surreal, as if she were still asleep and dreaming. She wanted to wake up.

Astrophil unclenched himself from her hair and trickled down her arm. She tugged on a pair of trousers and slipped into a work shirt. She pulled her hair back and jerked a tie around it. Astrophil took his place on Petra's shoulder, and she walked down the stairs for the second time that morning.

When Petra faced the door to her father's bedroom, she reached for the doorknob and just held it for a moment. She wanted to turn it. She did not want to turn it. Finally, Astrophil walked down her arm and tapped on the door with several legs.

"Come in!" The voice was faint, but surprisingly cheerful. He sounded almost the same way he had six months earlier, when Petra had rapped on this very door to tell him that a castle carriage had arrived to take him to Prague.

Petra pushed the door open. "Hello."

The light in the room was weak. Clean, white cloth covered her father's eyes. "Petra, come here."

She dragged a stool across the room and sat next to the bed. "Why did the prince do this to you?"

"Because he liked me."

"Don't joke about this."

"I was being serious. Well, mostly serious." He patted her hand. "If it's any consolation, the prince said I would be paid for my work. Eventually."

"As if I care about that!"

"Well, we all must care about something. Astrophil?" He spoke to the spider out loud, but this was for Petra's sake. With his affinity for metal and the ability to influence it with his mind, Master Kronos could have communicated with the tin spider silently, using only his thoughts.

"Yes, sir?"

"Have you been watching over my girl?"

"Of course, Master Kronos."

"And who watched over you, Father?" Petra said, frustrated. "Why won't you tell me what happened? Dita already told me part of it. I need to know the whole story."

"The whole story? Petra, even *I* don't know the whole story. What can I say? The prince always treated me very well. He is a bright young man. Very knowledgeable for someone in his teenage years. Very curious. He often invited me to dine with him in his private chambers. We got along splendidly. He showed me maps of the world, which change from day to day as explorers discover new countries. The prince employs several mapmakers, and they work terrible hours. As soon as one map is made, another river or waterfall or island or new world has to be added. The prince has his own personal map that's really ingenious. It took me several days to figure out how his chief cartographer, who is a skilled magician, made it. The prince keeps it in a locket, and it is the size of the head of a nail. When he tips the map into his hand—only into *his* hand, mind you—it grows until it spills across the floor. You can walk across the continents, and the oceans actually turn into small pools about two feet deep. It's a delightful invention."

"What is his library like?" Astrophil asked eagerly.

"Beyond words. And the prince gave me complete access to anything I wished to read. The library's silver ceiling is designed to look like the surface of the moon, which the prince showed me through a long tube with curved lenses on each end. You might not know this, but the moon is not as smooth as it looks. It is pocked with holes, and so is the library ceiling. Red-feathered birds live inside of the ceiling's holes and help preserve the books by eating bugs that get into the library and nibble away at the pages. Well, Astrophil, you might not like that part."

Astrophil bristled. "I am not a bookworm! I do not eat books! I am not a libriovore!"

Her father frowned. "Is that a word?"

"Does it matter?" Petra demanded impatiently. "Father, why do you make it sound as if you and the prince were *friends*? He *blinded* you!"

Mikal Kronos was silent. "Yes, Petra," he said slowly, "I am aware of that."

His voice was gentle, but Petra looked down, embarrassed by her outburst.

"Being at court was a very . . . exciting time for me," her father continued. "It was easy to like the prince. I was flattered by his enthusiasm for my work. He was so generous. If I had an idea, he praised it. If I needed assistance, he provided it. He introduced me to many of Europe's finest artists. They helped me construct some of the clock's most impressive parts—its sculptures, its gold-plated designs, and a decorative circle as large as a pond, painted with a brassica field that glows with sunlight during the day and blows in dark waves during the night. The stars on the clock twinkle, and they change position according to the season." Her father then fell silent. Petra waited.

"The clock is the most beautiful thing I have created. The prince insisted that it had to be more than just functional. It must also stun people with its sheer beauty. And it will, once it is unveiled to the public. I know it will, since it is one of the last things I ever saw. It is burned into my memory."

"But . . ." Petra hesitated. "I don't understand. If the prince was so pleased with the clock, why did he do this to you?"

"The prince said that it was an honor to give up my eyes. That I would betray my genius if I were ever to build a lesser object. I'm not quite sure *genius* was the best word for him to use, but then, it seems that the prince holds several points of view that are . . . questionable. When the soldiers tied me to a chair, the prince promised I would be well paid for the work I had done, according to our original agreement. Then he said that he envied the way I saw the world, that I must see it in a very special way to construct such a marvelous thing. I think . . ." His voice trailed off. He began again. "I think that he took my eyes for two reasons. First, he does not want anyone—he does not want *me*—to build another such clock or anything to rival it. Second, he intends to use my eyes. To wear them, you might say."

"*Wear* them? Is that possible?"

Her father shrugged. "Anything is possible. It just takes the right spell or the right piece of knowledge or the right flash of inspiration to make something work. If I learned anything from living six months at court, it is that our world is getting bigger and bigger, and that Bohemia is just a speck of yellow paint on the map. I know a spell was cast on my eyes that would allow the prince to wear them. I had never heard of such a thing before. But the prince's explorers are pushing into new corners of the world, into the Orient, the jungle, and mountains of ice where people ride wolves and eat only air. No doubt there are many spells and forms of magic we wouldn't recognize. No doubt the prince has gathered as much information as he can about these new kinds of magic."

"If the prince can wear your eyes, can he make things move without touching them? Can he build what you can build?"

When her father responded, his words were sharp. His voice held something that Petra recognized, but couldn't quite identify, for she had never heard him use it before. "He stole my eyes, Petra, not my mind."

Neither of them spoke for a moment, and the silence was awkward. Her father then said, more quietly, "Would you mind if I slept awhile?" He stroked her hand. "It's good to be home."

She kissed his forehead. "I'll come to see you later."

As she opened the door to leave, Petra suddenly realized what she had heard in his voice. She had often heard it in Josef's. It was bitterness.

3

Lightning and Wasp

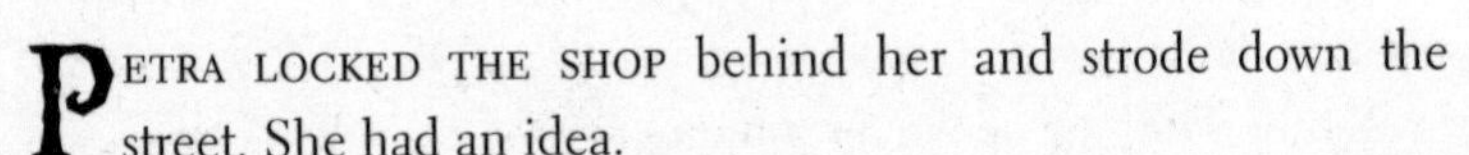

PETRA LOCKED THE SHOP behind her and strode down the street. She had an idea.

When she neared the center of Okno, the soft clapping of her footsteps echoed against stone walls. The street stretched before her in a straight, clean line. She passed the bakery, which was entering into its third round that day of preparing fresh bread. Petra glanced into an open window and saw strong arms thudding dough against a wooden table.

That everything was so normal seemed strange to Petra.

She reached the main road, where most of the artisan shops were arranged in a neat row. Wooden signs hung above the doors, each showing a different painting so that people who could not read would recognize the shop they wanted.

Mistress Jugo gave her a sour look and stepped back inside her toy shop, which was marked by a wooden board showing a spinning top. Although Petra's father had done his best to explain that his tin pets were made in limited numbers, and were just a sideline project in his metalworking trade, Mistress Jugo hadn't spoken to the family in years. She took Master Kronos's invention to be the beginning of a slowly unfolding plot to take over the town's entire toy production. Not to mention that Master Kronos's pets were a shocking display of his magical ability, which any self-respecting person (in Mistress Jugo's opinion) would decently keep to himself.

Petra marched steadily to the Sign of Fire, a shop that sold glassware. This store had large, glittering windows made from glass cut into many diamond-shaped panes and fitted together with crisscrossing lines of lead. A few colored bits of glass winked at Petra. A window over the door glowed with the name STAKAN in red letters. This was where her friend Tomik lived with his family.

Petra stepped into the shop, which was empty aside from a tin cat curled up near the doorway. He lazily opened one green eye and then closed it.

"Jaspar, I need to see Tomik. And Master Stakan. It's important."

The cat kept his eyes shut and purred. Or snored. It was hard to tell the difference.

Outraged, Astrophil raced down Petra's arm, but she cupped her hand over him and ignored the sharp jabs his legs made against her palm. The spider disapproved of Jaspar in general, and disliked the cat's bad manners in particular. "You'll only make things worse," Petra hissed.

"Who will make things worse?" Jaspar opened one eye again.

"Astrophil."

"Who?"

"Astrophil."

"Who?"

"Me!" The spider squeaked inside Petra's hand.

"Oh." The cat snuggled his head under a paw. "He's not important."

"But what I have to tell Tomik and his father *is*." She tried calling for them. "Tomik! Master Stakan!" The house echoed emptily.

"They're not here," Jaspar said. "But why don't you keep shouting, if you like the exercise?"

"Why don't you try to be worth the oil you drink!" Astrophil cried.

Jaspar yawned and his teeth glinted like jewels. "Speaking of oil . . . you wouldn't happen to have any, would you? I know where you can find Tomas and Tomik, but, sadly, my throat's a little too parched to tell you."

Petra sighed. "All right. Tell me where they keep the brassica."

The cat's silver needle whiskers were alert. "Try the wooden jug on the top shelf over there."

She fetched the jug and poured oil into Jaspar's dish. "Now will you help?"

Jaspar lapped up the oil and gave a metallic meow: "More."

"Where *are* they?"

Tomik and his father walked through the door.

"They're in the shop," Jaspar said.

"Thanks a lot." She put the jug back on its shelf.

"Aren't you an ungrateful girl." Jaspar curled up and went back to sleep.

Tomik was a year older than Petra. His sandy hair hung in his eyes. He pushed it back from his sweaty forehead. He looked at her uncertainly. Even before Master Stakan spoke, she knew that they knew.

"Is it true, Petra?" Tomas Stakan asked. "David's been to town and he's telling a strange story about your father. Is it true?" Master Stakan was as serious as stone as he listened to Petra explain what had happened.

"It's too much!" His fist slammed against the worktable. Bottles tinkled and one jumped over the edge of the table, smashing on the floor below. "Too much! One day the prince will regret the way he has treated his people! Even when he was a little boy he would send people to the gallows as easily as he would wipe his nose! One day he will—"

His thundering stopped almost as soon as it had begun. He glanced behind him nervously, as if someone might be watching him or hearing his rebellious words. He exhaled one long breath, and seemed to regain his calm.

"Maybe there's a way you can help my father," Petra said, and described the idea she had in mind. As she spoke, Master Stakan nodded occasionally.

When she finished, Tomik began to say, "I think that—"

His father held up a flat hand.

"I'll start working on it," Master Stakan said. "But it will take some time, and probably a lot of trial and error. What you're asking for isn't simple."

But it was possible. Petra felt hopeful, so she didn't really mind when Master Stakan shooed them away as if they were little children tugging at his work apron. "Now you two go find something to do with yourselves." He flapped his hands at them. "I have enough to do without worrying about you breaking something in the shop with your games."

"If you didn't notice, *we* didn't break anything!" Tomik protested.

Before Master Stakan could respond, Petra tugged Tomik up the stairs. He followed her, grumpily stamping on the worn steps. "Apprentice? Me, his apprentice? Bellows-blower, is more like it. Pot-scrubber. Window-washer. Floor-sweeper. What does he need me as his apprentice *for* if he won't let me do *any*thing!"

They entered his room in the attic. Tomik slammed the door shut behind them. The ceiling was low and the day was hot, so they sat with crossed legs on the floor.

"He's never even thought about the things I can do." In a low, eager voice he added, "Do you want to see my latest invention?"

"Of course," Petra said. Curious, Astrophil stood on his tiptoes.

Tomik leaned back on his elbow and dragged a beat-up box out from under his bed. He opened it, revealing dice made from pig knucklebones, a set of stubby charcoal pencils, and countless marbles. But as Petra looked more closely, she saw that two marbles were different from the rest. They were slightly larger, and something flickered inside each one. Tomik plucked the two glass balls from the box and held them out to Petra. She took one and discovered it was light and hollow. A star of bright light pulsed inside. "What is it?"

"A bit of lightning. It wasn't easy to get inside the glass, but easier than you might think."

"What do you mean?" Petra asked.

"It's pretty simple to manipulate lightning with magic. You see," he explained confidently, "lightning and magic are kind of similar. Like cousins."

Petra studied him. "How do you know this? It sounds as if . . . as if you've been taking lessons."

"Hardly," he scoffed. "Who'd teach me? No, that stuff about the lightning was something your father said."

"My father? To you?"

"Something I heard him say. *Overheard*," he clarified. "You know how distracted he gets when he's working on something. Before he left for Prague, I went to the Sign of the Compass one day on an errand for my father. Master Kronos was staring into space, talking to himself. He said something like, 'I'll start with the lightning. That will be the easiest step. The kinship between magic and energy. The kinship between kinds of raw power.' I didn't mean to eavesdrop, Petra." He searched her face to see if she disapproved. "It's just . . . I haven't been getting any help about how to use magic from *my* father. So I've been paying attention to yours."

Petra was unsure how to respond. Tomik's words immediately made her wonder if she had been paying enough attention to her own father. All she remembered of their conversations before Master Kronos had left for Prague was cogs, gears, dials, and pendulums. But lightning and magic? What did *that* have to do with making a clock?

"Anyway," Tomik continued, "hearing Master Kronos gave me the idea to try my experiment with lightning first. And I did it! But designing this sphere was nothing compared to trapping *that* fellow." He lifted the second ball. Inside, a wasp darted back and forth and rapped its stinger against the glass: *ping ping ping.* "I thought I could use them for a prank on Mistress Jugo. The idea is that when you break the glass, whatever is inside the ball will multiply a hundred times."

"Do they work?" Astrophil asked.

"Well, the one with lightning does. This is the second one I've made of that model. I tested the first one in a clearing in the forest and was really lucky I didn't burn down any trees. There was also an aftereffect of thunder, which I didn't think would happen. But I'm not sure whether this one works." He carefully lifted the wasp marble. "I'm not even sure I *want* to know. I'd have to break it to make sure it works and . . . well, the wasps are supposed to attack whoever's closest to the broken ball. But after making it I realized there was no one I disliked *that* much that I would send one hundred wasps after him. Kind of excessive, isn't it? I mean"—he paused and listened to the wasp *ping ping ping*—"one is enough. Plus, this wasp might remember me and decide I'm a more interesting target than whoever's closest by."

"Remember you?" Petra scoffed. "Don't be silly. Wasps don't have brains to remember *with*."

He grimaced. "It's not its brains I'm worried about."

Petra took the ball from him. The thin glass buzzed under her grip, which tightened as she peered at the insect's stinger. "Not a pretty sight," she agreed, and passed both spheres to Tomik, who tucked them back into the box.

"I thought of it because Lucie kept pestering me to make earrings for her in the shape of butterflies. Father told Lucie and Pavel that they could make the trip to Prague this year to sell our wares. Lucie wants to impress the city-folk. And Pavel." He rolled his eyes.

Lucie was his older sister. She was pretty, plump, and married to Pavel at the age of eighteen. She, Tomik, and Petra used to explore the woods together when they were younger. But the trio split up after Tomik and Petra suggested that Lucie wade in a muddy creek. Though they swore that they didn't know the creek was full of leeches, Lucie was hysterical when she discovered little black blood-sucking globs stuck to her pale legs. Wailing, she jumped from the water and rolled on the grass, shoving at her brother and Petra as they tried to peel off the leeches. They finally convinced her to let them help, but tears poured down her face and she whimpered as every torn-off leech revealed a bruise-colored mark. After this incident, Lucie decided Tomik and Petra were not so much fun to play with. Frankly, they felt the same way about her.

"I have better things to do than make her some ridiculous earrings," Tomik continued, "but then I thought, What if I used *real* butterflies? That'd be pretty—but also pretty useless. Then I realized that breaking something takes energy, and I could use that energy to multiply whatever was in the shattered glass. But a hundred butterflies? That's not so interesting."

"A hundred times prettier and a hundred times more useless than just one."

"Exactly," Tomik agreed with a laugh.

"Have you considered putting water inside?" Astrophil suggested.

Tomik rubbed his chin. "There's a thought. Smash the ball on a wall right next to somebody and they'd be completely soaked."

"You'd have to make sure the water multiplies more than a hundred times, though," Petra pointed out. "One hundred drops of water isn't very much. That's not even enough to fill a small pitcher."

"True. Hmm . . ." Tomik's eyes became unfocused as he considered how he might increase the magnifying power of the spheres. Then his gaze sharpened as he looked again at Petra. "But the concept is a good one, isn't it? There are so many possibilities. I could multiply almost *anything* this way. What do you think?"

"I think I'm jealous."

She meant this in an admiring way. Magical ability was extremely rare—that is, it was rare if you were not born into a noble family. And it was even more unusual for Tomik to be able to use his talent at a young age, since such talents did not typically begin to show themselves until about the age of fourteen. This was the age of adulthood, when the Academy tested children who were the sons and daughters of lords, high-ranking military officers, well-connected people, or those rich enough to make huge donations to the right people. Someone like Tomik would never be examined by the Academy, let alone admitted.

Tomik closed the box with a snap. "I keep trying to show Father, but he stops me dead in my tracks every time. He's either too busy or too tired. One minute he tells me that I'm too young to do any magic. The next minute he warns me that I'd better stop fiddling around with magic. He told me that his own magical abilities have brought him nothing but trouble, that his life would be a lot easier if he were a normal glassblower. I guess he lost some friends in the Guild."

Most cities and villages had a separate guild for each trade. Guilds were organizations that shared their trade secrets among themselves and established rules for how to craft an item and sell it. Usually, each town had a Glassblowers' Guild, a Leatherworkers' Guild, and so forth. But Okno was so small that if there had been a Glassblowers' Guild, Tomik's father would have been the only member. The same was true for many other artisans, including Petra's father. So in this village there was only the Guild. Its members worked with one another—or mostly did. A leather shoe crafted by Mistress Chistni was cinched with a metal buckle made by Petra's father. But Mistress Chistni's leather was made supple by hours of labor, not magic. This was a fact that she was willing to forget when she worked with Master Kronos. Not all members of the Guild shared her attitude.

So when Tomik stowed the box back under the bed and said, "Maybe we should keep this a secret," Petra was not surprised.

4

Earth and Sun, Sun and Earth

IT WAS DUSK when Petra left the Stakans' home. The sun had set, and the clouds blushed pink. Above them, a dark blue nestled into the dome of the sky. One bright pinpoint of light twinkled like the lightning in Tomik's sphere. Petra's father had told her that bright stars like that were planets, just like earth. Just like earth? she wondered. Were the hills and valleys the same? Did people have the same problems? Maybe on that planet, things were different, and no one ever took what didn't belong to them.

A dog barked, but then the streets of Okno were quiet. The farmers had returned from the fields, and one window—the kitchen window—glowed with firelight in almost every house. She should hurry home to supper. But she hovered by the fountain in the center of town, and dipped her hands in the cool, dark water.

Over the bubbling of the fountain, Petra heard the cries of swallows. The birds swooped in circles above her, seeking their evening meal.

Astrophil burrowed deeper into her hair.

"Scared, Astro?" Petra teased, trying to shake off her somber mood.

"Merely cautious," he whispered.

"Do you think some skinny swallow is drooling for a tasty treat like you? Silly. Metal insects give birds indigestion."

"I am *not* an insect. I am an arachnid. There is a distinct and well-observed difference between the two."

"Astrophil, has anyone ever told you that you sound like a stuffy old schoolmaster when you're afraid?"

"Thank you. But this is not fear. This is irritation." A swallow flapped close to Petra's head and Astrophil squeaked. "Now can we go home, please?"

When petra entered the kitchen, Dita was standing by the fire, scooping boiled carrots with strings of thyme out of the large iron pot that hung over the logs. Josef and David were sitting at the oak table that was so thick that thudding your fist against it would make you feel the same way as striking the ground. You would only be aware of just how little an impression you were making on it.

Josef was rather like the table at which he sat. He was a big man, muscular and brown. Deep lines marked his face. Petra's father said that you could tell how old a tree was by counting the rings in a trunk that had been cut open. One ring meant one year. But if Petra were to count the wrinkles on Josef's face in the same way, he would be ancient. And he was not even forty years old. He glanced at Petra and continued chewing. He was about as talkative as the table, too.

Dita scraped Petra up and down with her eyes. She clearly wanted to yell at her for being late. But then, with a slight shrug of her shoulders, she seemed to decide that the day had been an unusual one, and allowances could be made for Petra's behavior.

Petra sat across from David. He shoved an enormous chunk of carrot in his mouth and looked disappointed that Petra wasn't going to get in trouble.

After they had finished eating, Dita warmed a generous helping of chicken and carrots in the pot over the smoldering fire. She then arranged the food on a plate and dressed it with pickled onions. She passed the plate to Petra. "Take that down to your father."

Petra was worried that she might find him sleeping or, worse, wake him up. But he was alert and pleased when she walked into his room. "I have found a name for my enemy: 'Boredom.'" He beckoned her to his side. "You will make him run and hide."

They didn't discuss the fact that he would make a mess of things if he tried to feed himself. He simply straightened up and she sat down beside him with the plate on her knees. It felt very strange to be feeding her father, like writing with her left hand. But he chatted between mouthfuls as if they were sitting across from each other in the kitchen, having an ordinary meal. He asked about Tomas Stakan and laughed when she told him about her encounter with Jaspar, but she didn't mention Tomik's glass spheres or why she had visited the Sign of Fire.

She did, however, tell him about Master Stakan's angry explosion, and then added, "I just don't understand something. *He* knew that the prince was a terrible person. Why didn't you? Why did you accept the prince's offer to build the clock?"

He did not reply right away. "Well, Petra," he began slowly, "you need to give people the benefit of the doubt sometimes. Of course, there was that awful incident during the year of the drought when we lost several good people. They were friends of mine, Petra, people I wish you knew now. But the prince was a twelve-year-old boy then, and controlled by his father's counselors in Prague. All decisions were made by them until he turned fourteen."

Bohemia was its own country, but remained part of the Hapsburg Empire, which was under the reign of the prince's father.

Emperor Karl ruled from his court in Vienna, and had three sons. When each was born, he gave him a country. The eldest, Prince Maximilian, ruled Germany. Hungary belonged to Prince Frederic. And the youngest, Prince Rodolfo, had Bohemia. When Karl felt his death to be near, he would choose which of his sons would become ruler of the entire Hapsburg Empire after him, judging how well each had managed his own country.

"It's easier," Mikal Kronos continued, "to blame your sorrows on one person than on a group of them. Then you can believe that if only that person were to disappear, everything would be different, better. Maybe that's true sometimes. But more often than not it's just wishful thinking. Let us say that the prince *had* given the order to imprison, even kill, the people plotting rebellion when the fields dried up. It was a brutal choice. But how could I hold a young man accountable for a decision he made as a child?"

"He was the same age I am now."

"I am old," her father said, sighing. "And I still make mistakes in judgment."

Petra did not like to hear him say that. Her father's straight salt-and-pepper hair flowed over his shoulders, and Petra only had to look at it to admit that there were more gray hairs than black. She knew that he had been older than most fathers when she was born. She had not been his first child. Her mother had given birth to three sons. Each had been stillborn or died soon after he was born, and the third had been Petra's twin. There had been no midwife or doctor in the town then, or now. There was only an old woman, Varenka, who brewed medicine and helped deliver babies, though she was not particularly good at either.

"Of course, I had my suspicions about the prince," her father said. "If you remember, I went to Prague to meet with him first before agreeing to take the job."

"But how could you have agreed? Look what he did to you. How could you have met him and not seen him for what he was?"

"It is not always easy to see people for what they are. I hope you will be better at it than I have been. Prince Rodolfo is charming and persuasive. He seemed keenly smart and friendly. I was ready to believe, after that first meeting, that people had misjudged him and blamed him for things that he could not control, like the weather or the decisions of his advisers when he was younger. Also"—her father paused—"I was intrigued by the project. When it was suggested to me, I couldn't let go of the idea. It haunted my mind, and I had so many visions that I simply had to realize them."

Petra was silent, because she had the sense that although what her father had told her was true, the pause he had taken before he spoke meant that what he had said wasn't the whole truth. "It's just a clock. You could have built one for the mayor of Okno if you had wanted to."

"But such a clock? With such resources and talent from all over the Empire? No, never. Because . . ." He bit his lip. "Petra, you must be very careful not to tell anyone what I am going to tell you."

She was curious. "Of course I won't."

"No one!" He gripped her hand. "Not even Tomik."

"I won't. I promise."

His hand relaxed a little, but still held hers. "The clock is more than what it seems. You know, don't you, that the relationship between the weather and time is a very close one. What we call a 'month' is the time it takes for the moon to wax and then wane. The moon controls the tides, and the tides change the shape of the land, sometimes taking pieces of it away, sometimes giving pieces of it back. The tides bring rain clouds, and then winds push them over the land. For years we have thought that the sun moves around the earth, but I learned at the prince's court that it is not so. The exact opposite is true: the earth revolves around the sun. And we split the time that we see the sun and the time that we do not into hours. And it is the sun that decides how hot it will be."

Petra's head was spinning. What *was* he talking about? The earth goes around the *sun*? That made no sense whatsoever.

"The prince had an idea. You must admit it is an ingenious one. I never would have thought of it, but once he suggested it I saw its potential. I saw how much better it could make Bohemia. And I felt sure then that the prince could not have a bad heart. That if he had made wrong decisions, he wanted to make up for them. You see, he wondered if it was not possible to make a clock powerful enough to influence the weather. The elements of weather—the sun and moon—affect time. So perhaps we could make the very opposite happen. We could reverse the path of influence and make time change the sun and moon. The prince said that with a clock like this, there would never be another drought. The weather could be monitored to make the exact amount of rain, sun, and cloud needed to produce bumper crops of brassica every year."

So this was why her father had been so preoccupied with lightning and magic before leaving for Prague. As Petra listened to her father, she felt worse and worse. One of the things she had always loved about him—the way he would mutter to himself as if no one were around, or dip a quill into a glass of milk and not notice because of some idea in his head—was starting to seem like not such a good thing at all. He often worked on projects so much that he didn't see the world around him. But never before had this resulted in something dangerous.

"I wasn't even sure I could do it when I took on the project," Mikal Kronos continued. "I promised I would try, nothing more. I promised I would provide him with a clock able to stun all of Europe with its beauty, but as for producing something that could control the weather . . . well, that's a tall order, to say the least. As far as most people are concerned, the new clock in Staro Square will just tell the time."

"So it can't control the weather, then?" Petra asked with relief.

"In fact, it can. Or, rather, it could."

"But, Father . . ." She hated to say this, but forced herself: "Don't you think that maybe the prince won't use the clock to make sure the harvest is perfect every year? What if he does the exact opposite?"

"That thought did occur to me"—his fingers strayed across his face and touched his bandage—"afterward. But, Petra, the prince has nothing to gain from failed crops. The wealth of his country relies on brassica production.

"And the prince relies too heavily on his own cleverness. The clock's ability to control the weather lies in one final part, which still needs to be assembled and installed. This part is like a puzzle. But no ordinary person could solve it. Assembling the part requires more than intelligence—it demands intuition, and the power to see the metal pieces as I do. Does Prince Rodolfo wish to prove that he possesses all of these things? Does this eighteen-year-old want to outshine his older brothers and be chosen as the next emperor? Of course he does. Blind as I am now, I can't believe how blind I was to these facts before. 'I will finish the clock *myself,*' the prince told me. 'I respect your talent. I admire the way you see the world. You have an eye for beauty. But you are no longer necessary.'

"I have to believe that what he said isn't true. Prince Rodolfo stole my sight, but he is not *me*. The clock could work to control the weather, Petra, but the prince will not understand how to *make* it work."

5

What the Spider Said

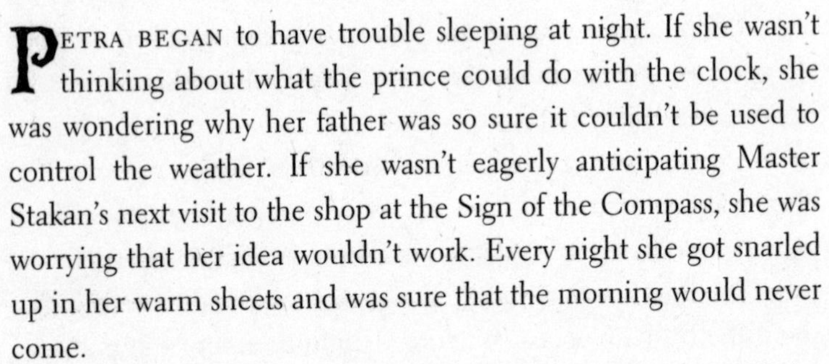

PETRA BEGAN to have trouble sleeping at night. If she wasn't thinking about what the prince could do with the clock, she was wondering why her father was so sure it couldn't be used to control the weather. If she wasn't eagerly anticipating Master Stakan's next visit to the shop at the Sign of the Compass, she was worrying that her idea wouldn't work. Every night she got snarled up in her warm sheets and was sure that the morning would never come.

"Life is much more interesting without sleep, anyway," Astrophil promised.

She groaned. "You just don't know what you're missing, you cold-hearted insomniac. I do."

But Petra had to admit that they did have fun in the evenings. She would sit on her windowsill with her long legs dangling in the night breeze and Astrophil would teach her the constellations, pointing out Cassiopeia in her chair, the belt of Orion the Hunter, and how to find the North Star. She taught him how to play cards. Since Astrophil could not hold his cards very well (there is a reason why the cards you are dealt are called a "hand"), Petra passed them to the spider with her eyes screwed shut and the cards faceup on the floor. But she always ended up seeing them anyway, even if she didn't want to. So their games were not really games as such, but lessons where Petra taught the spider the finer points of betting and bluffing.

Dita, who usually complained about Petra's love of sleeping in, began to look with concern at her young cousin's sunken eyes. Then one day when Petra was helping Dita pit and boil cherries for jam, Petra passed Dita salt instead of sugar. The batch of jam was ruined. They jarred it to eat later anyway, since Dita did not like waste. Petra did not like the thought of salty cherry jam, but everybody has his or her own priorities.

This is why, when Dita found a small army of candle stubs hidden under Petra's bed, she scolded the girl for her extravagance. She ordered Petra to make more candles, which is very boring work. Petra sat by the kitchen fire, where a small pot of melted beeswax simmered. She dipped a long string into the wax, lifted it up, let the wax dry, and then dipped it back in again. And over and over. The string got thicker and thicker with the creamy wax. The smell of melted beeswax was not that bad—it had a honey perfume—but Petra grew sick of it. Her arm got tired, her back got stiff, and she sweated from the combination of the late-summer heat and the fire.

When there was just an inch-deep smear of wax at the bottom of the pot, Dita set it aside for sealing jars. That night she made Petra drink a cup of warm milk with marigolds. The next night it was cool violet water. Petra thought Dita's concoctions tasted nice, but they did not help her sleep any better. So she refused the night Dita handed her a boiled willow branch to chew.

One evening, Petra managed to doze off for a few minutes. She woke to find that Astrophil was gone. She walked across the hall to her father's library with its uneven walls, crooked corners, and stuffed shelves, but she did not find the spider. So she slipped down to the ground floor, feeling her way along the dark staircase until she reached the constant hum and clank of the shop. The pets squealed delightedly, but she ignored them and cracked open her father's door. His room was pitch-black.

"Astrophil?" she whispered, wishing she knew how to communicate with him silently, like her father could. She had tried this many times over the years. Astrophil always just laughed at the way her face twisted into an expression of fierce concentration. "Are you there, Astrophil? Father?"

"Yes?" said the spider.

"Yes?" said the man.

"Is the noise from the shop keeping you up, Father?"

"No," he replied. She wished she could see his face. "I enjoy the sound."

Then something occurred to her. She could have kicked herself for not thinking of it earlier. "Why don't I buy one of Master Stakan's Worry Vials?"

He probably smiled. "How about buying two?"

THE NEXT MORNING, Petra went to the library to fetch some krona to pay Master Stakan. She sprang up each step.

The library was lined with bookshelves much taller than Petra. Years ago, Master Kronos had built a ladder that hovered in midair. To make it work, you snapped your fingers and, like an obedient (if slow) dog, it would glide to wherever you pointed. When Petra asked her father how he had made it, he had replied vaguely, "You just have to understand a magnet's emotions. Magnets are very affectionate, but they can be stubborn if you offend them, so building the ladder was really just a case of making friends." Which may have been why the ladder was always quicker to obey her father than anyone else.

When Petra entered the library, she snapped her fingers and pointed the ladder into the left-hand corner, where one wall of books met another. Then she climbed the rungs, noticing along the way a dried-up apple core her father must have left on the fourth shelf more than half a year ago. When Petra reached the top shelf, she pushed aside a number of books on how to build a water fountain.

Growing out of the wall was a dandelion. It was a fuzzy white globe, the sort you blow apart to see every seed carried on little white wings. But the fluff of this dandelion was actually fine filaments of silver. Petra leaned forward and blew on the flower three times, two longs breaths and one short. The globe gently fell apart. The seeds drifted down. They fell into holes in the wooden floor that were so small Petra could not see them, though her father had assured her that they were there. Then there was a whisper as each seed, now invisible, turned in the same direction.

A floorboard slid away, revealing a mound of krona and smaller piles of foreign money. Petra counted out as much as she needed to pay Master Stakan for two Worry Vials.

She paused, looking at the mix of gold, silver, and copper coins. It struck her that there were very few glints of gold. And the piles had eroded over the months. Most of the family's savings had come from the ordinary work her father would do every day, like fitting horseshoes and making iron hoops for barrels. How would their life change now that he could no longer work?

The question weighed on Petra like a heavy hand on the back of her neck.

She reached past the coins and flipped open a little trapdoor. There was another dandelion, but a springtime one. It was yellow and made of bright brass. The petals prickled against Petra's finger as she pushed it like a button.

She pulled her hand out of the hiding place and the floorboard slid shut. Like a flock of miniature birds, the silver dandelion seeds lifted out of the floor, soared up the bookshelves, and swept around their green stem. They formed a perfect sphere once more. Petra climbed up the ladder again to rearrange the books. When the flower was covered, she raced out of the library, down the stairs, and out the door.

Master Stakan greeted her cheerfully. "Petra! I was just going to see your father." He patted a soft leather bag on his worktable. "Shall we go together?"

"Yes! But before we leave, can I buy something from you?" She dug the coins out of her pocket. "Two Worry Vials, please."

"Hmm." He hesitated. "Having bad nights, are you? Well." He hesitated again. Then he turned and lifted two bottles down from a wall of shelves stocked with every shape and size and color of glass bottle you can imagine. The Worry Vials were short, fat, and clear. The opening to the bottle was wide, and sealed with a big cork. "Just be careful where you keep them, will you?"

"Sure," she said.

He clapped his hands together. "Then let's go."

At that moment Tomik came in through the door, carrying a loaf of bread. His eyes fell on the leather bag. "They're ready?"

"Yes," his father said, and pocketed the bag. "Petra and I are going to the Sign of the Compass. You stay here in case anyone comes to the shop."

Tomik's fingers punched through the bread crust. "I'm coming, too."

Master Stakan drew in an angry breath.

"You just don't want me to see," Tomik growled.

"I want Tomik to be there," Petra said. There was a firmness in her voice, as if she had forgotten she was only twelve years old.

Master Stakan exhaled gustily. His gaze wavered between the two children. Then he said, "You needn't mangle the bread, son. Come along."

But his face was that of someone acting against his better judgment.

THE THREE OF THEM CROWDED AROUND Master Kronos's bed in the little room on the ground floor. When Master Stakan explained why he had come to visit, Petra could tell that her father was excited, though he tried not to show it.

Master Stakan opened the leather bag and tipped two small glass balls into his hand. Though Petra had known what was in the leather bag, she still felt an odd pull in her stomach when she saw the two eyes—for that is what they were, two white glass eyes with silver irises and black centers. They were her father's eyes—*No*, she told herself, *they're just copies*. But still, she blinked at the glass eyes on Master Stakan's palm and felt unnerved.

With his other hand, Master Stakan reached for her father's bandages. Petra averted her gaze. When Master Stakan had placed the glass eyes, he said, "Well?"

Petra turned to her father. He looked so normal, so *whole*, that Petra realized she had not really seen her father's face for more than seven months.

Mikal Kronos sighed with a disappointment he could not hide. "I see nothing."

"Ah." Tomas Stakan's eagerness drained away. "You know, I thought I might have to give it a few tries. It's much more complicated than crafting eyes for the tin pets. Don't worry. I'm sure I'll come up with the right way to do it."

"I'm not worried, Tomas. I know you will. Thank you."

Master Stakan shook his head. "He has a black soul, the prince does. To send you home like this, with not a krona in your pocket to show for it."

"The prince promised to pay me in a couple of years."

Master Stakan snorted. "That's a long way away." Then, abruptly, he said farewell. His feet shuffled. Petra walked him and Tomik to the door, her hand briefly holding her friend's before he and his father stepped outside the Sign of the Compass. Through the window, she watched Master Stakan walk away with the haste of someone eager to escape his own failure.

He had left something unfinished.

Petra made a decision. She returned to her father's bedroom. Wordlessly (because she did not trust herself to speak) and quickly (because she was too scared to do otherwise), she stepped toward the bed.

Still sunk in his disappointment, Mikal Kronos didn't notice anything until his daughter's fingers were on his face. He felt her reach for the glass eyes. He seized Petra's hands.

"Please don't," he said.

Petra hesitated.

"Get Dita," he ordered.

Petra imagined what she would see: two sickening holes, red like something scoured, and the rough stitches that lashed the flesh together.

Her father's voice grew harsh. "Do as I say."

She did.

Soon, Dita was in her father's room. The bandages were back on Mikal Kronos's face. And the glass eyes were in the leather bag on the wobbly pine nightstand.

THAT EVENING, Petra closed her bedroom door behind her with relief, hurt, pity, and the nagging sense that she was overlooking something important, something that didn't fit. But her emotions were so tumbled together she wouldn't have been able to see it for what it was. She would have only been able to say that she felt confused.

She wanted to light a candle, but then she imagined Dita lecturing on the evils of waste. So she leaned out the window and watched clouds blow across the young moon. She said to Astrophil, "I don't understand something."

"Go on."

"Why did the prince take his eyes but still promise to pay him? If he could do something like this to Father without anybody caring, he didn't have to send him home or pay him."

"Perhaps what your father said was true. Perhaps the prince respects him."

"It's a strange way to show it."

"Evidence suggests that the prince is a strange individual." The spider flickered a few legs, and they glinted in the moonlight. "Your father has always prized learning."

Petra frowned. "What does that have to do with it?"

"Take me, for example. I am a very inquisitive spider."

"So what if you are?"

"I enjoy reading throughout the entire night. I have studied foreign languages. I hope to learn how to write one day. I try to discover new things, even if it makes me what you call 'nosy.' "

"Well, sure. I learned how to read at a young age, too. I don't exactly share your fascination with reading every moldy book under the blazing sun, but it's only natural that you would be advanced for your age. You belong to me."

"Precisely. And your father made me. Do you not think," he began slowly, "that there is a reason behind my interest in learning?" If a spider can shrug, Astrophil did. "Let us face facts. I am made of a metal called tin. It is unusual that I like to know exactly how many words begin with *z* while Jaspar—who, as a later model and a more complex animal, could be expected to be more 'advanced'—lazes around Master Stakan's shop and even *naps*! But ultimately I am a construction. I am what your father made me, and he made me—as you have just mentioned—to belong to you."

"Astrophil, you don't really *belong* to me. If you wanted to, you could walk out of this house." She said this fearlessly, but did so because she knew the spider would never want that. "Anyway," she pressed on, "each pet has a different personality. Isn't it possible that what you like and how you behave just developed naturally?"

"Possibly. I do not know, however, if 'nature' applies in my case." The spider waved a front leg, dismissing the idea. "Let us stop talking about me. Let us address one fact about which we both agree: your father thinks very highly of study.

"Perhaps Master Kronos was simply interested in the project. That would be very like him. But is it not possible he had other reasons for building the clock? What if the prince offered your father something more than money? Something Master Kronos could never afford and, even if he could afford it, would never be able to make happen because of his place in life? He is a mere artisan. He is a skilled one, and fairly well off because of it, but he is no lord."

"Astrophil, I don't think—"

"Of course you do. Because it is clear that the prince must have offered your father a place at the Academy. For you. Master Kronos said the prince would pay him in a couple of years. In two years you will be fourteen."

"But I would never, ever go!" Petra slapped the windowsill. "How could he think I would let him send me away to be trapped for years in a damp stone block filled with obnoxious rich brats trying to develop their magic? I couldn't learn anything there that Father couldn't teach me himself here."

"Perhaps. Perhaps not. He is self-taught. Who knows what his skills would be like if he had had some training?"

"Well, who knows if I have *any* skills? And that would be perfectly all right by me," she blustered.

"It is hard to imagine, given your father's and mother's abilities, that you yourself would not be gifted. And if you are, it is also entirely possible that your form of magic will be different from your father's, in which case he would not be able to help you hone it."

Everything Astrophil said made sense, and it made her feel sick. True, she had always longed to be able to communicate with Astrophil using only her thoughts. But now a muted anxiety buried somewhere deep inside her warned that she might not *want* to have her father's gift for metal. She might not be ready for the consequences. Especially now that she had seen some of those consequences. She thought about something the spider had said: *it is also entirely possible that your form of magic will be different from your father's.* What he did not say was that this meant she could have inherited her mother's magic: seeing the future. A gift she would never want.

A wave of weariness hit her. She remembered Master Stakan's Worry Vial. "I need to sleep, Astrophil."

"Well, if you must."

She walked across the room and lifted the vial. She cupped its bulging sides in her hands and climbed into bed. She removed the stopper. Remembering Master Stakan's instructions, she put her mouth toward the bottle's wide opening. She began to whisper. As her hushed words flowed into the bottle, the glass glowed green, brown, violet. Petra then reached for the cork and shoved it in, closing the vial. The colors inside the glass continued to change, but then settled into a deep purple, like the color of a bruise.

Petra leaned back against the pillows. Finally, her mind felt clear. Her eyes closed, and before she drifted off to sleep, another idea occurred to her.

6

Sudden Storm

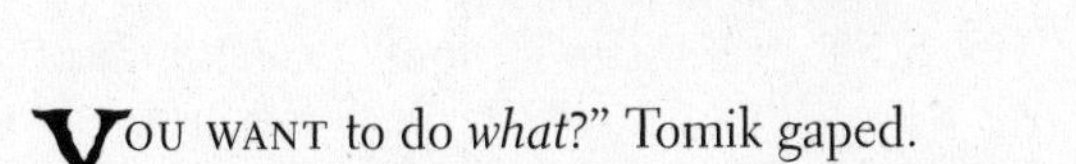

"YOU WANT to do *what*?" Tomik gaped.

"It's not such a bad plan," Petra protested.

"You want to go to Prague, sneak into Salamander Castle, and steal back your father's eyes?"

"You don't have to make it sound like I'm crazy."

"The word 'crazy' doesn't do you justice. I was thinking something more along the lines of 'rampaging lunatic,' 'mad as a ship of fools,' 'scryer-cracked,' 'fairy-touched,' and just plain 'bone-headed'!"

They were sitting on a heap of moss in the forest. Astrophil had wandered away, expressing an interest in studying the habits of ants. Petra and Tomik heard the chopping of trees in the distance. Summer was over. It was September, and the brassica harvest would be finished soon. The men in the village were beginning to set aside wood for winter.

"It's a risk-free plan, if you think about it," Petra said.

"Hmm. Let me think. I'm thinking. And you know what? I can't figure out how in the name of heaven and earth this is risk-free."

Petra struggled to keep her temper. When she spoke she strove to sound rational, but her voice was tense. "All I have to do is go to

Prague. It can't be that hard to get hired as a servant in Salamander Castle. The castle has hundreds of servants. The prince probably needs three of them just to wash his socks."

"You want to wash his dirty socks?"

"*No*. I'll get a job doing *something* in the castle, like"—Petra racked her brain, trying to remember any skills she had—"like mopping floors," she finished lamely. Then, with new spirit, she said, "Do you think my father lived in the castle for six months without someone noticing that he suddenly disappeared? People talk. I will listen. And then I'll find out where the prince hid my father's eyes. If I think I can, I'll steal them. If I think I can't, I'll just come back to Okno."

"Doesn't sound too risk-free to me."

"I don't care if it is or isn't." She gave Tomik a look that he recognized well. It was the steely expression of Petra at her most stubborn.

"I'll come with you, then," Tomik said.

She had hoped for this. "Really?"

"Absolutely. I can't let you be crazy on your own. Madness loves company."

But Petra grew thoughtful. "No," she said reluctantly. "You need to help your father design a pair of glass eyes that work. You know that I might have to return to Okno empty-handed. You have to help your father come up with a solution."

Frustrated, Tomik flung his hands back as if he had burned them. "He'd never listen to me. It would be easier to make the emperor hop like a dancing bear than to make my father hear anything I have to say about magic."

"Then don't *say* anything. Just show him."

"Easier said than done."

"You could at least try. What you did with the glass spheres is something I've never heard of anybody doing. If you got your father to look at them, even he would have to be impressed."

"Well, maybe." She could tell Tomik was pleased that she respected his abilities. "But I don't like the thought of you going to Prague on your own." His face clouded.

"Aren't Lucie and Pavel going to the city soon? Didn't you say they plan to sell wares from the Sign of Fire?"

"They leave in two weeks. They're not sure how long they'll stay, though. It depends on how the sales go. You'd have to figure out fast how you're going to get inside the castle." Tomik was focused, the way he always was when presented with a problem to solve. "I suppose you could tell Lucie that your family needs to buy medicine for your father."

Tomik's suggestion made sense. Though Okno was a prosperous village, they did not have an apothecary. Varenka, the old, rail-thin woman with brown-spotted skin who had delivered Petra, could brew some drinks that were supposed to cure headaches and fevers. But you do not want to know what Varenka put in her drinks. Let's just say that powdered chicken bones, crushed fly wings, and snail slime were some of the less disgusting things the woman used as "medicine."

"Say your family thinks you need a break from home, and you have an aunt to visit in Prague, too," Tomik continued to counsel. "That way you don't always have to be at the inn where they're staying. But you should spend nights with Lucie and Pavel. You don't want to wander around Prague after dark. It can be dangerous." Tomik had visited the city once with his father. "Never leave any krona in the inn. It will get stolen. Keep your money pouch well hidden on your body, under your clothes. And whatever you do, don't let anyone know where you've hidden it. There are a lot of Gypsies in the city, and one of their favorite tricks is to jostle you in the street. Then you touch wherever you've put your money, to make sure it's there. And then *they* know where it is. When you think you're safe, one of them will trail after you and nick your pouch when you're not looking. In fact, you should avoid Gypsies altogether.

"Lucie doesn't keep secrets, so we can't ask her to take you and not tell," Tomik continued. "And if we told her beforehand, pretending that Dita said it was all right, Lucie would be sure to mention it to somebody. So the best thing to do is for you to wait at the edge of Okno. When Lucie and Pavel ride past, you run up to them. You can fake Dita's handwriting pretty well, can't you?"

"Naturally." Petra leaned back against a tree, folding her hands behind her head. "I sign Dita's name better than she does herself."

"So write a letter from her asking Lucie and Pavel if you can ride with them to Prague. That should work."

He nodded, satisfied. Then he said that he should be getting back to the Sign of Fire, so they stood up and dusted off their trousers.

"Astro!" Petra called.

"I think that . . ." Tomik looked at her. "You should. That is," he began again, "leave your Worry Vial at home, Petra."

"Why?"

"The Worry Vials have a flaw." Tomik's blond hair hung in a short curtain around his face as he looked down. "Father designed them so that the problems and fears people whispered to the vials couldn't be known to anyone else. When the bottle turns different colors it's because there are tiny crystals lining the inside, and they bite into the worries like little teeth. The whispers turn green and brown as they're broken down into fragments. Then the glass turns purple as it absorbs the pieces. The more you use the vial, the darker it gets. But each time you open it, there's nothing inside, and even if you break the glass, the worries never escape. They stay in the pieces of the glass. But I recently discovered that there's a way in which you can actually *hear* whatever somebody told a vial."

Petra immediately saw that this was a big problem. "But you've sold hundreds of them! And to *members of the court.* I bet they've told their vials lots of things they don't want anybody to hear."

"Exactly. When I told Father, he was so embarrassed. I don't know what bothered him more—that there is a flaw, or that I was the one who told him about it. He hasn't decided what to do. If he tells everybody, it could ruin our business. It would be all right if people who bought the vials just demanded their money back. But what's worse is that they wouldn't trust the Stakan name anymore. And if Father stops selling the vials, people might begin to wonder what's wrong with them, and somebody besides me might actually figure out how to extract the secret worries."

"How *do* you extract them?"

"It's simple, really." Tomik shook his head miserably. "Lucie decided to use her Worry Vial as a vase for flowers from Pavel. No one thought anything of it when she poured water in the vial, and the glass stayed the same color it was before. It was violet, because Lucie doesn't have enough worries to make the vial a darker color. The next day, the flowers were withered and Lucie was sad. I was in the kitchen when she poured the water out. I heard her say, 'That's odd,' and turned around to see that her Worry Vial was clear again. Then I realized that the water had somehow sucked the worries out of the glass. The *water* had been violet, not the vial. I did some experimenting, and discovered that if you put water in a Worry Vial, and pour it out later, the water's different. It's dark. It'll evaporate eventually, like water always does, but vial water leaves behind a light dust. When you stir the dust with your finger, you can hear the whispered worries again."

"Most people aren't like Lucie," Petra comforted. "Who would think of putting anything inside a Worry Vial but worries? Your family is so used to having the vials around that they don't seem special, but they're very valuable to everyone else. They wouldn't treat it like an ordinary bottle. Has anyone ever complained to the Sign of Fire?"

"Not yet," Tomik said gloomily.

"At least someone will *know* if his vial has been tampered with. If you walk into your bedroom and see that your purple vial has become clear, you know that something's wrong. Somebody would have contacted the Sign of Fire if this had happened."

"I guess that's true."

"You should come up with an antidote. Then offer it for free to anyone who has bought a Worry Vial."

"An antidote?"

"Yes . . . you know, something that will stop the water from pulling the secrets out of the glass. Maybe you could mix a sort of syrup that you pour into the vial after the glass has absorbed the worries. The syrup could seal the worries into the glass, like melted wax."

"Hmm." Tomik became pensive, and they were quiet until a cuckoo called from the trees, breaking the silence. "Hey, where *is* that spider of yours? I have to go home."

"Astrophil!"

The spider twinkled toward them, walking across a bed of moss. "The organizational skills of ants are really quite impressive."

As he approached, they heard a shatteringly loud crack. Astrophil squeaked and jumped to Petra's shoe, ducking under the hem of her trouser leg.

"Was that a tree falling?" Petra said uncertainly.

"Too loud." Tomik peered up between the trees.

A flash of light stitched across the blue sky. Thunder shuddered.

"But it's a beautiful day!" Tomik protested. "This is bizarre."

Not as bizarre as what happened next. Light brown grains began to sift down through the trees, hissing across the leaves and settling onto Tomik and Petra.

Tomik rubbed a hand through his hair. He stared at his fingers incredulously. "Is it . . . is it raining *sand*?"

As if startled by Tomik's voice, the sandstorm stopped.

Tomik kneeled to inspect the sand-sprinkled moss, muttering in disbelief. Petra and the spider were silent, but they were both thinking about the same thing: the prince's clock.

7

Greensleeves

PETRA SECRETLY BEGAN preparing to leave the house at the Sign of the Compass.

She worked harder in the shop than ever before. She made sure that the gears were well oiled, with not a speck of rust. She convinced a merchant passing through town to buy the tin monkey. She felt a pang when she told him that the pets were one of a kind, and that her father would not make any more. Master Kronos was feeling better, and enjoyed sitting in the shop and chatting with the customers. He liked the merchant, who had a gloomy voice that became excited when he first saw the monkey. But after that day, Master Kronos decided that he would give the remaining tin animals to his family and friends.

Dita said, "No, thanks," when her uncle offered her one. "David's Stella is enough for me."

Josef surprised them all by choosing a mouse, dipping his large hand to scoop up the one with the tiniest paws and longest tail. "Thank you, sir." Josef put the mouse in his pocket and never said what he had named it.

Petra asked Mikal Kronos if she could give the last puppy to Tomik, and he readily agreed. "I'm not sure she'll get along with Jaspar, though," her father warned.

Petra had not seen Tomik in a while. They each had to work during the day. At night he was preoccupied with trying to figure out how to fix the flaw in the Worry Vials and how to make a working pair of eyes for Petra's father. Tomas Stakan had finally agreed to let his son help him in designing the eyes, but they had no luck. Two more leather bags sat next to the first one on Mikal Kronos's nightstand.

When Petra walked the puppy to the Sign of Fire, the pet sniffed at the wind, drooled green oil when she saw a pigeon, and zigzagged every which way to look inside a shop or down an alley. Petra was glad that she had thought to put a leash on her.

The walk to the Stakan shop seemed to last forever, but when she arrived she was rewarded by Tomik's delighted face as the puppy wriggled in his arms and he named her Atalanta.

Soon, all the pets had been given away. Some people, like the mayor, were miffed that they had not received such a gift from Master Kronos. But those who welcomed a tin creature into their homes treasured it, treating it as tenderly as if it were a baby—which was exactly what Mikal Kronos wished.

One day, when Petra noticed the first fallen leaf lying like a flake of copper on the ground, Mikal Kronos spent the empty hours in the shop quizzing his daughter on the properties of metal. She was making an unusual effort to do well. She remembered the more ordinary properties—metal's ability to conduct heat and cold, for example. But she also was quick to recall aspects of metal that not many people knew, because her father alone had discovered them. Astrophil sat on Petra's shoulder. He knew the answers to all the questions, and sometimes bounced impatiently when Petra was slow to respond, but he had been forbidden to answer.

"When is iron at its most dangerous, Petra?"

"When it bears a grudge."

"Good. How do you teach metal not to be afraid of fire?"

"You must sing to it."

"Which metal is said to have the best memory?"

"Silver."

"Why?"

"Because it is still in love with the moon. Silver tries to be like the moon in all things."

"*All* things?"

"Well, except—"

The door to the shop swung open, and a grandly dressed woman stepped inside. As her gaze fell on Petra with her tangled hair and Master Kronos with his bandages, she instantly regretted coming here. Petra could tell from the way the two pink petals of her lips twitched. A footman followed his lady inside, and looked around the store with contempt.

The woman's bell-shaped skirt floated across the rough wooden floor. Petra heard the clip of small shoes that were made to sound exactly like that. "Good afternoon," Petra said.

The woman did not return the greeting. "I hear," she said in a voice as light and delicate as a porcelain cup, "that you sell silver animals."

"Tin, my lady," Petra's father replied. "But I am afraid they are all gone."

"Can you not make more?"

"As you see, my lady, I cannot."

She looked again at Master Kronos's face. She turned to Petra, clearly displeased. Then her eyes narrowed, for she had caught sight of Astrophil. "But what is this? A tin spider? So you do have one such creature left."

Astrophil immediately disappeared into Petra's hair. Petra was about to order this graceful, horrible woman out of the shop when her father said, "Unfortunately, he is not for sale. He belongs to my daughter, and has for six years."

"I am willing to pay a very good price for it."

"I am very sorry to repeat that he is not for sale."

"I will pay even more. I know how you artisans operate. You will do anything to drive up the price."

"Perhaps I can interest you in something else? A music box?"

She waved a gloved hand. "I have many."

"But I doubt you have a Muse Box. Petra, show her."

Petra used a footstool to reach the row of Muse Boxes on the topmost shelf. She stepped down and thrust the box at the woman.

"It plays whatever you need to hear," Mikal Kronos said, and nodded at his daughter. "Petra, go ahead."

Petra opened the box. It began to play a merry jig of a pipe and two fiddles. It took Petra a moment to recognize the tune. It was called "The Grasshopper." When Petra was nine, or perhaps ten, it had been played on the night of the annual May bonfire. Ever since Okno survived the Black Plague centuries ago, the men in the village would head into the woods on the first day of every May, cut down the tallest poplar tree they could find, and carry it through the village streets. Everyone else followed behind in a long parade, and one child was chosen to sit on the tree as it traveled through the village. When the procession reached the town square, the May Child was lifted to the ground and handed a torch to light the bonfire once the poplar had been chopped into pieces. As Petra listened to the music box play "The Grasshopper," she remembered how everybody was dancing but her. She watched the Tree of Life burn and felt angry that yet again, one more year, she hadn't been chosen to be the May Child. Her father asked her to dance. And she forgot her disappointment.

Petra closed the box.

"This music means nothing to me," the woman said, and turned to leave.

"It was my daughter who opened the box. Do try it yourself, my lady."

With a look of amused disbelief, the woman lifted the lid. A quick, longing melody flowed from the box. Petra didn't recognize it.

The woman listened, staring at nothing.

"It is not a Czech tune," Petra's father said. "Am I right? I believe it is an English song called 'Greensleeves.' "

The woman shut the box. "I know the song. But I did not wish to hear it."

"It plays what you *need* to hear, not what you want to hear."

The woman's eyes glittered. She ordered her footman out of the shop. Then she paid much more than the asking price for the Muse Box. She gripped the box in both hands as she left the Sign of the Compass.

That evening, when Petra bid her father good night, she hugged him and said, "You know I love you very much."

"I do know that," he said, and placed his wrinkled hand on her knotted hair.

"Do you know . . . did you hear that it rained sand last week? With thunder and lightning? On a clear day?"

"Did it?" His voice was indifferent, but in a practiced way.

She whispered, "Aren't you worried?"

He paused, and Petra saw that he was. Still, he tried to persuade his daughter that everything was all right. "If the prince caused this, it only means that he cannot control the clock's power. Perhaps he has been able to assemble the last part to some degree. That is possible. Lightning would be the easiest thing for the clock to produce. But I never designed the clock to rain sand. This suggests to me that he cannot assemble the last part properly."

"But he's trying."

"Petra." Her father's voice was stern as he gripped her shoulders. "The clock is no longer our concern. Do you understand?"

"Yes." His white bandages confronted her. She nodded, although she knew he could not see her. "I do."

8

Firefly

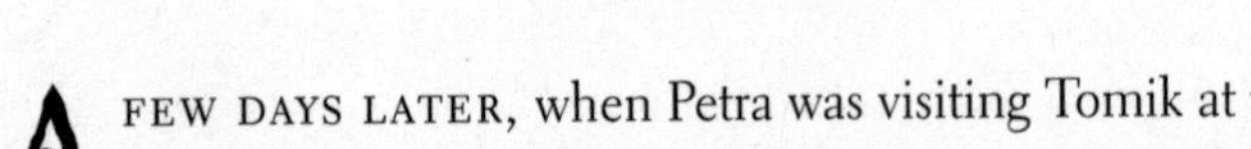

A FEW DAYS LATER, when Petra was visiting Tomik at the Sign of Fire, he hissed at her so Master Stakan wouldn't hear: "Lucie and Pavel leave tomorrow morning. Dawn. I'll be there."

Petra practically ran home.

Through the twilight, she saw the sign with a compass that looked like a flower transformed into a machine, or a machine transformed into a flower. Petra veered. She sprinted around the house to the back. She took off her shoes and loped through Dita's small garden.

Petra had avoided coming here. Not because of Dita's rows of green plants, but because of the building not far from them. It was her father's smithy, with its forge and a water-filled slack tub for cooling red-hot iron. A little over a month ago, the sight of the smithy would have been disheartening. But tonight her mind burned as brightly with excitement as any piece of fire-tempered metal. Ever since Astrophil had suggested that her father had lost his sight while trying to secure a noblewoman's education for her, Petra felt a heavy guilt. She wanted to turn that feeling into the glow of pride.

For twelve years, she had not been what the villagers might call an impressive girl. Petra attended classes at the schoolhouse, but found them dreadfully boring, and received average marks. She was lean, not exactly pretty—she had high, wide cheekbones and the odd silver eyes of her father. Mikal Kronos always claimed she had a knack for metalworking, but she'd never really applied herself to learning what he could do. Now that she was old enough to become her father's apprentice, and at least learn the more ordinary aspects of his trade, there was so much that he was unable to do, unable to show her.

But these things would change.

Petra entered through the back door. She went to the library and scooped a protesting Astrophil off the pages of a book about geometry. Then she walked into her bedroom, shut the door behind her, and raised her right palm to face the flustered spider.

"Time for bed," she announced. "We're leaving tomorrow. Will you wake me two hours before dawn?"

He didn't reply at first. Then he said slowly, "Your plan to go to Prague is brave, Petra, but is it wise?"

"What could happen to us? We'll be with Lucie and Pavel. Besides, we're just going to explore the option of rescuing Father's eyes. This will be a preliminary investigation. You know I wouldn't do anything dangerous."

If Astrophil had eyebrows, he would have raised them in disbelief. "This adventure could be like a riptide."

"What do you mean?"

"A riptide is when you swim in the sea, close to the shore, never intending to go out very far, and then an underwater current sucks you out far into the deep water."

"How poetically *grim* of you, Astrophil. First of all, Bohemia is *landlocked*, remember? We have no seas. So we've nothing to fear from riptides."

"You are deliberately misunderstanding me."

"And second, you're forgetting just how much we can *learn* from this experience."

The spider noticed which word she had stressed. "You are deliberately tempting me."

"Think about everything that Prague has to offer. The most learned scholars in Bohemia live there. And what about the prince's library? Wouldn't you like to at least see it?"

The spider was quiet, thinking. Then he said, "I suppose that someone must look after you."

"Four o'clock in the morning, then?" Petra said cheerfully.

"If you actually manage to get out of bed at four o'clock, I will eat my spiderweb."

Petra pulled a thick burlap sack from a drawer and filled it with a jug of brassica oil, the little wooden box containing Astrophil's spoon, a knife, two pairs of trousers, three drawstring shirts, and a work smock. With a grimace, she added a brown skirt that was stiff from having never been worn. She thought a moment, and then tossed in clothes for winter: a hard leather coat and a woolen scarf Dita had knitted for her. Pavel and Lucie might not stay long in Prague. But that didn't mean she had to leave the city with them.

She blew out the candle. She would pack the rest of what she needed in the early morning, when she was less likely to draw the attention of the rest of her family. David, she was sure, was still awake in his room on the top floor, above hers.

Petra struggled to fall asleep. She thought of how happy her father would be when she returned with his stolen eyes. She would suggest new tin pets to craft, like a firefly. She imagined a green light blinking on, off, on, off, and on again, until finally everything was dark and she slept.

ASTROPHIL HAD TO PINCH her several times before she sat up. "Ow! *Astro!* Is that really necessary?"

"Perhaps. Perhaps not. But it is entertaining."

Petra dragged on her clothes, still sleepy. She took a sheet of paper down from a shelf, along with a goose quill and a pot of ink. She forged the note from Dita to Lucie and Pavel. She blew the ink dry. Then Petra ripped a scrap from the empty bottom of the page, and tucked the forged letter in her bag. Inking her quill, Petra bent over her desk again. On the scrap of paper she wrote:

Dear Father, Dita, Josef, and David,

I'll be back soon. Don't worry about me.

Love,
Petra

Petra shouldered her packed bag. She softly stole across the hall to her father's library, then began riffling through books and papers.

"What are you doing, precisely?" asked Astrophil.

"Looking for drawings or notes about the clock," she replied. Her father's loss was connected to the clock, and she needed to have as much information about it as possible.

When false dawn began to brighten the library, filling it with the gray light that comes just before the sun rises, Petra gave up. Her father must have left any papers about the clock in Prague, probably in the hands of the prince.

There was one thing left for her to do. She unlocked the safe in the floor and took some krona—not much. Then she resealed the secret compartment.

She was ready to leave the room when something about the floor caught her attention. In the smooth wooden board hiding the safe she saw the pattern of extremely tiny holes. She wondered why she had never noticed them before. Perhaps they could be seen only by dawn light. Certainly she had never been awake this early to gaze at the floor of her father's study—or to do anything at all, for that matter.

"Ahem." Astrophil tapped one leg impatiently.

Petra ignored him. She inspected the floor more carefully. She noticed a dusty rug at the foot of one of the bookshelves. She pulled it aside and saw, to her excitement, a constellation of holes smaller than the point of a needle bored into the gleaming wood.

She climbed up the ladder to the dandelion for the second time, her heart beating. Shifting aside a book on water fountains, she blew once on the flower. The seeds did not budge. She shook the stem, but it simply bent back and forth without shedding any of its seeds. Nothing worked.

Astrophil said, "Again I must ask: *what* are you doing?"

"I'm not sure," she admitted. Petra glared at the dandelion. She felt like shaking it again just to relieve her frustration, but instead she pushed the book back into place.

But as she did so, something occurred to her. Nestled next to the book on water fountains was another one about precious stones. She gnawed her lip in anxious consideration, and then uncovered the dandelion again, taking in its round, silver shape.

"Petra, do you want to go or not? Because we need to leave *now*."

She leaned toward the flower. Then she said, "Marjeta." This was the word for pearl. It was also the name of Petra's mother.

The flower's sphere collapsed. The seeds whirled down to the spot on the floor where the rug had been. Astrophil squeaked as a panel slid away to reveal a hiding place he hadn't known was there.

That had been too easy. Petra grinned and shook her head. She would have to tell her father to change the password when she returned.

Kneeling by the hole in the floor, she stuck her hand inside and gasped when it hit something hard. She touched cloth and dragged it into view. It was very heavy to pull. It was a sack tied with twine. She opened it quickly and saw—nothing. Bewildered, she thrust her hand inside and yelped when she hit that same hard something yet again. She shook away the pain and then felt inside the bag more gingerly, tracing the outline of something long and cylindrical, with a sharp, pointed end. Suddenly she realized what it was: a screwdriver. It was one of the invisible tools her father had made years ago. No wonder she could never find them in the shop! Her hand passed quickly over the tools, feeling several of them. What were they doing here?

She had no time to consider the answer. She roughly tied the bag again and shoved it back to where it had been. Then she continued to grope for anything that resembled papers or a notebook. When her fingertips touched a smooth vellum binding, she pulled it into sight. She did not pause to look inside the book but thrust it into her pack. As Astrophil tugged at her sleeve she fumbled for the hidden brass flower, pressed it, and was already dashing as quietly as she could out of the room when the panel in the floor slid shut.

TOMIK WAS WAITING for her by the road that led from Okno to Prague. "Where were you? It's already dawn! Lucie and Pavel will be coming along any minute. Here." He thrust a small cloth bag at her. "A little going-away present. Use them well. Actually, don't use them unless you have to, since the effects will be . . . dramatic."

Petra opened the bag and looked inside. Three glass balls winked up at her. "You didn't," she said.

"Oh, but I did. Sir Wasp is all yours."

"What's the third one?" She reached inside, fished around, and brought out a ball that did not contain an angry insect or a sliver of lightning. She lifted the sphere, and a small jet of water splashed inside.

"One Marvel, made to order. It was your idea to put water inside, remember?"

"Actually, it was Astro's." She shook the ball and stared at the water's lovely dance.

"Indeed it was my idea." Astrophil drew himself up to his full height.

"But she made some key suggestions," Tomik told the spider. "Now, Petra, seriously: try to avoid breaking one unless you need to for protection from something. You know I haven't tested the Hive." He tapped the sphere with the wasp. "And I haven't tried out the Bubble either. So don't break them unless you *have* to."

"What's the one with lightning called?"

"Not sure. Any thoughts?"

Petra recalled what she had been thinking about before she fell asleep the night before: a lightning bug. "What about 'Firefly'?"

Before Tomik could respond, they heard the clopping of horse hooves and the rattle of a carriage. He gave Petra a fierce hug. "See you in a couple of weeks!"

He broke away and began to walk swiftly into the trees. "Not sticking around for Lucie and Pavel?" she called.

He turned around. "I see enough of them as it is. By the way, take care to keep Astro hidden when you're in the city. He could get stolen. And take care of yourself, too."

SO FAR, SO GOOD. Lucie and Pavel didn't look at the letter twice, and the young blond woman was thrilled to have Petra for company. Petra sat in the back of the cart, which chimed with glassware whenever the cart rattled against a bump in the road.

Lucie talked nonstop. She pointed out where poppies had

grown along the road earlier that summer. "But they're all gone now." She sighed. "They were so red and pretty."

Pavel looked lovingly at her. When a snake squiggled across the dirt road, the horse whickered and Lucie squealed. Pavel patted her arm. Petra rolled her eyes.

For most of the trip, Lucie hung her arm on the bench and twisted around to chat with Petra. The younger girl nodded along to whatever Lucie had to say, but she was impatient to look at the book she had taken from the secret panel in her father's library. As the day grew darker, she stole a few glances at the pages. It was enough to confirm that the sketches were indeed of a large clock.

"May I read it?" Astrophil asked. Petra propped it open for the spider. His green eyes glowed in the twilight. He walked quickly across the page, scanning the scribbled notes. Soon he reached the bottom of the page, and then slipped beneath it. A bump appeared in the paper as Astrophil pushed it up from below. Then the page flipped over as if an unseen hand had turned it.

"I don't like the dark," Lucie said.

"Don't worry," Pavel replied. "We should reach Prague before true nightfall. And if we don't, we'll be able to see by my Little Lantern."

Petra snorted, then coughed to hide her noise of disgust. "Little Lantern" was Pavel's nickname for Lucie, whose name meant "light." Petra's own name couldn't have been more opposite.

When each of Marjeta Kronos's sons had been born, she had given him the same name, showing a stubborn streak that Petra might have appreciated. Born years apart, the boys were named Petrak, which means "rock." The first two sons each lived as long as a cut lilac branch in water. For a week, they breathed shallowly, barely cried, and refused to nurse. Varenka massaged their limbs with oil and wine, and rubbed honey on their gums. She offered to concoct a drink of mummy. This is a syrup made from body parts dug up from graves and then boiled. Mummy is supposed to ward off death. But Marjeta refused each time Varenka offered, saying that nothing could save the babies and she would not make their brief lives painful in any way, including forcing them to drink a vile liquid that wouldn't work. Varenka was offended, but didn't argue. After all, Marjeta Kronos could tell the future.

When she became pregnant for the third time, her spirits got heavier as her body grew. Her older sister—Dita's mother—and all of her friends did their best to help her through this difficult pregnancy. But Marjeta Kronos was no longer the cheerful woman they knew. Her husband had been distressed by the deaths of his first two sons, but he refused to give up hope for his third child. He pressed his wife to tell him what the matter was. Marjeta always grew distant and tired when he asked, and shook her head with the decision of someone who knew that what she said would not be believed, or would do no good.

When she gave birth, it was to twins. The first child was a son. He was stillborn, but Marjeta said he was to be named Petrak anyway. The second child was a pink, healthy, squalling girl. She was wrapped in clean cloth and given to her mother, but by then Marjeta was too weak to even hold her. Mikal cradled the girl in his arms instead. Marjeta opened her eyes and spoke to the infant, "I worry for you. The future is not clear, love." And then she added, strangely, "The horseshoe makes its own luck."

When Marjeta died, Mikal wanted to name the baby after her. But his sister-in-law Judita suggested the name Petra, saying that she thought that this was what Marjeta would have wanted. And so Petra became who she was.

"Petra." Lucie leaned over the bench. "In Prague you can't walk around looking the way you do, half boy and half girl. Maybe people in Okno don't care how you dress, but in Prague people will look at you oddly. You should comb your hair and wear something more suitable, more ladylike."

Petra considered this. "May I borrow a comb, then?"

Lucie handed one back to her. Then she turned around and faced the road, settling into her seat with the satisfaction of someone whose words, after many years, have finally been listened to.

When Lucie's back was turned, Petra dug the knife out of her pack. She opened it and proceeded to saw away at her tangled hair, cutting so it fell just to her shoulders, like Tomik's. Petra worked the comb through her newly short hair, screwing up her eyes in pain. But when she had untangled most of the knots, she enjoyed the way her hair swung about her neck. She felt lighter, freer.

"Thanks, Lucie," she said to the young woman's back, and passed the comb.

Lucie turned around with a smile that got stuck somewhere along the way. She gasped. "*Petra*," she whispered in horror. "You look like a *boy*."

Pavel, who had been keeping his eyes trained on the road, stole a glance over his shoulder. He let out a long whistle.

"Dita is going to *kill* you," said Lucie.

"What else is new?" Petra shrugged, and tossed her cut hair out of the cart for the birds to make nests with.

9

The Golden Spiral

THIS WAS PRAGUE?

Her first vision of the city had filled her with wonder. When Lucie, Pavel, and Petra reached the outskirts of Prague, night had fully fallen, and the city glimmered with lights. The Vltava River flowed like quicksilver in the moonlight. Boats bobbed along in the water. The castle spires on top of a tall hill pierced the black clouds.

Lucie had fallen asleep by then, her head resting on Pavel's shoulder. When they reached the inn, Petra helped him try to wake her up. Lucie flickered open her long, fair eyelashes for one good look at Petra. "Who are you?" she murmured confusedly, and fell back asleep, her cupid-bow mouth open. Pavel and Petra managed to get her upstairs to their room. The innkeeper brought an extra pallet for Petra. The girl plopped down onto it, and tried to ignore the bedbugs. At first, she was too excited to sleep. The pattern of the city lights, not quite wild and not quite orderly, burned behind her closed eyes. She decided she had never seen anything so beautiful as this city.

But morning light can be unforgiving. At dawn in the common room downstairs, several of the inn's guests slurped down bowls of lumpy gruel. Petra decided to skip breakfast. She hurried away, telling Pavel and a still sleepy-eyed Lucie that she had been to Prague before and knew the way to Aunt Anezka's from the inn. Pavel was thinking of all the things they had to do that day, so he simply told her to meet them at the inn before dark and let them know then if she planned to sleep at her aunt's or with them. Lucie, half awake, nodded without really understanding and stirred her gruel with a spoon. Petra shouldered her pack, which contained the things she could not bear to have stolen: her father's book and Tomik's Marvels. She tied her purse around her waist, inside her shirt.

The first thing that happened on her first day in Prague was that Petra stepped into a pile of something very unpleasant. She looked down and grimaced. "Ew."

Astrophil peeked over the edge of her ear. "It looks like someone just emptied a chamber pot in the street," he said disbelievingly.

Across the street, a pair of hands appeared in an upper-floor window to prove Astrophil's theory. The spider and the girl shared a moment of shocked silence.

"That is *not* what I would call the practice of good hygiene," Astrophil declared.

Petra walked, trying to ignore the squish of her right shoe. She stayed in the middle of the street, where it seemed less likely for her to be pelted by things people were tossing out of their windows. Soup bones and empty bottles rained down from above.

There were no trees in the city, and no space between the buildings. The houses and shops were jammed together. Many of the buildings looked very ramshackle. They leaned, they sagged, they towered, they tilted.

Petra spotted a trough of water and pushed past a few horses to reach it. Bits of green stuff and a number of bugs (dead and alive) floated on the water, but Petra didn't care. She plunged her right foot into the trough.

"Do you have to hang on to my ear, Astro? It tickles."

"Your hair is too slippery now for me to hang on to that. Perhaps it would help if you did not wash it for a while."

"Believe me, no one would notice if I didn't." Petra eyed a young boy who looked as if he had never had a bath in his life.

And then the unexpected happened. Petra smelled something delicious. She followed the scent until she turned down a street crammed with shops. Dozens of wooden signs swung, showing oxen, candles, necklaces, dragons, flying horses, and countless other things. It was a challenge for Petra to figure out what exactly could be bought at some of the stores. Surely one could not buy a dragon?

Petra could have discovered the answer to that question if she had peeked inside the shop at the Sign of the Fire-Tongued Dragon. But she had only one purchase in mind at that moment, and it had everything to do with the sugary scent that pulled her along the road. She turned a corner and faced a large square packed with rows of small stalls. To Astrophil's delight, many of them were heaped high with books of all shapes, sizes, and colors. "Ooh," he said. "Let's go closer." He gripped Petra's earlobe excitedly.

"Astrophil!" she hissed, trying not to attract attention, for now several people milled about them, mostly scholars in long black robes that identified them as students at Karlov University. "If I wanted to get my ears pierced I would have asked Dita to stick a needle in them a long time ago."

A bookseller with a long, scraggly beard gaped at her. For the millionth time she wished that she was able to speak to Astrophil with her mind. Carrying on a conversation with him meant that everyone around her would think she was talking to herself.

"Sorry," Astrophil said. "But can we get closer?"

"After we buy breakfast." She had identified the source of the sweet scent, and it was a stall selling pastries. Several people were in line. Petra stood behind a young man in a Karlov cloak. The line advanced slowly. Petra impatiently scratched some bug bites on her arm.

When only the Karlov student stood between her and breakfast, a girl and a boy walked toward them. They wore Academy robes made of dark green velvet with a golden spiral stitched on the right shoulder. They paused right next to the man in the Karlov robe, and Petra was surprised to see that they expected him to let them step in front. She was even more surprised when the student stepped back and waved them ahead.

"Oh, I cannot decide." The girl stared at the row of cakes and cookies and honey breads. "Kolachki, perhaps? I do love their apricot jam centers. Or gingerbread?"

"Just pick one, Annie. We have to get to class." Then the boy said to the woman behind the stall, "Apple strudel. A big one."

"*Anna.*" The girl glared at him. "Remember to call me Anna. We are adults now. You should act like one."

He rolled his eyes.

"Is it not splendid that we are in the same class?" she said. "Mother and Father are so pleased. To think that we can start fires with a snap of our fingers! I cannot wait to begin seriously practicing."

"I guess."

"You speak like a commoner, Gregor."

"Look, if you don't pick your pastry now I'm going to go to class alone. If you're so blazing pleased about being in the Academy, you can try not to get us kicked out after only a week."

She sighed. "I will have two kolachki." She nudged her brother, and he pulled a large purse from his robe. "I wonder what the prince's talent is. They say that he was in private lessons for all four years at the Academy. His talent is a state secret, of course, since our enemies would know his weakness if they knew his magic."

"You talk such nonsense." He paid the woman. "Bohemia doesn't have enemies. We're part of the Empire."

"Why hide his talent, then?"

Gregor shrugged and began to walk away. "Maybe he doesn't have any and didn't want anyone to find out. Maybe that's why he didn't take classes with a group of students."

Petra heard someone behind her gasp. The pastry seller looked scared.

"Or maybe"—the girl grabbed her brother's arm and glared at him—"he has more than one magical ability and therefore needed special attention."

He shook off her hand. "Don't be stupid, Annie. Nobody has more than one magical ability." He stalked away. His sister trailed after him, protesting.

The student in front of Petra shook his head. "Reckless. What a reckless thing for him to say."

Petra bought a hoska, a braided bread made with almonds and raisins. She tucked her purse back inside her shirt, but she put the change from the bread in her pocket, so that she could reach the coins easily. Then she walked away slowly, mulling over what the brother and sister had said. The girl had been right about one thing, Petra thought: knowing what the prince's talent was would help her get what she wanted. And she supposed that she *was* the prince's enemy.

Listening to their conversation had only confirmed her bad opinion about the sort of students enrolled at the Academy. The Academy was, above all other things, exclusive. Petra's father had explained the meaning of the spiral stitched onto their robes. If you stand above or below a spiral, you can see how it spins out from its center. But if you stand inside the spiral and look straight around, you see a line, like the horizon. Using magic, her father explained, was like seeing a spiral from every point of view. Most people see only the results of magic, like seeing a spiral from above or below. But having the ability to use magic meant being able to not just see its effects, but to be inside of it, to see an infinite line of possibility.

The coins jiggled inside Petra's pocket as she walked, reminding her of more ordinary subjects. "Things are more expensive here," Petra said.

"Perhaps," Astrophil replied. "But I think the pastry seller simply cheated you."

Irritated, she stopped and put her hands on her hips. "Astro! Why didn't you tell me?"

"I wanted to see if you would realize it on your own."

Petra was groaning in exasperation when someone interrupted her.

"The uncle stole your cloth, missus." Petra heard a high voice. "I seen him. His hand is on the silks."

At first, Petra could not tell where the voice was coming from, but at the mention of a thief she instinctively touched the spot where she kept her purse. Then she remembered Tomik's advice about pickpockets and cursed herself for being so thoughtless. But when she looked around, she saw that no one was paying attention to her. Everyone on the street corner was gazing at the girl with the high voice. "The uncle stole your cloth," she repeated.

"Poor thing," someone next to Petra murmured, and tossed the girl a small coin.

The girl was about Petra's age. She was dressed in rags and had large, sunken eyes that stared straight ahead. "I seen him," she said, showing a broken tooth. "His hand is on the silks."

It was clear to everyone in the small crowd that the girl's mind was in ruins—broken, probably, by a scryer. People with the Second Sight, like Petra's mother, can see into the future without any outside aid, but only into the future. Scryers, on the other hand, can look only into the past or present. They differ from someone with the Second Sight in another way: a scryer can never have a vision by him- or herself. The power always has to be channeled through another person, and a child is the best medium for a scryer. The scryer asks the child to look at a shiny surface like a mirror and say what he or she sees. The younger the medium, the better. The problem is that being a medium makes your mind very fragile while under the control of a scryer. And scrying is not an exact science, but one that offers conflicting images and false leads along with grains of truth. There were many stories of scryers who, impatient with results they couldn't understand, forced children to stare into a mirror until their minds collapsed.

"I wonder who she was before," Petra whispered.

"A person who could be used and thrown away," Astrophil said pityingly. "I have read that there are thousands of orphans in Prague. She was probably someone who would not be missed."

"Even if nobody misses her, I bet she misses the person she used to be." Petra laid her hoska at the girl's bare, dirty feet.

And that was when she felt invisible fingers dip inside her shirt and snatch away her purse.

10

The Long-Fingered Thief

Petra spun around and caught a glimpse of a dark blur ducking around a corner not far ahead. "Hang on," she told the spider. She sprinted down the street. She was swift and nimble. She would have been pleased by how easily she jumped over obstacles and swung around corners if she hadn't been so worried about losing sight of the boy running ahead of her. He had stolen just about all the krona she had.

The Gypsy was twisting and turning down the narrow lanes, hoping to lose her. But, as his bad luck would have it, he ran down streets that Petra knew from this morning, and she remembered very well how this area was laid out. Suddenly he turned right. Petra gave a satisfied half smile. He had just disappeared down a blind alley. His only way out of the street would be to slip brazenly into one of the shops or homes. Petra sped up to prevent him from doing exactly that.

When she turned down the alley, he gave her the look of a hunted animal. She seized him by the arm. "Give it back!"

"I ain't got nothing of yours!" he shouted. "Let me go!" He kicked at her, but she gripped him firmly.

"What's going on here?" The belly of an officer turned the corner of the alley, soon followed by the man who owned it. He trundled toward them. "Did I hear some shouting? This little Gyp stole something from you?" He looked with disgust at Petra's prisoner.

The squirming boy froze, and stared at Petra with an expression of utter fear. It was the first time she saw his face clearly. His dark skin was scarred by the pox. The notch across his left cheek had probably been made by a knife. Beneath brows that looked like they were drawn by two strokes of a thick goose quill drenched in ink, his tawny eyes stared. Petra's first impression was that they were cracked, because their yellow color was marked by so many flecks of green.

What do they do to thieves in Prague? she asked herself. In Okno, men and women were thrown into the local prison for various periods of time, but children who stole were usually left to the mercy of their parents and sometimes had to labor for whomever they had wronged. From the boy's expression, however, Petra gathered that the law here didn't send boy thieves out to the orchards to pick fruit for grocers. So she said, "Oh, no, sir. No, we were just playing a game."

"Is that right? Thought you'd waste an officer's time, then? Cause a big fuss for nothing? Get everyone worked up?"

"I'm very sorry, sir. You're right. We weren't thinking. We were playing Catch the Pig Tail." She glared at the boy for remaining silent. Why did she have to come up with all the excuses? She kept a good grip on him with her right hand, for she suspected he wouldn't think twice about running away at the earliest opportunity—and with her purse, which he must have tucked away somewhere inside his clothes.

"Hill-folk and their idiot games! I have a mind to take both of you in just for annoying me." The officer's red beard quivered as he frowned. "Unless you got a good reason why I shouldn't." He looked at Petra meaningfully. To her surprise, the boy did the same. They both seemed to expect her to do something.

"Well, yes. Um, I'm really, really sorry. Both of us. We're—" she stammered.

"Petra." Astrophil's hushed voice in her ear was tired, as if he couldn't believe he had to explain. "He wants a bribe."

"Oh! Of *course*." The officer and the boy relaxed as she reached into her pocket with her left hand and pulled out two small coins. She dropped them into the man's outstretched hand.

"That's it?" His face fell.

"Well, my people, they're just poor brassica farmers." She gave the boy a look that she hoped said "I can catch you again," and slowly let him go. She reached into her pockets and turned them inside out to show their emptiness. The boy did the same.

"Street urchins," the officer harrumphed, and turned to lumber back out of the alley.

When he had left, Petra pounced on the boy and ducked both hands inside his shirt.

"Hey!" he shouted. "You foul-handed harpy!" She plucked her purse out from under his armpit. "I was gonna give it back! Give a lad a chance!" He stumbled away from her, his stained and sweaty shirt askew. She glared at him and then glanced inside the pouch to make sure everything was in it.

The boy drew himself up and smoothed down his shirt. "Now, normally I'd expect you to buy me breakfast, seeing as how you almost sent me to the gallows. But"—he grinned, catching her outraged eyes—"since you're a lady and I'm a gentleman, I suppose it ought be my treat."

As THEY WANDERED down the crammed streets, she asked the boy, "Am I so obvious?"

"What, that you're fresh from the hills, like the scratch said? Too right you're obvious!" He had an odd way of speaking, and an accent she'd never heard before. His voice had a swing in its step, like someone walking in the city on his day off.

"No. Is it so obvious I'm not a boy?"

"Well . . ." he drawled. "It's not like you're the only one to have that idea. When we first arrived in Prague, my sis thought it'd be easier to move around the city alone as a boy than as a girl. Her getup worked for about five seconds. But she's a real stunner, a drop-dead good-looker. She takes after me. Don't worry, though. You do all right in a pair of trous, but I got a sharp eye."

They reached the door of a pub called the Shorn Lamb and the boy led her through a maze of stuffy rooms. He brought her to a table in the corner and ordered two big bowls of stew from a woman with more blue tattoos on her arm than teeth in her mouth.

After she left, the boy stuck out his hand and pumped Petra's when she took it. "Name's Neel."

"I'm Petra," she said.

She still had her doubts about Neel, however, and so decided to warn Astrophil. She would try communicating with him silently. *Yeah, right*, she told herself, *like that worked the last thousand times you tried it.* But she concentrated. She felt something tickle in the back of her mind. Had she imagined it? She followed the slight buzzing sensation and focused on it. It was like the almost-silent hum of Astrophil's internal gears, a sound she heard so often in her ear that she forgot about it. But the humming in her mind now was something she *felt*, as if Astrophil were inside her head. Certain she would not be heard, she nevertheless thought hard, *Lie low. If he discovers and takes you, he could sell you for more krona than he can imagine.*

The hum skipped. But Astrophil controlled his surprise, and

sent this stern thought to Petra: *There is no need to worry about me. Keep your eyes on him.* I have *been lying low, in case you did not notice.*

An astonished, elated feeling washed through her. *Astro! Astro?*

What?

You can hear me! I can hear you! I did it! I did it!

Yes, yes. You did. But we can celebrate later. For the moment, I beg you to be sensible and pay attention to that street thief you have inexplicably decided to befriend.

Neel was studying her. Excitement had illuminated her face. "You're a moody one," he said. "Glowering one moment and glowing the next." He paused. "And you're quick, for a kitchin."

"A what?"

"A kitchin morte."

"Um . . ."

"A *girl*. A kitchin is a girl."

"Oh. So . . . is that word from your language? Your voice sounds different. Of course, no one here talks like folk in Okno, but you . . . are different," she finished lamely.

"Kitchin morte is Cant. I got my own language."

"What is Cant?"

"Cant's what the Company of Rogues speak. The Company's like a . . . like a guild. A group of no-good-doers who work together."

"You mean thieves."

"Thieves, sure. And jugglers, tinkers, actors, hucksters, ruffians, coney-catchers, cardsharpers, play-beggars, hey-passers, potwhippers, fortune-tellers, and the like. And their kids."

"Are you part of the Company of Rogues?"

"Nah. I got my own people."

"You're a Gypsy."

"The word *Gypsy* . . . well, it's not exactly in a crate."

Petra paused. "Do you mean 'inaccurate'?"

He swallowed a mouthful of the stew and then pointed at her with his spoon. "It ain't right, see? *Gypsy* means 'Egyptian.' I don't come from Egypt. We call ourselves Roma, and we speak Romany. It's a funny thing . . ." he trailed off, looking at her. "It's strange you caught me lifting your purse. Roma are flash thieves. And I have *never* been caught." He was silent for a moment. Then he lifted his right hand and pinched his forefinger and thumb together.

Petra yelped and dropped her spoon. She rubbed her left arm, which had been resting on the table several feet from Neel.

"Interesting." He lifted his hand again.

Petra resisted the urge to slap it away. "It is not so interesting if you're the one getting pinched."

"Very interesting," he pronounced, lowering his hand. "You weren't supposed to feel that."

"What did you do? *How* did you do it?"

Neel lifted his hand again. Petra's spoon lifted into the air and plopped into her stew. "Eat up."

She stared at him. "Can you move things with your mind?"

"Nah. It's more like . . ." He flexed his hand. "Like I've got extensions. Like my fingers are real, real long but you can only see a little bit."

"Doesn't that get in the way? When you eat with a spoon, are you grabbing it with the tips of your real fingers? Are the invisible parts hanging around and jabbing into your face?"

He laughed. "That'd be awkward! No, the ghosts come and go. If I feel myself wanting something, like a fine ribbon for my sis or to play a joke on someone, my fingers just kind of grow longer. The ghosts go away when I don't need 'em. It's very useful."

He took in her expression of rapt attention. Then he leaned forward across the table.

"Did you ever hear that people who lose a leg sometimes feel the part that's missing?" he asked. "That they can twitch their ghostly toes and feel an ankle that ain't there?"

"No. Is that true?"

"Of course it is. Why, I met a rogue who'd got his leg crushed by a horse. The mangled bits were chopped off below his knee, but he swore he could still feel jolts of pain in his ghost limb and had dreams of walking."

"How do you know he could really feel the leg that wasn't there? I've never heard of such a thing."

"Just because you don't know something doesn't mean it's not true."

"I didn't say I didn't believe you." Petra was uneasy at the thought that someone might still feel a missing part of the body. Could her father feel his phantom eyes? Did they cause him pain? He had never mentioned it.

"I don't care if you do or don't believe me. Just pretend to believe me for a spell. Course, if you don't want to hear my story, a Roma story that normally someone who isn't Roma wouldn't hear . . ."

"Tell me."

Neel smiled. "Hundreds and hundreds of years ago, our people lived in the desert. They trained horses and elephants. Now, both are beasts you can train and ride. But they sure don't think alike. If a horse loves you, he loves you across hot coals and battlegrounds and buggy swamps. But an elephant needs to know *why* you want something. He has to agree that what you're doing makes at least some sense.

"The Roma used to be split into three tribes, not four like we've got now. The Ursari is the tribe best at training animals. Fact is, they still sell animals to the *gadje*."

"What's the *gadje*?"

"Outsiders, you know. Like you. Now, there was one Ursari

tribesman named Danior who was better at handling horses and elephants than the rest. He also had a clearer way of seeing things than most of the Ursari. It gets hard to like someone who's always better than you, and the Ursari leader especially didn't like Danior. Soon he began to downright hate him. So one morning Danior woke up alone in the desert. His tribe had left him high and dry. He had his tent, but no water and nothing to hunt with. And that's sure death in the desert.

"He plodded along in the burning sand, looking for water. You can't last long like that. Soon he lay down and waited to die. Then it struck him that he could hear something. It was the sound of many hooves. He thought maybe his tribe had come back for him, so he hefted himself up.

"But it wasn't the Ursari. It was a group of *gadje*, and pretty important-looking ones at that. Seven mean-eyed warriors on horses were in the lead. Behind them walked an elephant carrying a man who was the most important one of all.

"Now, Danior recognized most of the horses and the elephant, too, because he had trained them. And who was the *gadje* on the elephant? It was none other than the desert king, who had a gold-glittering wife and eleven pretty children.

"Danior raised his hands, asking the warriors for help. They stared straight ahead, like he didn't exist. Then Danior begged the horses to help him. The horses, though, loved their masters like Danior trained 'em to. So the horses listened to their masters and ignored him.

"Then came the elephant. The desert king tilted back and forth on top, in a little house that was strapped onto the elephant's back. Danior saw that one strap was loose and dangling down, and he reached for it.

"The desert king looked down, drew out his sword, and slashed it, cutting off every single finger on Danior's hands."

Petra gasped. "What happened then?"

"The elephant knew Danior for who he was, and she didn't agree with the desert king's treatment of him. So she reared up. She shook off the house and the wicked king with it. She reached out with her long nose and wrapped it around Danior. She ran off fast, faster than the horses and faster even than you, Pet. She took him to an oasis, where she lowered him into the water. She scooped up mud and patted it over Danior's hands to stop the bleeding.

"The funny thing was, after his hands healed he discovered that the ghosts of his fingers were far better than his real ones. The ghosts were longer and dead quick. They could flash out and grab a desert hare by the ears. Danior hunted, and he learned to use his new fingers.

"But Danior had a score to settle with the wicked king. When he rode out of the oasis on his elephant, he headed straight for the capital city, where the white palace stood tall like a hard flower.

"That night, he snuck toward the palace. His invisible nails clicked open locked doors. Soon, he was in the nursery, looking at a row of princes and princesses snug in their beds.

"Danior was a fair man. He led away only ten of the wicked king's children, one for every missing finger, and left behind one son. That prince grew up to hate the Roma for stealing his family, but he also hated them for not wanting him, too.

"When Danior reached the city gates, he loaded his new children into a big wagon, promising them kindness and freedom. He hitched the wagon to the elephant, and the great gray beast galloped over the sand.

"That's how Danior began a new tribe of Roma called the Kalderash. They're a secretive lot. Also too snobby for my taste. But that's what comes from thinking your great-great-great-great-whatever-grandda was Danior of the Ursari, and that your relations were princes and princesses."

"What did Danior do to the Ursari?"

"Do?"

"Well, they left him to die. He avenged himself against the wicked king. Didn't he avenge himself against his tribe?"

Neel looked at her as if she had suggested the sky was orange. "You can't avenge yourself against your own people."

Petra saw what he meant. It was hard to say who had been crueler to Danior, the wicked king or the Ursari. But family is family, even if they abandon you in the desert.

"Are you a member of the Kalderash tribe?" Petra asked.

"Nope. The Lovari. We're players—you know, we act and sing and juggle and fiddle and the like. But it sure doesn't pay well."

"You have magic skills." She looked at him with respect. "And you're so young."

"I'm not. I'm older than you."

Petra was skeptical. He was a few inches shorter than she was. "How old are you?"

"Well . . . I don't know."

"What do you mean, you don't know?"

He shifted uncomfortably and began eating again. "Truth is, it's not uncommon to have long fingers like I've got."

Petra considered pressing him to explain why he didn't know how old he was, but then it occurred to her that she also had things she didn't want to share. Instead she said, "Really? Lots of Gypsies can do what you do?"

"Roma."

"Sorry. *Roma*. Are they all long-fingered?"

"Nah, not all. But plenty. The Gift of Danior's Fingers runs strong with the Kalderash, but it pops up everywhere in the Roma, 'cause of marrying across the tribes. It's very useful for us Lovari, since I can pick a pocket or two whilst my cousins put on a puppet show. Though other people aren't supposed to *feel* it when you use them. Which makes you"—his yellowy eyes narrowed—"right odd."

They were both quiet for a moment. Neel ducked his head down and continued eating his stew in silence.

Perhaps, Astrophil offered, *he is wondering what he has gotten himself into. Might you not do the same?*

Neel settled back in his wooden chair and patted his stomach. There was still a very small portion of stew left in his bowl. "That was good. Well, I'd better find the privy. I'll finish eating when I get back." He winked.

Petra looked at the bowl and suddenly remembered, as Neel was getting up, the empty pockets he had shown the officer. He started to turn away.

Her hand flashed out and seized one of Neel's wrists. "You can just go in your trous," she said angrily. She was sure he was about to leave her behind. He would slip out the back and she would never see him again. She would have to pay the bill and walk out of the Shorn Lamb alone, and wander this crowded, stinking city alone.

Astonished, Neel sat back down in his chair and shook off her grip. He hissed, "What's the matter with you? Always resorting to a ruckus. You're attracting attention, jumping around like you're full of fleas. And that"—he wagged his finger at her—"will always get you caught. Always."

Petra glared. She was in no mood for a lesson in thievery.

"Listen, I'm sorry," Neel said. "I'll let you leave the pub first. It's harder to leave second, 'cause then you leave an empty table and folks notice. It's true it wasn't decent of me to leave you in second, because I'm more experienced. So you go on ahead and I'll follow after." He gestured toward the exit in a manner that might have been called courtly.

Petra felt a little better knowing that he had not been planning to trick *her*, but she was still troubled. "What about the people who work here? Don't they deserve pay?"

He sighed. "Maybe those who can't look after what they got don't deserve to keep it."

Neel's words made her think instantly of her father and his stolen eyes. By Neel's logic, her father's blindness was not a cruel torture. It was something he had brought upon himself.

Petra had not cried once since the day her father was brought home in the cart, and she refused to do so in front of this lithe and untrustworthy thief. She had to get out of the tavern. Right then she felt like a sheet of thin paper soaked with dirty water, and just one more drop could make her disintegrate into shreds.

Petra reached for her purse and beckoned to the tattooed woman. "I'll pay. Just go."

He stared. Then, to her surprise, he ducked under the table and seemed to rummage for something. Just as the woman reached them, he straightened up and held out a filthy coin. "We'll go halves." He smiled at her expression. "Always keep your money in your shoes, Pet. It's nigh impossible to nick it that way."

After they had paid, Petra walked quickly through the airless rooms, eager for the open warmth of the sun. Neel was close at her heels. When the heavy pub door slammed shut behind them, he continued to trail after her. She wasn't sure which way to go, but she didn't care.

"What's got you so riled?" he shouted at her as they pushed past a swell of people. It was noon, and the streets of the city were bursting with noise and bustling bodies. "I paid, didn't I?" When Petra did not respond, Neel's voice rose in frustration. "Fine, I get it. You got some high-minded ideas about what's right. That's because you can afford them. Me, I got a family of fiddlers and puppeteers, and only my sis can get real work because her skin is light enough. So I'll take what I can get and if that's stew that's fine by me. I'm glad that you told the scratch what you did and saved me from a hanging, but I've got no need to keep company with some hoity-toity type."

Petra stopped abruptly. "Then why are you following me?"

Neel spread his hands. "I just happen to be going the same way as you. Aren't I allowed to go meet my sis? 'Cause she'll tear my hide if I don't."

Petra did not want to reveal that she did not know where she was going. So instead she asked, "Where are you meeting your sister?"

"Why, at the castle. That's where she works."

Petra paused. "Your sister works at the castle?"

"That's what I said, ain't it?"

They had stopped in the middle of the street. People milled around them, jostling their sides. "Keep moving!" shrilled a woman with rash-red cheeks.

Neel tugged Petra to the side of the street, where they stood against a wall that smelled of wood rot. Petra asked the boy, "Is Neel your real name?"

"Well, no." He shoved his hands in his pockets and looked away.

It was as Petra had thought. He couldn't even be trusted to be honest about the most trivial thing.

He continued, "It's Indraneel. It means 'blue.' But I'm not blue, and 'Indraneel' isn't easy to wrap your mouth around. So it's plain 'Neel' for me."

Petra then said, "Would you introduce me to your sister?"

11

Crossing Karlov Bridge

THEY SOON REACHED the Vltava River. There they crossed the Karlov Bridge, which was a magnificent construction lined with statues of Bohemia's heroes. The bridge was brand-new. Prince Rodolfo had commissioned it to celebrate his graduation from the Academy. He had named the bridge after his father. Some might say that this was unnecessary. After all, he had already changed the name of Argos University to Karlov University when he was thirteen or so. But one can never flatter an emperor too much.

Neel had no idea who any of the statues were supposed to be. He confessed that, like many Roma, he couldn't read, and didn't know much about Bohemian history. "Who cares about *gadje* history anyway? My people got better stories."

Petra had to admit that this might be true. But she gladly told him about the statues. It was rare for her to be in the position of teaching anyone something.

"Who's that moony-eyed lass?" He pointed to a statue of a woman holding a pail of water high.

"That's Lady Portia. Eight hundred years ago, people used to burn anyone with magical powers at the stake. She convinced the

Tribunal of the Lion's Paw that this sort of thing had to be outlawed."

"What's the Tribunal of the Lion's Paw?"

"It's Bohemia's highest legal court. It's made up of seven judges, who are picked by the prince. They have almost the final say on any legal matter in the country."

"Who gets the final say, then?"

My goodness, has he been living under a rock? Astrophil's words buzzed in her mind.

Don't make fun of him, she ordered the spider. She told Neel, "The prince. The Lion's Paw recommends laws to the prince, and he decides whether he likes them or not. After the law was passed, Lady Portia revealed that she herself had magical talent. At first, people thought that she had pushed for the law only to protect herself, but it turned out that her talent was the ability to withstand any heat. She could suck on hot coals like candy. No one would have been able to burn her at the stake anyway, so it's clear that she fought for the law only out of the goodness of her heart."

Neel shrugged. "They could've drowned her instead."

Next came Florian, Duke of Carlsbad. "He founded the Academy," said Petra. "Then he left tons of money after he died to enlarge the school's castle. They added running water, Turkish baths, a theater, three hot-air balloons, and a lot of other things they keep secret."

They saw Emperor Vaclav the Clever, who looked shorter than Petra had always imagined. "He's the reason why you can't attend the Academy unless you belong to the gentry," Petra explained. "His tribunal passed that law almost two hundred years ago, when he was only the prince of Bohemia. This led to the Peasant Rebellion, which was basically suicide for the hill-folk. Vaclav flattened the rebel forces. Their surrender was only accepted because they met the most important condition of the agreement: the rebels named everyone they knew with a magical power. Those people were arrested and never seen again."

"That's why we Roma live in wagons," Neel said. "They're pretty useful for getting well away from a situation that's gone all kinds of bad."

They came to the last statue, which was of Emperor Karl, who looked particularly handsome.

"What'd he do?" Neel asked.

"I think he's most famous for how he became emperor. When his father the emperor was alive, Karl had one brother, the prince of Hungary. Karl was the prince of Austria. The prince of Hungary and his father loved fried frog legs. One night they ate sixty fried frog legs and drank half a barrel of beer. They were dead the next day. The cook was accused of poisoning them and was executed. Then Karl became the emperor. I guess we're not supposed to think of that story when we look at his statue. But I can't remember anything else about him."

They had reached the other side of the Vltava and began walking up the hill. Neel said that this area of Prague was called Mala Strana. The air was fresher here. The shops had signs that were in writing only, with no pictures. The shopkeepers apparently thought that all their customers could read. Or the shopkeepers did not *want* any customers who couldn't read.

A young boy was sweeping up the street trash. The houses had red ceramic-tiled roofs, not ones made of thatch. The walls were painted in many soft colors: pale green, buttery yellow, pink, and sky blue. Stone angels decorated the corners of houses, which had glass in every window.

Petra was awed, but when she commented on how beautiful everything was, Neel just said, "I wouldn't mind getting inside one of those houses. Bet there's a lot of shiny stuff to steal."

I do not feel very well, Astrophil suddenly murmured.

What's the matter? Are you hungry? Do you want some oil? Petra asked, focusing on the buzz in her mind that she recognized as Astrophil's presence. Anxiously, she realized that the buzz was fainter than it had been earlier. What was wrong? She had given him his usual dose of brassica oil that morning.

No, I am not hungry. I feel . . . I do not know. Dizzy, perhaps? I am finding it hard to hang on to your ear.

Petra wasn't sure what to do. This had never happened before. She wanted to pluck the spider down and carry him in her hand, but Neel was very perceptive. She didn't want to take the chance that he would see Astrophil.

Just try to hold on a little longer, Petra told the spider. To Neel she said, "Can we go faster?"

"What's the rush?" He looked at her quizzically. Then he noticed how anxiously she was biting her lip. "Yeah, I guess we could hurry along some." Their pace quickened.

Astrophil was quiet.

When they reached the castle grounds, Neel pointed out Golden Alley, a row of tiny houses. Neel said that this was where the prince's foot soldiers lived. Normally, Petra would have giggled at the fact that people were living in homes that looked like painted henhouses. But she barely heard what Neel said.

When they reached an impressive building with three large doors and soaring windows, Petra asked, "Is this the castle?"

Neel laughed. "It's the stables. One of our Ursari cousins works here. My sis and I usually meet here, so if one of us shows up earlier than the other, we can chat with Tabor." They stepped inside one of the smaller doors. Petra heard the low snorts of well-fed horses. As her eyes adjusted to the darkness, she saw a young woman in a gray-blue dress talking with a broad-shouldered man. Neel waved and rushed over, calling, "*Sar san, Pena?*" Petra trailed behind slowly, not wanting to jostle Astrophil. The dark-skinned man clapped Neel on the shoulder and then walked away, shovel in hand.

As Petra approached, Neel's sister seemed to be a dream that she could see with increasing clarity. Her black hair was braided and pinned up in a crown, showing the smooth lines of a slender neck. Her skin was light—not as pale as Petra's, but a deliciously creamy color. Her eyes tilted up slightly at the corners, and were the shiny color of black lacquer.

Neel spoke rapidly in Romany, gesturing toward Petra. She could hear him repeat one word over and over again: *Pena*. He seemed to be calling his sister this, so Petra assumed that this was her name. When Neel paused and said in Czech, "This is Petra," she held out her hand. Feeling proud of herself for understanding part of their conversation, even if it was just a little bit, Petra said, "Hello, Pena."

Brother and sister broke into peals of laughter. The young woman managed to regain control first and shook Petra's hand. "Hello, Pena," she echoed Petra's words.

"*Pena* means 'sister,' " Neel said, still snickering.

"Don't worry, Petra," said the woman in a musical voice that gave no hint of an accent. "It's a nice way to be greeted. If everyone thought of me as a sister my life would be a very happy one indeed. My name is Sadira, but you can call me Sadie. After all, we are now like family. Neel says that he stole your purse, but that you didn't turn him over to the law. I'm not sure which I find harder to believe: that you caught him or that he's not now rotting in a jail cell." She frowned at her brother. "You shouldn't take such risks, Neel."

"I didn't!" he protested. "She was easy prey! She was flashing where she kept her purse to all and sundry, and wasn't paying attention to anything but a beggar girl! If I hadn't pinched her purse, someone else would've."

"Obviously she's not such easy prey, if she managed to catch you."

"But how could I know that?" He spread his hands. "She looked fresh from the hills, like it was her first day in Prague."

"Well, it is," Petra admitted. "I'm hoping to find work here."

"Yes, Neel said you wanted to meet me. He said you seemed interested that I work at the castle. Is there something I can do? I would like to repay you for keeping my little brother's neck out of the hangman's noose." Sadie pinched Neel's cheek hard and he made a face.

"Could you help me get a job at the castle?"

At that moment, Petra felt Astrophil flutter on her ear. *Petra, I—* he began. Then he fell, tumbling over her shoulder like a shooting star. Petra snagged him out of the air and stared with a panicky feeling at the spider on her palm.

Sadie and Neel peered in amazement at the spider. "What is it?" Sadie breathed.

"What's it doing?" asked Neel. The spider's legs were twitching.

"I think . . ." Relief flowed over Petra like cool water as she suddenly realized what Astrophil's problem was. "I think he's sleeping."

12

The Clearing in the Forest

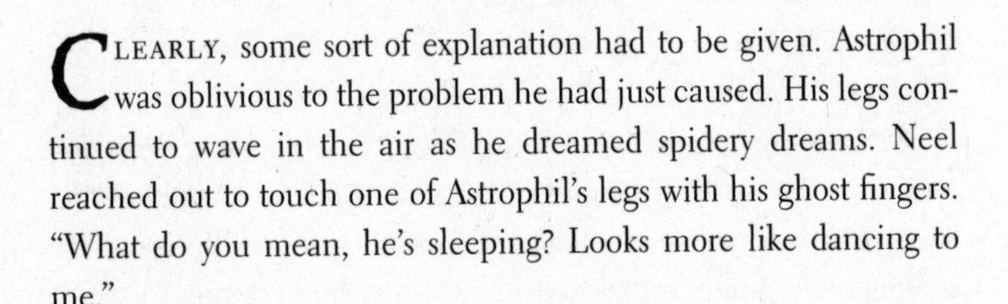

CLEARLY, some sort of explanation had to be given. Astrophil was oblivious to the problem he had just caused. His legs continued to wave in the air as he dreamed spidery dreams. Neel reached out to touch one of Astrophil's legs with his ghost fingers. "What do you mean, he's sleeping? Looks more like dancing to me."

Sadie looked up at Petra. "Well? Will you tell us what it—he—is? Or would you prefer to keep your secrets?"

Somehow, the fact that Sadie was offering Petra the chance to put Astrophil in her pocket and not say another word made Petra want to tell them everything. But a stable boy was already looking in their direction with far too much curiosity. "Not here," Petra said. "Can we go someplace more private?"

Neel spoke to Sadie in Romany. She nodded. "Join us for the midday meal, Petra, if you like. This is my day off. Neel came to walk home with me. These days, we live on the other side of this large hill, down in the forest. There we can talk openly about your silver spider and finding work for you. Come meet our family. If, of course"—for the first time she looked awkward—"you want to."

Petra tucked Astrophil in her pocket. "Let's go."

• • •

THE FOREST ON the other side of the hill was thick, and had provided many generations of Bohemian princes with good hunting. Petra saw several deer as they walked among the trees. Acorns crunched beneath their feet. It didn't seem to Petra that they were following a trail, but Neel and Sadie strode ahead confidently.

Soon, the smell of burning wood and roasting meat teased Petra. They heard the bell-like sound of a hammer on an anvil. When they reached a clearing in the forest, Petra saw ten large wagons ringed around a campfire. A dog with fanged teeth ran up to them, barking. He licked Neel's and Sadie's hands. Petra stood stock-still while he sniffed hers.

Several children wearing brightly dyed clothes were clustered in a group near the campfire, building a house out of stones, sticks, and tree bark. A woman in a full-skirted orange dress was roasting a haunch of venison on a spit over the fire. She looked at them with surprise, and seemed to ask Neel and Sadie a question.

The musical ringing stopped, and a muscular man with a short beard and a gold hoop in one ear appeared from behind a wagon. He held the hammer in his lowered left hand. His intense stare swept over Petra. Then, ignoring her and Neel, he turned to Sadie. He was smiling, but something he said made her face pinch with anger. She replied shortly and stalked to the largest wagon. She opened the door and stepped inside, slamming it shut behind her.

The man looked at Petra with open hostility. Neel said something to him in a voice that was amused but not nice. The man shrugged as if to say, "It's your problem, then," and sauntered away. They soon heard again the ringing of metal on metal, but this time the beats were quicker and louder.

"What was that all about?" Petra asked Neel.

"Emil ain't happy you're here."

"I could've figured that out on my own. What did he say to Sadie to make her upset?"

"He called her a *rawnie*."

"What's that mean?"

"It means a lady, very high-class."

"That doesn't sound so bad."

"Yeah, but you use it to mean an outsider. Sadie's father was a *gadje*, you see. Normally there'd be problems with her being fully accepted by any tribe except the Kalderash, because they're all mixed up anyway from the start. But our ma's the leader, so everyone's got to treat Sadie like she's one and the same as a full-blooded Roma."

"Your mother's the leader of the Lovari?"

"Are you kidding? Look around: there's thirty-nine of us here. Well, not now. Most of us are working in the city. Some are hunting or gathering mushrooms and nuts and berries. Thirty-nine isn't the whole Lovari tribe. My ma's just the leader of our group."

"Why is Emil here, then, and not off hunting or working?"

"You might've noticed that Roma aren't exactly the most popular people around. Some people don't like our color, some people don't like our ways, and some people . . . well, we've got to have enough warrior types around at all times. Emil isn't the friendliest sort you'll come across, but he's got brains and is good with a sword and dagger. He's always had a problem with Sadie, though, and that's a hard thing to figure. You've seen her: she's as sweet as an apple. I can't figure why he doesn't like her."

"What if," Petra suggested, listening to the hammer and anvil, "he likes her too much?"

Neel stared at her as if she had just hopped on a fast horse bound for the madhouse. He started to speak, stopped, and finally just muttered something in Romany. He looked at the wagon Sadie had disappeared into and said, "Sadie's been talking to our ma a long time."

"Maybe I should've stayed in the city."

"Don't feel sorry about being here. We wanted you to come. Emil likes to stir up trouble. And my ma and sis got other stuff to talk about than you." He scuffed his foot in the dirt. "We're in something of a fix here."

"What's the matter?"

"Our horses caught some plaguey thing. Most of them died. And we can't move the wagons without horses."

"So you're stuck here?"

"Like flies in honey. Except it might actually be nice to get stuck in honey. Instead, we're in Prague."

"What's so bad about that?" Although Petra thought parts of Prague were stinking and dirty, she was enjoying her first day in the city. After all, one could find delicious pastries, overhear fascinating gossip, and meet interesting people.

"One, there don't seem to be any Ursari in the area, so we can't sway them into loaning us some horses. And we can't afford to buy more from the *gadje*. Two"—he was ticking off the reasons on his fingers—"we should be heading south by now to escape the worst of the winter. This part of Bohemia heaps up snow right quick, and then the roads get blocked as good as a sick kid's nose. Three, we happen to be sitting in the prince's hunting grounds. Which isn't exactly law-abiding of us. This means that just about any money we make goes to bribing the prince's gamekeeper not to tell all and sundry that we're here. We pay him to tell the prince that if he wants to shoot deer, they're real thick in a part of the forest miles from here. So we not only don't have any horses, but it also looks like we won't be buying any anytime soon. Unless some miracle happens, like Ursari trooping through Prague when we know they're already heading south toward Spain, we're well and truly trapped."

Sadie opened the door to her family wagon. "Neel? Petra? Ma wants to talk to you."

Neel and Petra walked up the three hanging steps to the wagon door. When they were inside, Neel took off his shoes and set them on a straw mat. Petra did the same. The wagon was about the size of a large room. Two round, glassless windows let in light, which flickered over a raised platform covered with bright cloths and silk cushions. Beneath an iron lantern was a woman with a stern face, sitting cross-legged.

Neel, Sadie, and Petra sat down on the cloths around her. Sadie resembled her mother, but the older woman's face was narrow, her chin pointed, and her skin dark and lined. "Petra," Sadie began, "this is our mother, Damara. She would like to hear whatever you were going to tell us about the spider, if you don't mind."

Petra gently took Astrophil out of her shirt pocket. The other three leaned closer. *Astrophil*, she thought. The ticklish sensation in the back of her mind was faint, but it was there.

The spider continued to slumber.

ASTROPHIL.

His green eyes blinked and stared at Petra. *How strange.* He didn't seem to notice that he and Petra had company. *I was just completing a painting. It was a landscape, and I was using oil paints that were coming out of the tips of my legs, one color for each leg. But where has it gone? It was a masterpiece.*

Astrophil, you were dreaming.

That is absurd. To dream you need to sleep, and I never sleep. By the way, where are we? And how did we get here? And— He finally turned around and saw Neel, Sadie, and their mother. *What exactly is going on, Petra?*

Well, we went with Neel to meet Sadie and then you fell asleep. You fell out of my hair and they saw you. Then they invited us to come to their home for lunch and I decided that was a good idea.

I am starting to believe that I have *been sleeping. Because if I had been conscious, I would* never *have allowed you to do something so extraordinarily foolish.*

"This is Astrophil," Petra introduced the spider. "He was made by my father." Then she took a deep breath and began to tell them why she had come to Prague.

13

The Hour Strikes

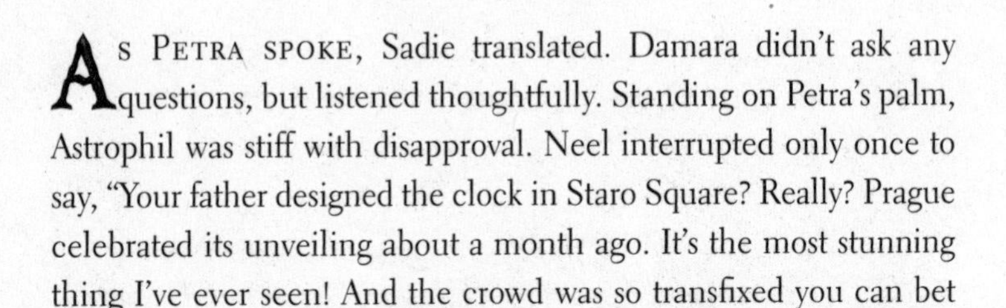

As Petra spoke, Sadie translated. Damara didn't ask any questions, but listened thoughtfully. Standing on Petra's palm, Astrophil was stiff with disapproval. Neel interrupted only once to say, "Your father designed the clock in Staro Square? Really? Prague celebrated its unveiling about a month ago. It's the most stunning thing I've ever seen! And the crowd was so transfixed you can bet they weren't looking at their purses. Got a *good* haul that day."

Petra told them almost everything, except about the clock's hidden powers. She had promised her father to keep that a secret. And Astrophil might have had a spider's equivalent of a heart attack if she broke that promise.

She concluded, "So now you see why I want to get a job at the castle. I have to figure out how to get my father's eyes back. They don't belong to the prince. He stole them. My father loved his work, and the prince stole his happiness."

Sadie translated for her mother. Then she said, "Don't worry, Petra. I'm sure I can find a job for you. The castle employs hundreds of people, and the head housekeeper is constantly looking for someone to do one job or another. They think well of me there. I'll introduce you to the housekeeper."

Then Damara asked something. Sadie said, "My mother says

that you will be risking your life to find your father's eyes. She wonders if your father would not prefer blindness."

"My father has done everything for me. Now it is my turn to do something for him."

After Damara listened to Sadie she frowned. Then, with the slowness of someone choosing her words carefully, she said that she understood how Petra felt, but that she could not believe her father would agree.

"Why not?" Petra replied. "Neel could get hanged for picking pockets, but you let him do it to bring in money. Why is this any different?"

Neel scratched his head. "Uh, Sadie, maybe you better not put that bit into Romany."

Sadie looked at Petra, who said, "Tell her." Sadie shrugged and did.

Damara's black eyes snapped and she spoke fiercely, glaring at Neel.

"She says that a green fairy must have sucked Neel's brains out of his ear when he was a baby, because she certainly didn't raise him to be so stupid." Neel rolled his eyes. "Come on, Neel. She's right. You may think stealing is a game, but—"

"I don't! We need the money! Don't tell me we don't need the money!"

Sadie started to say something but Damara cut into the conversation, this time in a gentler voice. Her children fell silent. Sadie translated, "Ma says that she knows Neel is trying to help. And there's nothing she can do to stop him."

"Darn right," he muttered.

"She has always had confidence that he wouldn't be caught. His ghost fingers make that impossible. Or, at least, we thought it was impossible. But she points out that you, Petra, don't have the Gift of Danior's Fingers. How can you hope to succeed?"

Petra felt the glow of a sudden idea. "What if Neel were to help me? If the prince doesn't value my father's eyes, he'll keep them someplace where they'd be easy to steal, and I could do that on my own. But he wouldn't have gone through the trouble of taking them if he didn't think they were special, so he probably keeps them someplace hard to break into. If that's the case, then I'm sure he locks them up with other valuable things. If Neel helped me, he could take some of those things and sell them. Then you would have enough money to buy your horses."

Her proposal was met with silence. Astrophil stared with incredulous green eyes. Sadie crossed her arms. "I'm not translating that."

"If you won't, I will!" Neel began to speak excitedly to his mother in Romany. She raised her eyes to the ceiling as if asking it for help. She shouted something that Petra was willing to bet anything meant "Even if I was in my grave I'd rise out of it to tell you no, never, not in a million years!" Or something to that effect. Damara pounded her first against the cloth-covered floor. Their voices grew louder and louder. Finally Sadie shouted, "*Dosta!*"

Damara exhaled one long breath. When she spoke, her voice was calmer but strong.

Sadie said, "My mother says that if you want to risk your neck, Petra, that's your business. She respects your decision if not your sense of self-preservation. But her son will not take part in your plan. She says you're welcome to stay here for the midday meal, and to return anytime you wish. But you will no longer be welcome if you try to drag Neel into your plan." She glared at her brother. "And I, for one, agree."

"And *I*, for one—" Neel stopped. He shrugged. "Well, I can't argue against the both of you, can I?"

Sadie looked relieved but a little suspicious. "All right, then. Let's eat."

• • •

AT LUNCH, Petra found herself the center of attention. Emil and a few others gave her disgusted looks, but most of the Lovari were kindly curious. Ethelenda, the woman who had been roasting the meat when they arrived, gave Petra a thick slice.

One of the little girls pointed to Petra and asked Neel a question, wrinkling her nose. He laughed. "She wants to know why your clothes are so ugly."

"Are they?"

"Well, brown and brown aren't exactly the liveliest colors. Makes me think of pinecones. Burned porridge. Rags after scrubbing down a muddy wagon. And horse droppings."

"I like pinecones," Petra said defensively.

Ethelenda offered to pierce her ears. "Um, no thanks," Petra said.

"You might actually want to dress more like a girl," Sadie said. Coming from Lucie, this advice always made Petra grit her teeth, but she listened to Sadie. "I can see why you wanted to walk around Prague in trousers. No one thinks twice about a boy being alone in the streets. But there's no point trying to convince people at the castle that you're a boy. In fact, I'd advise against it. The job that the housekeeper is always looking to fill only goes to boys, and you don't want it."

"What is it?"

"Cleaning out the privies."

"Oh. I see. Maybe skirts aren't so bad after all." Petra sighed. "So much for my short-lived disguise."

"It didn't work that well anyway," said Neel.

After lunch, a young man set up a wooden board one hundred paces away from the campfire. The target was a painted red circle the size of a melon, with a walnut-sized black dot marking its center. Damara slipped a dagger from her tall boot and was the first to throw, thwacking the blade's point into where the black spot met the red circle's border. Everyone clapped. Then the young people began taking their turns. Many of them missed the board entirely (everyone groaned) or just hit the plain wood. Two of them threw the blade respectably into the red. A girl complained that she couldn't even see the black spot at this distance. At that, Emil stood up and said he would show them how this game was done. With the grace of a snake rearing its head to bite, Emil leaned back and then threw, the shiny blade spinning from his fingers. He scored a direct hit on the black. Someone whistled admiringly. One woman shook her hand as if she had touched something hot. Emil grinned. Sadie rolled her eyes.

Then Emil said something to Petra that she didn't understand. His voice was friendly, but he smirked.

Neel said, "Do you want to throw?"

Now, Petra had only ever used knives for chopping vegetables, cutting meat, carving bits of wood into horses, and, most recently, cutting her hair. So she didn't have high hopes for her chances at hitting a target at one hundred paces. But Emil's attitude irritated her. If she refused, he would be pleased. If she missed, he would be pleased. If she managed to at least hit the board, she could walk away from the Lovari with her pride. She said she would give the dagger game a try.

"Ever done this before?" Neel asked.

"No."

"Let me show you a couple things." He pulled out his knife. "Now, if you start out like *this*," he said and cocked his hand, "you're liable to throw it so that the handle hits the board, not the blade. Watch." He threw, and the knife clattered against the wood and fell. The group made hooting calls.

Neel retorted in Romany, explaining (Petra assumed) that he had meant to do that. The onlookers laughed, shaking their heads in disbelief. They flapped their hands at him. He shrugged and seemed to say that they could believe what they wanted. He went to pick up the fallen knife and walked back to the campfire. The dagger floated below his hand. He was carrying it by the blade with Danior's Fingers. "Now, *I* can hold it like *this*." The knife lifted, hovering about a foot above his hand, the iron tip pointing at the board. Neel threw the dagger. It sang in the air and thwacked straight into the black.

The Roma were not nearly as impressed as Petra was. They had seen this many times before. One of Emil's friends said that Neel had used an unfair advantage.

"Unfair!" Neel muttered to Petra. "Even if you got the ghosts, you still got to learn how to use them. Danior did. It's not like I don't practice to be able to do that." Huffily, he fetched the knife for a third throw.

"You should hold it like *this*." He gripped the knife normally and tilted his wrist. He glanced at Petra to see if she could tell the difference between how he was holding it now and how he had held it the first time. To her surprise, she could. She nodded. He threw, and the knife went into the red.

Now it was her turn. When she held the knife, she was curious to find that it felt very natural. She seemed to sense the knife in her mind, like a tiny needle that pricked gently. She knew how she should hold her fingers, and how to angle her arm, her wrist, and the metal blade. It seemed as simple as adding grain to a scale until you could see the needle flicker to the exact weight you wanted. Petra squinted. The black center was about as big as a freckle. But when she threw, she knew the blade would hit the black. And it did.

Neel whistled and clapped Petra hard on the back. The rest of the Lovari had different ways of responding. Everyone looked at least a little taken aback. Sadie and a few others applauded, and many began speaking among themselves. Petra heard one word repeated: *petali*.

"What's *petali*?" she asked Neel.

"It means 'lucky.' They're saying you've got beginner's luck."

"Really?" Petra replied archly, and walked to pluck the steel dagger from the board. She liked this game. This time she didn't take so long finding the right position for the throw. She confidently let the blade spin from her fingers. She hit the black mark again.

She turned to Neel with a grin. "My family has always had a way with metal."

A COUPLE OF HOURS LATER, Petra said she had to go back to her inn. She and Sadie agreed to meet in the morning at eight o'clock in the castle stables. Petra shouldered her pack. "I'll walk you home," Neel said.

They set out through the trees together, heading for the center of town. They talked the whole way. Petra told him about the differences between Okno and Prague. She described her family and Tomik. Neel's voice painted vibrant images of the different places he had lived in, like Spain, Portugal, Hungary, and North Africa.

Once they crossed Karlov Bridge into the older part of town, Petra thought they would retrace their steps back to the Shorn Lamb and the market, but Neel led her in a different direction. "I want to show you something."

He brought her to a square that was flanked by soaring towers that prickled with spires. In the center of the square, people were massed around a tall, slender building with a pointed roof. They seemed to be waiting for something. Petra could see only the back of the building, but she guessed what it was even before Neel shouted, "Hurry up! It's almost time for the hour to strike!" They ran into the crowd and jostled for a good view.

Petra gazed in awe. The clock was even more beautiful than

she had imagined. As her father said, the clock's face showed a brassica field rippling in the breeze. Golden Roman numerals ringed the dial. Signs of the zodiac, also in gold, flashed in a constant circle as a flat, blue plate made from lapis lazuli spun below the face. Tiny green copper dragons peered down from the pointed roof above the clock's face. Their twisted tails were streaked with gold.

Then the silver minute hand and the gold hour hand reached the number five together. Jets of water sprang up in the air on either side of the clock, in the form of dripping lilies of the valley. Small children splashed in the water below. Melodious chimes rang. Above the clock's face, blue double doors folded open. Small statues appeared in one door. They turned to face the audience. Then they disappeared behind the second door. It was a parade of good and evil. First came the devil, then an angel, then a miser clinking his money bag, then a woman scattering brassica seeds, then Death as a skeleton. Last came Life, a young girl who looked like Petra. She slipped behind the second door. The blue doors shut. The wings of the copper dragons fluttered like leaves, and a red rooster statue at the top of the tower crowed.

Petra was speechless. The clock was unbelievably lovely, and must have been very difficult to design.

When they reached the inn's door, Neel said, "You know, I might be seeing you at the castle."

"You might?"

"Yeah. I've been thinking about what Sadie said. I decided it's about time I gave up picking pockets and tried my hand at a real job. Thought I'd see if Tabor could get me work in the stables." He sounded serious, but his yellowy eyes twinkled.

"But, of course, you wouldn't have to *stay* in the stables," Petra said craftily. "I'm sure that once you got a job at the castle, you could probably explore different parts of it pretty freely."

14

Genovese

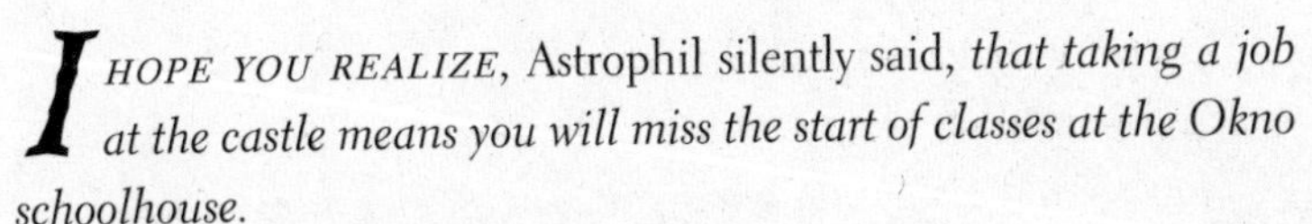

I HOPE YOU REALIZE, Astrophil silently said, *that taking a job at the castle means you will miss the start of classes at the Okno schoolhouse.*

And you can see how sad I am about it, Petra replied. She marched across the inn's common room, sat across the table from Lucie and Pavel, and announced that Aunt Anezka wanted her to stay with her for an entire month. "I'll move my things to her house tomorrow. She'll take me back to Okno."

"Well, if that's what your aunt really wants . . ." Lucie said. "We wouldn't be good company for you anyway. We're so *busy* selling our wares." And Lucie launched into a long complaint that Petra ignored. She ate her dinner quickly. Then she dashed up the stairs to their bedroom.

Petra had been aching to try something the moment she was alone.

She emptied her pockets, placed a copper krona on her palm, and stared. Anticipation thrilled through her. Could she move metal with her mind, like her father?

The krona lay motionless in her hand.

"Float, lazybones," she ordered.

The krona did not budge.

After a few minutes of staring at the stubborn coin, Petra placed it in her purse and sighed. Disappointment warred with a sneaking sense of relief. In the midst of everything else—a new city, a new ally, and a dangerous plan—she wasn't sure she was ready to use the more extravagant skills of her father's magic. She was not sure what using them might mean—about who she was.

"You are young, Petra," Astrophil spoke out loud. "Do not expect everything to come at once."

"It's just . . . I spent all these years thinking that I didn't care whether I had any magic or not. I never expected that I would actually have it."

"I never doubted you would."

"And now I don't know what I'm supposed to do about it."

"You should always do what you can. And I am not speaking about magic."

Petra pulled the notebook from her pack. After looking at it for an hour, she could make neither head nor tail of it. The sketches were intriguing, but they mostly showed either things Petra had already seen (like the clock's statues and water fountains) or things whose importance she didn't understand. Petra paused when she saw her own face, and ran a finger along the edge of her penciled features. She remembered the statue of Life trailing behind Greed and Death. But most of the sketches seemed to have little to do with the Staro Clock. Petra saw spring flowers (like crocuses) and winter berries (like holly and mistletoe). There was a drawing of their home in Okno, a thin sword, a ship that had gears that turned paddles in the water, a house that stood on chicken feet like the home of the fairy tale witch Baba Yaga, a human heart that seemed split into segments, and a lizard with the face of a man.

Some of the drawings looked like blueprints of the clock. They seemed fairly straightforward. Petra didn't notice anything particularly unusual about the measurements for the dials and the face. But what completely baffled her were lines and lines of equations. Petra asked, helplessly, "Do *you* understand it, Astro?"

The spider gave her a mournful look. "I studied the equations during the ride to Prague. But there are no explanations for any of the symbols. How can I figure out an equation if I do not even know what the symbols stand for?"

Petra heard Lucie's and Pavel's footsteps on the stairs. She shut the book and sat on the pallet. "Fat lot of good that did." She stretched out and yelped as the first bedbug bit her. "Astrophil, why don't you pretend to be a real spider and eat insects?"

"What an unpleasant idea," he said serenely. He curled into a little tin ball on the pillow by Petra's head and fell asleep for the second time in his life.

THE HOUSEKEEPER of Salamander Castle, Harold Listek, was a nervous man with watery eyes. Petra stood before the seated man, trying to smooth the wrinkles of her skirt.

Master Listek gave Petra a confused glance and turned to Sadie. "Well, what is it?"

"Excuse me?"

"Boy or girl?" He looked like someone who thought a trick was being played on him.

"A girl, sir. Her name is—"

"Viera," Petra interrupted. Her own name was not terribly common, and she didn't think it was wise to reveal anything of her identity.

"Well, if it's a girl, then what the devil has happened to her hair?" he cried.

"The pox," Petra said promptly. The disease usually made one stark bald, at least until the sickness had run its course and the hair had time to grow back. Petra imagined Neel completely bald and tried not to laugh.

But Master Listek caught her. "The pox is no laughing matter, girl! Why, anybody would think from the look on your face that pox was your favorite treat! Like kolachki! Not at all, not at all. It can make your skin look like a cheese grater. I could tell you a few tales about court beauties laid low by a bout of the pox. Marriage negotiations wrecked. Reputations ruined. Of course, the pox can leave just a few scars, and one can live with that. Indeed. But how miraculous that you seem to have escaped the worst fate of the pox. Why, your skin is quite smooth." He peered at her as if she were a horse he might buy. "I suppose that is a sign of good health, isn't it? And good health—"

"Yes, sir," Sadie gently interrupted. "She is a healthy, strong girl. I think she would be well suited to working with me."

"Out of the question, my dear, out of the very question! Why, a chambermaid is often *seen*. And what with her *hair*—"

Hair seems to cause humans quite a lot of problems, Astrophil told Petra. *I am glad I do not have any*.

"Perhaps a position in the kitchens?" Sadie pressed. "There she would have to cover her head with a cap anyway."

"Hmm. Hmm." Master Listek's finger quivered against his lips. "Yes. Yes. I suppose that would do. Mistress Hild can always use another hand. Now, Sadie, see to it that this girl gets her uniform and makes it to the kitchen without falling into the dungeons or getting lost in a closet, will you? Why, the last person we hired somehow got trapped in a suit of armor and we only found her skeleton!" He slapped his knee and laughed. "That's a joke," he wheezed. "A joke!"

Sadie smiled creakily but Petra didn't even bother.

"Thank you, sir." Sadie began to lead Petra away.

"And the best way to stave off the pox is worms, I say, worms. You have to dry and powder them, mix a little bit in your tea before bedtime. I never got the pox, I'm glad to say, and it's all due to the benefacting powers of worms—"

The door shut behind them.

"If I'm going to be working in the kitchen, I can always prepare a cup of bedtime tea for you, Sadie," Petra said wickedly.

Sadie grimaced. "No, thanks."

She led Petra down a dark hall. Petra didn't feel as if she were in a castle. Rather, it seemed as if she were in a labyrinthine cellar with many doors. After she had met Sadie at the stables, the young woman had led her straight to the servants' entrance, which was small and low. From that point on, Petra had seen only one underground room after another. Even Master Listek's office, though it was decorated with a sad red rug and a few unmemorable knickknacks, was disappointing. Petra had hoped to find more grandeur in the castle, especially after everything her father had told her. But she supposed that the prince didn't put much energy into beautifying the servants' quarters.

If she was looking for grandeur, she didn't find it in the vestiary, where Sadie helped her into a gray-blue dress that was her size, with an apron to match. The walls were lined with shelves of the gray-blue clothes. Imagine that every dress was one rainy day. The vestiary housed years of them. Sadie helped Petra tuck her sleek hair under the cap and said, "Take good care of your clothes. They are part of your wages."

"What?" Petra objected. "Couldn't they pay me with fur-lined boots? Or hot, saffron-scented baths? Or pastries?"

"Once a week you're allowed to have a bath."

"A hot one?"

"Er . . . it's lukewarm. Sort of. After all the older girls—like me—have their turn in it," Sadie said somewhat apologetically.

Petra groaned. She turned to the spider and pointed at her cap. "Well, get in."

"Surely not," said Astrophil.

"Where else are you going to hide?"

Astrophil crawled inside her cap and lay flattened against her head. "I am cramped," he complained in a muffled voice.

Sadie led her down yet another dark hallway that looked almost completely identical to the last dark hallway. But this one had a large door at the end of it. Rattles, bangs, and various steamy smells came from the door.

"There you go, Petra. I'll see you tonight. Enjoy your first day in the kitchen." Sadie smiled. "And try not to throw any knives."

The kitchen was a flurry of activity. Men and women were shaking pans over a brick oven fueled by wood-burning fires below. Several pots large enough to take a bath in hung in the fireplaces. Petra felt sweat spring immediately to her forehead. The other workers in the kitchen did not seem to notice the sweat dripping down their faces as they scurried around a large wooden table that took up nearly the entire room and was loaded with meat, vegetables, and cheese.

Petra asked a girl if she could speak with Mistress Hild. She was led toward a broad woman with a meat cleaver in her hand. Mistress Hild's face looked permanently irritated. Wrinkles fanned out from her small mouth. When the servant girl introduced Petra as the new kitchen maid, Petra uneasily noticed that Mistress Hild's right arm was more muscular than her left, the result of hours of chopping. When the woman set down the cleaver, Petra relaxed.

Mistress Hild placed damp hands on Petra's shoulders and pushed her toward one end of the table, where there was a mountain of dirty onions. Petra stumbled. One of the kitchen boys snickered.

"Peel them," commanded Mistress Hild.

"All of them? Alone?"

"Of course, you stupid girl. Everyone else is busy. Tonight there will be a great feast for thirty people, including ambassadors from Italy, England, and the Ottoman Empire."

Petra looked longingly at the other servants, who were stuffing small quails, chopping celery, grating cheese, and mincing meat. One lucky woman was blending butter, eggs, sugar, and a dark spice. Several of the kitchen workers gave her smug looks, glad to have escaped the worst task of all. Petra searched Mistress Hild's face for some trace of pity. She found none. "Where's a knife?"

"You will peel them with your fingers only. When you are done, you may have a knife to chop them."

Petra looked with despair at the huge mound of yellow-brown balls. "But what are they all *for*?" She couldn't imagine what dish required so many onions.

"Genovese."

"Jeno-*what*?"

"Jen-oh-vay-zay." She pronounced it slowly, like she was talking to someone who had been dropped on her head as a baby. "Genovese is made with onions and meat. It's a dish from Italy. You *have* heard of Italy, haven't you?"

A snicker came from a scrawny girl.

Petra shot a dangerous look in her direction, then replied, "Most of Italy's wealth comes from taxing ships that come into its ports. It often gets attacked by pirates." She paused, and Astrophil silently helped her. "Italy is composed of city-states. It is divided into several different regions, each run by a duke." Petra became aware that the noises of chopping and scraping had stopped. Everyone in the kitchen was staring. "Italy—"

"Enough." Mistress Hild pushed her into a chair and handed her an onion. "Peel."

When she had walked away, a freckle-faced girl leaned toward her and whispered sympathetically, "At least you get to sit down."

After a couple hours of peeling, Petra was covered with papery onion skins. Her fingers were black with dirt. The table now held countless bald onions. Mistress Hild passed by. She handed Petra a knife and an enormous pot. "Chop," she said.

Petra chopped. She cut the onions quickly and with a grace that was noticed by some of the girls around her. But Petra did not see their admiration, because tears leaked out of her eyes from the tang of the onions. She sniffed to ease the burn in her nostrils and wondered if the prison guards ever used this form of torture on the unfortunate people under their lock and key. She tossed the chopped onions into the pot.

She split open one onion and saw, instead of white rings, a pool of black, reeking goo. Its smell hit her like a slap in the face. Petra paused, wrinkling her nose. Then she deliberately (and naughtily) swept the bad onion into the pot.

Genovese, she discovered, must cook for many hours. After Petra finally finished her task, Mistress Hild set the full pot over one of the kitchen's fires, adding a few hunks of meat. Then she steered Petra toward a sink heaped with oily dishes. She tipped a kettleful of boiling water into the sink. "Wash," she said.

Petra washed. To say she was bored would be an understatement. But she was at least somewhat entertained by Astrophil's continued report on the details of Italy, and by imagining what would happen to Mistress Hild once the Italian ambassador tasted her Genovese.

But Petra was denied the pleasure of seeing Mistress Hild fired, or demoted to Dishwasher-in-Chief or Chamber Pot Scrubber Supreme. Mistress Hild passed by the bubbling pot and dipped in a wooden spoon. She slurped a spoonful. Gagging, she spat into the fire and grabbed a pitcher of water. She gulped at it, and water spilled over her stained apron. She coughed and spat again. Then she whirled around and saw the woman who had been in charge of selecting and cutting the meat. Mistress Hild whacked the woman's arm with the wooden spoon. The woman howled. "It ain't me, mistress! That meat was fresh, I tell you!"

"It was her!" The scrawny girl pointed a long finger at Petra. "She popped a black onion in the pot! I saw her do it!"

What is happening? Astrophil lifted the edge of Petra's cap and peeked out.

Mistress Hild faced Petra, the wooden spoon still in her fist.

Oh my, said Astrophil. *I think you are about to be fired.*

Petra grabbed a large glass of hot, dirty water and faced the cook. *Not without a fight.*

But Mistress Hild's chief assistant crossed the room and began to whisper in the cook's ear, darting her eyes in Petra's direction. As she spoke, the cook's mouth grew into a little smile. And this Petra decidedly did not like.

"You," Mistress Hild pronounced, "are going to the Dye Works."

15

In the Dye Works

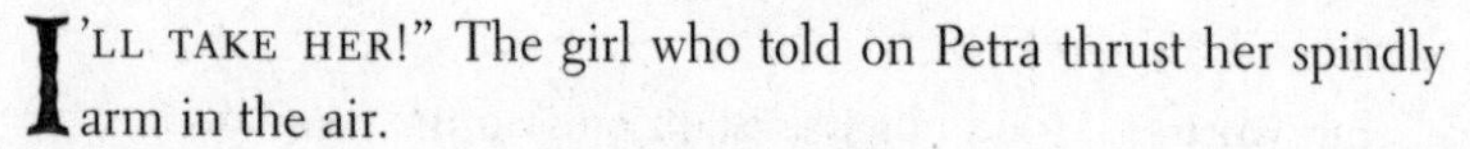

I'LL TAKE HER!" The girl who told on Petra thrust her spindly arm in the air.

"Me! Me!" cried a boy with pig grease on his fingers.

Several of the servants clamored for the right to take Petra to the Dye Works, whatever that was. Petra was wondering about the source of her newfound popularity when Mistress Hild's response clarified things.

"You all just want to get out of work," the woman sneered.

"I've finished my task," the freckled girl said timidly. The cream she had been ordered to whip was thickened into white, pillowy mounds.

Mistress Hild nodded. She scribbled a note, passed it to the girl, and jerked her head toward the door. Petra reluctantly set down the glass of oily water. She followed her guide out the door. Astrophil sighed in relief. *At the risk of sounding disloyal, I think a fight between you and Mistress Hild would have ended one way: with her turning you into mincemeat and serving you for supper.*

So long as mincemeat doesn't involve onions, I'd say that there are worse fates.

Once they were in the hallway, Petra sized up her companion.

The girl's greenish eyes and dappled skin made her look like a woodland creature. Her head was lowered, her eyes focused on her small feet. She seemed a little lacking in vim and vigor, but Petra was very glad to have escaped the company of Mistress Hild and her sidekick, Miss Toothpick Arms. "I'm Viera," she said. "What's your name?"

"Susana." Her country accent, like Petra's, was as thick as tree syrup. "You're from the hills, aren't you?"

"I'm from Okno."

Susana stopped looking at her feet and gazed at Petra with delight. "Really? I've always wanted to go to Okno. It's supposed to be so lovely. I'm from Morado, but I guess you've never heard of my village."

"Of course I have." Morado was not far from Okno. Petra had only ever heard of Morado as a town where you would never want to stay longer than the time it takes to ride through it. But she thought that saying so would hardly be polite.

My arm is getting tired.

A little corner of Petra's cap was still sticking up in the air, propped up by one of Astrophil's tin legs.

I cannot move. The spider poked Petra's head.

"Ow!"

"What?" Susana looked at Petra, confused.

"Nothing."

Being in your cap is boring. Let me out. If you will not be working in the kitchen any longer, you do not have to wear this ridiculous headgear.

Instructing the spider to crawl to the side of her head facing away from Susana, Petra pulled off the cap and shook her sweaty hair free. Astrophil happily took up his post on Petra's ear.

They walked up a flight of stairs. Guards waved them past when

Susana presented Mistress Hild's letter. Petra noticed that the air had grown fresher, and they even passed a window showing a cloudy sky. They were now aboveground. "Am I being promoted?" she asked cheerfully.

Susana gave her an apologetic look. "I'm afraid you're not going to like where you're going."

"Where am I going?"

"The Dye Works."

"I know that. But what's the Dye Works?"

"It's in the Thinkers' Wing."

"The wing? Are we going to visit a bird?" Perhaps Mistress Hild planned on having her fed to an enormous goose with a philosophical mind and a fatty liver.

"The Thinkers' Wing is a section of the second floor. It's a series of laboratories where the prince's magicians . . . experiment." Susana began to walk more slowly. "The Dye Works is where the castle produces all the colors it uses for cloth, hair, wood, and even stone. The woman who runs it has skin that oozes acid, and if she touches you . . ." Susana shuddered. "She's got a terrible temper and is always looking for a new assistant because she fires every one she gets in a matter of hours. She and Mistress Hild *hate* each other. We're told to spit in the sorceress's food. I guess Mistress Hild figures you'll either get burned by acid, drive the Dye Works witch crazy, or get fired quicker than you can blink. Or all three."

They turned a corner. The corridor presented many doors that echoed down the hall like two lines of dominoes. They reached a door that would have looked perfectly ordinary except that it had two handles, one made from plain iron and the other painted a vibrant red. "You see?" Susana said, pointing to the red handle. "She needs to have her own special doorknob. The iron one would melt under her fingers." She knocked on the door. Silence ensued. She knocked again and they both heard a screech: "Go away!" Susana looked like she heartily regretted volunteering to escort Petra. Petra, however, felt more curious than afraid. She gripped the iron handle and pushed the door open.

The room was like the moon in the middle of the month. It had a domed ceiling and was split into two halves, one sharply bright and the other as dark as a cave. A black velvet curtain separated the two sides almost entirely. It was not quite drawn, and as Petra squinted against the sunshine pouring in from skylights cut into one half of the ceiling, she thought she detected some movement in the shadows behind the curtain.

Susana gasped when a gray head popped through the opening in the curtain. Two circles of thick glass took up almost all of the old woman's small, pale face. "What?" the woman howled.

"Mistress—"

"I'm very busy! This is a crucial moment! If my lavender turns to purple you'll pay for it!"

"Yes, but . . . your new assistant is here," Susana explained.

"Ah, excellent! Dash the lavender! I can always make more later." She stepped past the curtain and snapped it shut behind her. "Let's have a look at her." As Petra walked forward, the woman pointed at Susana. "You! Go find something else to do! Shoo! Get out of my laboratory!"

Susana gave Petra a look that said "Sorry, but what can I do?" and scurried out of the Dye Works.

"Now, now, now. What have we here?" The woman stepped closer to Petra, but kept a distance of two feet between them. "Hands!"

Uncertain, Petra stood still.

"Hands, I say! Hold them out."

Petra lifted her hands and began to extend them toward the snowdrop-white woman.

"Not so close, cellar brat! There. Now flip them over. Ah. Good hands. Very good, I believe." She turned her attention to Petra's face. "Decent color. The nice pink of country life. You've got a healthy look about you."

"So I've been told." Petra thought of Harold Listek's ramblings. "What are you wearing on your face?"

"And the girl's polite, too!" The woman's eyes were two foggy pools behind the glass, but Petra thought she saw an eyebrow quirk. "They are spectacles. Are there no spectacles in your hinterland of a home?"

"What are they for?"

"For? They help me see, obviously. But these are no ordinary spectacles. Come here." She pointed Petra toward a table and tapped a metal pot filled to the brim with liquid. "What color is that dye?"

"Blue."

" 'Blue,' she says! Try again."

"Um, light blue?"

The woman whipped off her glasses and plunked them on the table. "Pick them up." They were heavy. "Now look."

Petra hooked the wire stems over her ears and gazed into the bowl. The liquid was swarming with spots of colors—bits of pink, streaks of white, sprinkles of green, and a nice fat glob of violet.

"You see?" crowed the woman. "There you have the exact proportions of the different colors that go into making that particular shade of blue. You may very well say that the bowl holds light blue dye, but think how many light blues there are! A robin's egg, a spring sky, and an aquamarine are light blue. But what a difference lies between the colors of all three!"

Petra watched the colors surge and mingle like strange fish. "It's amazing."

Perhaps the woman recognized in Petra's voice the true ring of someone who can judge good work and beauty, for she nodded. Petra placed the spectacles back on the table. The woman blinked, her eyelashes fluttering like two small dusty moths. Then she put the spectacles back on, turned to Petra, and paused.

She was looking into Petra's face so intently that the girl felt uncomfortable. But after a few seconds the woman averted her stare and twitched her mouth. As odd as it may seem, Petra felt as if she had passed some exam without even knowing what she was being tested for.

"I suppose they told you all loads of jibber-jabber about how I'm an old banshee who eats servants alive and has burning-acid skin."

If Petra had been intimidated by Susana's reports, she didn't feel an ounce of fear now. Maybe this was because when she had gazed through the woman's spectacles, she felt as if she were at home, as if she were visiting a colleague of her father's. So she said, frankly, "Yes, they did."

"Well, it's all true. Except the part about eating you alive. I promise I shall just fire you in the good old-fashioned way and maybe throw a pot of something at your head while I'm at it. No hard feelings, you understand. That's just the way things will be."

"As long as you don't mind if I throw something back, I can live with that."

"Cheek! Sauce! You're lucky that a touch of my hand could make the skin peel off your face, or I'd box your ears for that."

"So your skin really does ooze acid?" Petra was fascinated.

"What do you think I need an assistant for? Of course, it's not the case that my skin is *always* acidic, or I'd be wearing no clothes and there might not even be a floor beneath us, for that matter. Right now my skin is in a low-acid phase. But sometimes I have acid attacks, and it's difficult to say when they'll come. That's why the wires and frames of my spectacles, certain bowls in this room, a chair behind that curtain, and the doorknob are made of adamantine." She noticed the stunned look on Petra's face. "Oh, I constantly forget how many imbeciles lurk in this benighted pile of rocks they call a castle. Adamantine is—"

"The strongest metal on earth," Petra breathed.

"Why, yes." The woman did not hide her surprise. "But what would you know of it?"

How could you have missed that the doorknob was made of adamantine? Astrophil lectured.

Why are you accusing me? How could you *have missed that? Come on,* Astro, she thought defensively, *the doorknob was covered with enamel paint.* But she did feel a little foolish, for if she had not been so distracted by looking through the spectacles, she would have recognized the dull, dreary color of the stems.

"Adamantine is indestructible," Petra said out loud. "Swords made from it can't be broken or blunted. The metal can't be melted down. It's very difficult to find, and almost impossible to forge, which makes it—"

"Cost more krona than you can shake a stick at. Exactly. And while the prince values my talents, he's not going to foot the bill for every tool and bit of furniture in my laboratory to be made of adamantine. I could pay for it myself, of course, but why should I? Still, you have no idea how maddening, how heartbreaking, it is to achieve the perfect shade of coral orange and have the bowl suddenly melt in your hands. The dye splatters everywhere and is lost, or the acid gets into the dye and it turns black. So that's where you come in. You take my instructions. You be my hands."

"But if the doorknob is made of adamantine, why do you have two? The iron handle is unnecessary, isn't it? Even if you touch the red knob, the adamantine would absorb the acid. Everyone else can use it."

The woman was scandalized. "But it is *my doorknob*! What makes you think I *want* everyone to use it? Do you have any idea how many times a day you swampy servants wash your hands? I'll tell you: none! You'll use the iron one, you will!"

"Yes, Mistress . . ." Petra trailed off. She realized she had no idea what to call her.

"Iris."

"Mistress Iris."

"Just Iris, please. I don't have time for your mincings and suckings-up. Leave that for the court to do."

"Is that your first name or your last?"

"Well, if you must know, my name is Irenka Grisetta December, the Sixth Countess of Krumlov. But that really is an insane amount of syllables to say. You can call me Iris for short."

Krumlov! Astrophil's legs flickered against Petra's ear with excitement. *She is a member of one of the most powerful families in Bohemia! They are cousins of the prince. Krumlov is an enormous, splendid estate of land, and its main city is said to be a miniature Prague. Whatever is she doing here? She should be holding ball dances and scheming to get her nephew on the throne, not working as a maker of dyes.*

Petra knew that some of the most important positions in the castle were held by Academy-trained members of the nobility. But she, like Astrophil, was surprised to find someone of such high rank working like a normal person in a laboratory, adamantine doorknobs or no adamantine doorknobs. *Maybe she likes her job*, Petra suggested.

With the airy ease of someone who has told you her name but finds no need to know yours, Iris ordered Petra to fetch a mortar and pestle and a jar on the topmost shelf near a skylight. The jar teemed with little black insects. Petra brought them to the table.

"We are going to make a brilliant red dye. Crimson. It will be used to dye the velvet sash of the prince himself, so it must be perfect. These"—Iris pointed to the jar of bugs—"are kermes beetles. They have been harvested from evergreen oaks. You are going to crush them."

"But they're not red."

Iris's face looked strained, like she was just managing not to scream. "No," she said through clenched teeth, "they are not. But when you pulverize them alive, their blood *is* red, and a very special red at that. Now, when you tip them from the jar into the mortar, make sure that you grind them up quickly. They are devilishly fast."

And so Petra began her second job at the castle that day with a glad feeling in her heart. You might think that crushing bugs isn't much more enjoyable than chopping onions, and you might be right. But Petra could tell that working for Iris would be, at the very least, anything but boring.

PETRA'S EYES DROOPED as she walked with several other girls toward the women's dormitory. It was a long hall littered with many pallets, on which some people were already sleeping. She scoured the hall for another free bed, hoping to see Sadie or Susana. Eventually she spotted Susana, but she was curled up, sound asleep.

Petra was relieved when Sadie waved and patted the pallet next to her. Petra snuggled under a wool blanket. The pallet wasn't the thickest ever made, but it was fairly clean and comfortable. Someone blew out the candles. As a smoky, waxy smell filled the air, Petra told Sadie about her day in a low whisper. Sadie had spent most of the afternoon preparing bedchambers for the visiting ambassadors, so her own report was not as interesting as Petra's—just filled with the tedium of changing sheets and dusting.

Listening to Sadie's voice coming out of the blackness, Petra was struck by how perfect it was. She spoke Czech as if she had learned it from birth. Petra whispered, "How do you speak Czech so well? Neel has such a funny way of talking."

"He could speak like me if he wanted to," Sadie whispered back. "We're both very good at learning languages. We've lived in so many different countries."

"Were you born here?"

"No, I was born in Spain. When people ask why my eyes and hair are so dark, I tell them that my father was Spanish. And that's true. I say nothing about my mother. They assume that she's Bohemian."

"Was Neel born in Spain, too?"

There was a brief silence. "We think he was born in Bohemia."

"You *think* he was?"

Sadie was quiet, and Petra listened to the rattling snores of a nearby woman. Then came Sadie's hushed answer: "Neel was abandoned as a baby. He was left near our clan's campsite. Nobody wanted to take him at first, especially because he had no token around his neck."

"Token?"

"A string. Or a bit of leather with a ring or a stone on it. Anything, really, that means that a father has acknowledged a child as his. Neel was just wrapped up in a blue blanket, with no clothes or anything else. I was little at the time. I don't remember much about it. But my mother took him in."

"A blue blanket? Is that why his name is Neel? He said that it means 'blue.' "

"Well, yes. It does mean 'blue.' But his full name means some-

thing more like 'a stone that is blue.' 'Indraneel' means 'sapphire.' "
Sadie paused. Then she said, "Petra, don't mention any of this to him. He doesn't like to think about it. Or talk about it. I am his sister. Our mother is our mother. End of story. All right?"

"Yes." Petra sighed. It seemed that people were always telling her things she had to keep to herself. Sometimes it was hard not to feel like a Worry Vial with two legs.

16

Iris's Invention

MORE THAN TWO WEEKS PASSED. Petra hadn't yet had a free moment to even step outside of the castle, and the only sunshine she saw came in through the skylights of the Dye Works.

Her life fell into a steady pattern. She woke up at dawn. She powdered minerals or steeped flowers in water or scraped the insides of imported seashells. Dyes stained her hands with interesting colors. She ate lunch with Iris. She desperately tried to forget how the kitchen workers treated Iris's food. Petra ate dinner with the other servants in their eating hall. Sadie kept her close by, watching over her like an older sister. She taught Petra how to sew money into her skirts for safekeeping. One night Petra took a needle, thread, and Tomik's Marvels into the privy. There she hid the spheres in the hem of her dress, hoping they wouldn't break. Although Petra always hated wearing skirts, she now had to admit that they had their uses.

Many things began to weigh heavily on Petra's mind. Even though the servants were each allotted a small, locked wooden chest for their most valued possessions, she worried about keeping her father's notebook in a place that could easily be searched. And she wondered if Lucie and Pavel had left Prague already. Had her family yet learned that she was somewhere among the thousands of people in the city? She wished she could write a letter telling them that she was safe, but she was unsure how to send it. Anything mailed from the castle was subject to being read, and would be stamped with a salamander-shaped seal that would betray where she was.

What troubled her most, however, was that she was no closer to her goal. She had no idea where the prince kept her father's eyes. She hadn't even seen anything of the castle beyond the servants' quarters and the Thinkers' Wing.

One morning, Petra strolled down the Thinkers' Wing, humming a tune. The doors flanked her like silent soldiers. She idly gripped a doorknob. It rattled but would not turn. Petra stopped humming, because she suddenly recognized the melody on her lips. It was "The Grasshopper," the song she and her father danced to years ago.

A longing for home filled her heart. She tried to ignore it, staring down the Thinkers' Wing.

Surely her father had worked in one of these laboratories.

Petra tried the doors until she found one that was unlocked. She pushed it open and stepped inside. A shuddering wave of power hit her. Astrophil squealed and pinched her ear. She was thrown back into the hallway on her bottom, her teeth clattering. She stood up, dusting herself off. The closed doors looked smug. "I'm not afraid of you," she told them.

Speak for yourself, said Astrophil.

After Petra rattled several more locked doorknobs, one turned in her hand. She stuck a toe inside the room as if testing the waters of a chilly lake. She and Astrophil sighed with relief when nothing happened.

Inside this laboratory was a man with paint-smeared clothes. He was staring at a canvas the size of a wall. When he noticed

Petra's presence, he was friendly, and introduced himself as Kristof, an artist from Poland. But he spoke barely any Czech. Soon he forgot that Petra was in the room, and just resumed staring at the utterly blank canvas. Petra saw him use a brush to dab pink paint on the canvas. The color quickly disappeared, leaving the surface as empty as it was before. Kristof looked pleased, but Petra was confused. She didn't see how an absentminded artist and his absent art would help her quest, so she did not return to Kristof's studio.

Every day she tried the locked doors, but with no further luck. She attempted to take the stairs to the next floor of the castle, but was rudely stopped by guards. As Iris's assistant, Petra had a pass that gave her access to the Thinkers' Wing. But she was not allowed beyond that.

She began to feel that her idea to seek a job at the castle in order to rescue her father's eyes was a mistake. It didn't make her feel better that the one person who said he would help her was nowhere to be seen. Neel was as invisible as if Kristof had painted his portrait. She supposed that Neel, despite what he'd said, had never bothered to get a job in the stables.

There was never a moment's rest when Petra was in the Dye Works, and she was surprised to find that this suited her. Working to meet Iris's demands distracted her from thinking about how her plan was proving to be a failure. And as she slowly learned how to prepare and mix pigments, Petra felt like she was atoning for something: for not trying harder to practice her father's trade. In the Dye Works, she strove to do well. Iris criticized Petra's work, but the girl knew that she was deft at carrying out Iris's commands. Although Iris complained, Petra began to suspect that her words were really praise given in a grouchy tone, such as "You ground that ochre too finely!" Petra could tell the difference between this kind of comment and words expressed with real irritation, such as when Iris grumbled about receiving orders for hair dyes.

"As if I didn't have enough to do! As if my highest priority was keeping Lady Hortensia's hair a sunny yellow! If you ask me, it would be far easier for her to catch an eligible husband if she were to buy a new brain. But no! Everybody has to look as fine as possible for the prince's ball, and they don't care a whit that I am on the brink of an important discovery."

The prince, Iris revealed, would soon turn nineteen. An elaborate celebration would be held in his honor. Her gift to him would be the invention of a new primary color.

"Currently there are only three primary colors: blue, yellow, and red. Every other color is a mix of these three. Except white, which doesn't count as a color."

White is the absence of color, Astrophil informed Petra.

I know that, Petra thought back.

"Imagine," Iris continued, light gleaming on the lenses of her spectacles, "imagine that there was another primary color. It would open a world of possibilities. You can mix red and yellow to get orange. Red and blue make purple. But what would happen if you mixed a new primary color with red? What would you see?"

Petra was less interested in the invention of a new primary color than she was in the birthday celebration. Perhaps while everybody was busy, she would be able to skulk around the castle. "Will the celebration take place here?" she asked. She hoped that the prince would decide to have it in a hunting lodge hundreds of miles away.

"Of course. And you will get to see some of it."

"Really?"

"Oh, yes. Prince Rodolfo is good to his people. He believes that everyone should join in his happiness."

It amazed Petra that a woman as intelligent as Iris could think well of somebody Petra knew to have a black heart. But one day, while grating a madder root, Petra asked the following question: "Do you make Kristof's paints?"

"Kristof!" Iris frowned. "I suppose you mean the Pole down the hall."

"Yes. I met him last week."

"Did you? Well, I would advise you not to keep his company. You are *my* assistant. If anyone is going to get rid of you, it will be me."

Petra didn't understand what she meant by that, but she could tell that Kristof wasn't on Iris's list of favorite people. Though she had a hard time imagining who *would* be on that list, except maybe the prince. "So you don't make his paints."

"I most certainly do not. I told Prince Rodolfo somebody else would have to do *that* disagreeable job." She pursed her lips at Petra's baffled expression. She said testily, "Kristof *makes things disappear.* That is his talent. Of course, it has its limits like anything else. He can only make living things disappear, though I assure you that is quite enough. Let's say he wanted to make *you* disappear. He would need to make a brush that included a strand of your hair, and paint mixed with your blood. Then he would paint your portrait. Since people don't exactly leave their blood lying around, there are only a certain number of poor, foolish people he can paint. Thank heavens."

Petra thought about Kristof, about his unlocked door and sweet manner. She thought about how the prince had tricked her father into thinking he was a friend. If you would like to know how easy it is to overlook evil, to see it for something else, Petra could tell you: it is the easiest thing in the world.

SERVANTS AT SALAMANDER CASTLE were allowed one day off a month. Petra was eagerly looking forward to her first free day when, unexpectedly, it came early. She got a sick day, of sorts. But she was not the one who was ill. Iris had an acid attack.

One morning, Petra pushed open the door to the Dye Works and was greeted with a strange sight. Footprints had melted into the stone floor. The puddlelike holes trailed from the bright side of the room and disappeared into the dark half, where one part of the velvet curtain was burned away.

"Iris?" Petra called. "Are you there? Are you all right?"

"Of course I am!" Iris was hiding behind the remainder of the black curtain—naked, Petra guessed. "I just got upset."

"But you always get upset."

"This is different!" Petra heard the sniff of somebody whose handkerchief had disintegrated. "When I get very, very angry or depressed my skin churns out acid like your grandmother's best cow makes milk."

Petra decided not to mention that she had neither a grandmother nor a cow. She was concerned about Iris, because it probably wasn't so entertaining to be naked and trapped in an adamantine chair behind a curtain. "Well, are you angry or sad?" It didn't seem too difficult to tell the answer to the question, since Petra had heard more than one snotty sniffle. But she thought she would ask.

"I'm *both*!" Iris pounded the arm of her chair. "The moment I give that hedgehog Hortensia her hair dye, what do you think happens? I'll tell you: twenty-six of her closest friends and enemies march in here wanting the same exact color! *Twenty-six!* Do they stop to think that they're going to look like a row of identical, dotty daffodils? No! Why oh *why* does the court become a playground for flirtation between the rich, magicless, and brainless?"

Petra knew the answer as well as Iris did: there was no place else for them to go. When aristocratic children failed the Academy exams, they packed up their fripperies and went straight to Salamander Castle. There they usually tried to make one another miserable, arrange a suitable marriage, amuse themselves with drinking and dancing, or some combination of the above. If Iris's attitude was anything to judge by, the Academy-trained researchers of the Thinkers' Wing had little patience for the young courtiers.

"And I am no closer to inventing a new primary color! It needs to be ready in advance of the celebrations, so that we can use the color to dye the prince's robes. I promised Prince Rodolfo that the color would be ready soon. Why was I so *confident*?" This last word was a wail of shame.

Astrophil was unsympathetic. *What a prima donna. You would think that the entire world revolves around her invention.*

Petra saw his point, but felt sorry for Iris. She understood how easy it is to put so much emotion into a project. "Iris, don't worry. You still have several weeks before the prince's birthday. You have time."

Iris sniffed.

"Can't you just turn your magic off? Go into acid retirement, maybe?"

"Retire!" Iris snorted. "You can't just wish away your magic. Anyway, my gift has its compensations."

"Like what?"

"Well, for example, if I get emotional enough and touch a patch of phosphorus, I can make a green so bright it would make your eyes sing."

"It doesn't seem worth it. What's the point of a magical talent that makes your skin ooze acid every time you get angry or sad?"

Iris chuckled. Slowly, at first. Then she laughed as if Petra had just said something hilarious. "Oh, you little *lamb*!" she wheezed. "Clearly no one has ever attacked *you*. No one has ever done you an ounce of harm in your life. Am I right?" Her laughter died away and was replaced by an earnest voice. "I do hope that I will con-

17

The Menagerie

PETRA PASSED BY her locked wooden chest and then made her way to the stables. She found Neel outside the building, trundling a wheelbarrow full of manure. His expression was as sour as the smell surrounding him.

"What are you doing?" Petra made a face.

"What do you think? The only job I could get was mucking out the stables." He set down the wheelbarrow.

"But I haven't seen you anywhere in the castle. I've been looking for you at dinner."

"Where Sadie would be? My sis? Who's not supposed to know I'm here?" Neel shot Petra a hard, irritable glance.

She bit her lip. Of course Neel wouldn't have been at dinner. Petra felt embarrassed, and this made her belligerent. "Well, Sadie doesn't go into the men's dormitory." Petra's voice rose. "I've been sneaking around the entrance to that room every night, and you're never there."

Neel laughed mirthlessly. "You think the rest of the servants would let *Gypsies* eat with them? Sleep with them? Not on your life. Tabor and I are only good enough to clean up after the horses. Even if I weren't keeping clear of Sadie, I'm not the right color to break bread at a *gadje* table, or sleep on a *gadje* bed. Tabor and I go back home when the working day's over. Come on, don't tell me you're surprised."

This was the second time in one hour that someone had treated Petra as if she didn't understand the way the world worked. Annoyed, she frowned and was about to say something when Neel cut in: "I don't need your pity."

"I wasn't going to give it!" she flared. "You'd probably rather spend the night with your family anyway!"

"Well, yeah! But that's hardly the point, is it?" He shook his head and picked up the wheelbarrow again, walking away from Petra. For a moment, she stood there. Then she spun on her heel and began striding away.

Petra, you are overreacting, said Astrophil.

I am not! I'm tired of getting nowhere. All I do is work day in and day out in the bowels of the castle. And when I'm finally free, I go to see somebody who's supposed to be my friend. And the only thing he does is yell at me!

Are you sure you did not yell at him first?

Petra slowed her pace. But she defended herself. *He was being impossible! He said he would help, and he hasn't even bothered trying to get a message to me. And he's been working here the whole time!*

Exactly. He has been working here the whole time.

Petra stopped in her tracks.

Do you think, the spider continued, *that he would be shoveling horse manure if he did not really want to be part of the plan?*

Petra hated it when Astrophil was right—which was very often. But she turned around and ran to catch up with Neel. The boy glanced at her and looked away. He continued to push the wheelbarrow until they had reached a corner of the grounds reserved for drying manure in the sun to sell later as fertilizer.

"At least it's not hot," Petra ventured. She had been stuck inside the castle for so long that she had not realized that the weather had truly changed. The air was chilly enough to make the tip of her nose cold. A brisk wind blew across the dusty yard. "The stink would be really bad in summer. And the flies."

Neel tipped the horse droppings into a large pile. "So I'm supposed to be grateful, then?"

Maybe you can find a cheerier subject to discuss than manure, Astrophil suggested to Petra.

Petra pulled her father's notebook from under her shirt, where she had tucked it into the waistband of her skirt. "Neel, I want you to do something for me. This is one of the most valuable things I own. It can't be found, but I don't have a good place to keep it. Would you hide it for me, please? There's no one else I can trust." She held out the book.

He wiped his hands on his trousers and took it. He flipped through the pages. "It's just a bunch of signs and drawings."

"It's my father's. It's about the clock. I don't really understand what it all means, but it could be important. I don't think the prince knows it exists, but if he did"—Petra took a deep breath—"he'd probably do just about anything to have it."

Petra knew she was taking a risk. If what her father said was true, if the prince truly didn't know how to use the clock, then the book could indeed be very valuable to him. She couldn't leave it in her locked chest. She was sure that the servants' lockers were regularly searched by the housekeeper. If Harold Listek found the notebook, he might not think it was important. But if he did . . .

Petra hoped Neel would hide it. The tricky thing was, now that Neel knew the book might be important to the prince, he might try to sell it for the price of several horses.

Neel looked at her. She could read the same thought in his tawny eyes. She almost snatched the book out of his hands. He glanced away, peering at the pages again. He lifted a brow. "Huh."

"What?" she snapped. She should never have shown him the book. What was the point of trying to win the trust of someone you cannot trust?

"Your da understands the idea of zero."

"*What?*" She looked over his shoulder to see which pages had caught his interest. They showed strings of equations. *Oh*, those *pages*, she thought. "What's 'zero'? Is that a Romany word?"

"*That* is zero." He pointed to a symbol shaped like the letter O. "You know your numbers, right? One, two, three, four—"

"Yes." She glared.

"Well, zero comes before one."

That had to be wrong. "Nothing comes before one."

"That's kind of the point."

He ruffled his hair and turned a page. Petra balled her fists in frustration.

Astrophil spoke up, addressing Neel. "Are you trying to say that zero operates as a placeholder for calculations? That it represents nothingness?"

Neel nodded. "But the *gadje* don't use it. It's stupid that you don't. You can't do knotty math without it."

"Do you understand what the equations mean?" Astrophil asked.

"No, but I can guess that Petra's da was trying to measure energy, not blocks of wood."

Petra was speechless. It was a good thing Astrophil wanted to do all of the talking.

"How do you know this?" the spider asked Neel.

He shrugged. "Zero comes from the same place as my people. Even if it hadn't, we would have picked it up along the way. It's a neat idea. The best thing about wandering everywhere is that you can choose what you like of a place and take it with you, like almonds off the tree."

"How is it possible that the Roma are interested in complex mathematics and yet your people cannot read?"

"It's not that we *can't*. Why should we read?"

"Well, to pass along information. To record your history."

"Information should be shared by people, not things. These pages are just dead trees." He frowned at the spider. "Any history worth having should be alive."

Petra held up an irritable hand. "Are you two talking philosophy? Because if I wanted to listen to that I would be sitting on a splintery bench in the Okno schoolhouse. Neel, will you hide my father's book or not?"

The boy weighed the book in his hand. Then he put it under his shirt. "Yeah, sure. I'll hang on to it for you." Then he seemed to guess her wish to change the subject. "You seen the menagerie?"

"No. What's that?"

"The prince's animal collection. Come on, Petali." He tugged at her sleeve. They walked across the grounds until they reached a locked door. Neel held his hand a few inches from the keyhole and twisted his fingers. The door clicked, and he pushed it open.

The garden was a paradise of green geometric shapes. There was an elaborate maze and enormous flowers that Petra had never before seen in her life. Some of the blossoms were as large as her head. She was astonished that so many flowers were growing. It was, after all, already October. Butterflies fluttered like scraps of colored paper. A tiny, needle-beaked bird with wings that were a constant blur ducked in and out of the flowers.

"That's a hummingbird," said Neel. "Looks like a flying blue-green jewel, doesn't it? Hummingbirds don't live in Bohemia. And you'd never see all these flowers blooming about in one spot at the same time. Guess the prince had 'em magicked."

He led her to a series of large cages. Monkeys screeched and clambered upside down at the top of one cage, swinging themselves back and forth. In another cage, they saw a bewildering creature with shiny fur, webbed feet, and a duck's bill. "It lays eggs, just like a spider," Astrophil informed them. This just made the animal seem even more bizarre.

They saw a tall, spotted animal with long legs, an impossibly long neck, and two short antlers on its head. It was busy chomping leaves hanging from the trees above.

"Look"—Neel pointed to another cage—"it's an elephant."

The gray creature had huge curved tusks. Its eyes were tiny beads surrounded by a mass of wrinkles. The black eyes fixed on Petra and Neel. Then the animal ignored them. It wrapped its powerful trunk around some leaves, ripped them away, and then stuffed them in its mouth.

"Ain't she pretty?"

Pretty was not the first word that sprang to Petra's mind as she gazed at the animal. But she had to admit that it had a hefty kind of grace. It looked noble. Petra looked at the bars of the elephant's cage with sympathy. She, too, felt trapped.

Petra told Neel everything that had happened since she began working in the Thinkers' Wing. She explained how she had tried to explore other levels of the castle but was stopped by guards. She described Iris and her acid condition. She told him about the prince's birthday. "Someone like him *would* have his birthday on Halloween. Think he'll come to his party dressed as a devil?"

"You're supposed to dress like something you're not, so I wager you a krona he'll come as a normal person." Neel looked thoughtfully at the gray animal. "What you need to do, Pet, is make Iris give you the nod to go anywhere in the castle. She can't be walking pell-mell down every hall, can she? She could have one of those—what do you call 'em—acid attacks. If she's so set on inventing a new color, well, you just tell her that you need to get something for her that's in a different part of the castle. She's some sort of lady, right? She can give you a pass or a seal or something so you can go past the guards. It won't be easy for me to snoop around the place, though I got my ways. The best thing for you to do is figure out where the prince stashes his goods. Then we break in the night of the party."

Neel's plan was good. It was artful. It was downright devious. But it also presented Petra with a challenge. Could she think of a way to contribute to his idea? To match its cleverness? Even as part of her wondered why she needed the respect of a thief, she searched for a way to gain it. A thought struck her. "The castle must be huge. I can't look into every single room and cupboard for my father's eyes. So you know what we need to do? We need to find someone *who feels guilty*."

Neel gave her a confused stare, so she explained what she had in mind.

After he had heard her plan, he nodded. "That'll do. That'll do all right. But you're not going to break into a room alone. There's no point using your boot to crush a snake's tail when my bare foot'll stamp out its head just fine."

She looked at him.

"That is: leave breaking and entering to the experts."

They turned to leave the garden. The iron door swung behind them and locked in place.

A tall man stepped from behind a row of trees several feet away from the cages. He walked out onto the path and stared at the shut door. He recognized the boy: he was one of the Gypsies working in the stables. As for the girl: she looked like every other servant girl in her gray-blue dress, though her hair was shorter than usual. He hadn't had a good view of her face. But something told him that he *should* know who she was.

Whoever she was, she and the Gypsy had no right to be in the garden. When he was watching them from behind the trees, their low-voiced conversation struck him as suspicious. But he hadn't been able to make out what they were saying.

He approached the cage. *What were they talking about?* he asked the elephant.

Well, I suppose I could tell you. The gray beast munched its leaves and swung its trunk up to snare another mouthful. *But I don't think I will.*

Jarek sighed with exasperation. Elephants are such difficult creatures.

18

The Reader and Rodolfinium

PETRA AND IRIS were behind the black curtain, working in almost total darkness. This was where they handled light-sensitive materials or conducted experiments with colors that you can see only in the dark. Shelves were stacked with bottles of delicate dyes. Some of them glowed. On the other side of the table where Petra and Iris worked, their backs to the curtain, was a door. Once, Petra had tried to open it and Iris snapped, "Who magically transformed you into *me*, that you think you can sashay your way anywhere you please in *my* laboratory?"

The Countess of Krumlov was now seated in her adamantine chair, watching Petra mix powders and set flames under various brass bowls.

Petra said casually, as if she were just making conversation, "I noticed that we don't have any heliodor on the shelves."

"What the devil would we do with heliodor?"

Petra's father worked mainly with silver, copper, tin, iron, and sometimes gold. These are most commonly thought of as kinds of metals, and indeed they are. But they are also part of a vast system of minerals that include jewels and semiprecious stones, like amethysts, jade, diamonds, and other kinds of crystal and rock. Minerals can be decorative, or they can be made into useful things, even dangerous things. Arsenic, for example, is a mineral as well as a poison. Mikal Krono used to quiz his daughter about the many different kinds of minerals, not just common metals. Petra decided to put this knowledge to good use.

"Well," she said offhandedly, stirring a maroon mixture, "I've heard that heliodor can make liquids sparkle if added in the right way."

Iris was silent.

"We don't have a lot of minerals on hand," Petra continued. "I haven't seen any jordanite in our stores, or hematite, dravite, xenotine—"

"We can't have every chunk of rock that's been scratched out of the earth! Some of these things are quite difficult to come by. And their usefulness is by no means proven."

Petra lit a fire under the bowl of reddish-brown dye. She stirred quietly. Then she said, "Well, if you don't want to try . . ."

"I don't want to waste my time!"

The brick-colored liquid thickened. Iris peered into the bowl and said, "Add some chalk."

Petra tipped in a spoonful of the white powder and said, "We could do some research beforehand, couldn't we? Isn't there a library in the castle?"

Ah, the library! Astrophil sighed dreamily in Petra's mind.

Iris pursed her lips. "Well, I suppose you could fetch me a few books on the properties of minerals. After we're done with this batch of Mayan red."

After they were finished, Petra left the Dye Works and waited outside the closed door. She did not want to arouse Iris's suspicion in any way, so she thought she would make it seem as if a pass to enter another level of the castle was the furthest thing from her mind. After a good few minutes in the dark corridor, she opened the door and complained, "The guards won't let me pass."

"Oh, bother." Iris grabbed a sheet of parchment and a pot of ink. She wrote, "Third Floor Clearance." Then she signed it and stamped it with the Krumlov seal. A design of a white ermine now marked the paper.

"Will the library let me take books out?"

"Bother!" Iris scribbled a postscript.

Petra strolled toward the door with the note, as if she were not interested in the slightest in going to the library.

"Well, hurry along, won't you? You're not made of molasses!" Iris called as Petra shut the door behind her.

THINGS WERE VERY DIFFERENT on the third floor. The hallway ceiling was golden pink and the blue carpet was plush. It took Petra a moment to realize that the carpet was rippling under her feet in gentle waves. The wallpaper on either side seemed plain blue, but as Petra walked farther she could see a many-sailed ship floating off to her right. She heard a gull screech. She stroked the marble that bordered the doors. The stone was riddled with holes. Some of them were tiny bubbles. Others were deep enough for Petra's finger to wiggle inside.

That is travertine marble, Astrophil informed her. *The fissures were made by water.*

Many of the doors that appeared in the stretch of sky-colored wallpaper were shut, but as Petra passed she peered into rooms where the doors stood ajar. She saw a salon with long, silk-colored divans. She gazed into an immense ballroom with cathedral windows. Many servants fluttered around the ballroom, and several gray-blue men and women were crouched on its wooden floor, polishing it until it gleamed.

Soon she reached a large double door made from oak. The word *Bibliotheca* was carved above the doors in blocky Gothic letters.

There it is! cried Astrophil. He bounced up and down on her ear.

Calm down, will you?

Across the doors was a large carving, showing an old man sitting in the dirt with a stick in his hand, drawing something. Far behind him, soldiers were crashing into one another with swords and shields. And right behind the man was a muscular soldier with a raised sword.

What's that all about? Petra was curious. The scene had nothing to do with books.

That is Archimedes. He was a Greek scientist and mathematician. See: he is so preoccupied with his idea that he is writing notes in the dirt while the Greeks and Romans war behind him. He was so dedicated to his work that he did not even notice that a Roman had come to kill him. He died for his idea.

Was the scene supposed to be a warning? Or was Archimedes supposed to be some kind of role model? Whatever the case may be, Petra did not like the carving. She pushed open one door. It swung widely.

She stood in a room the size of a large closet. Directly in front of her sat a man in a high-backed, stuffed brocade chair. His desk was short, small, and bare aside from a long bar that read, SIR HUMFREY VITEK, ESQ. The man was heavyset, and about her father's age. He wore a wig, spectacles, and a black robe trimmed with scarlet piping. He hadn't noticed Petra, but was staring into space, his eyes flicking left, then right, then left, then right.

The door Petra had opened began to groan backward. It thudded into place. Sir Humfrey jumped. "What? What?" Then, adjusting his spectacles, he focused on Petra. "Well, miss, who might you be?"

"Viera."

"Well, Miss Viera, I don't mean to be rude . . . but are you quite sure that you mean to be here? You see, I was just reading some exquisite Persian sonnets about a desert flower called the selenrose. I was feeling so restful." He wrung his hands, folded them, and sighed. "If you don't have a library pass I shall have to call the guards, which would disrupt my sense of tranquillity. The rules say I must call the guards in cases like these. But it seems to me to be an unnecessary action to take for such a little thing as yourself."

"I'm looking for the library." She scanned the room, but it was utterly empty. There were no other doors besides the ones she had just stepped through. "Is this it? Where are the books?"

This is most disappointing, said Astrophil, hurt.

"All the books are here, in a sense," replied Sir Humfrey.

Petra glanced again at the blank walls. "Sure. *Right.*"

"They are here." He tapped his forehead. "At least, one copy of everything except books specifically banned by the Lion's Paw to the eyes of anyone but Prince Rodolfo. I have a delightful job, really. I get to greet lovers of literature and history. And when no one comes, I am never lonely. I can read away." His gaze drifted from Petra and he stared off into space as if there were an invisible page before him. Then he looked at Petra again. "But you shan't make me call the guards, I hope? That would be so unpleasant."

"My mistress sent me." Petra held out Iris's letter. "Won't this work as a pass?"

Sir Humfrey's eyes widened when he saw the ermine stamp. "Is this from the Countess of Krumlov?"

Petra nodded.

"Oh, my." He stared at the letter in Petra's hand. He reached out a finger and then drew it back.

Realizing what made him so hesitant, Petra said, "If she had been acidic when she wrote it, the letter would have burned up. There's nothing wrong with the paper."

He looked a little sheepish. "Yes, of course." He took the letter and studied it. "All right, then. Yes, everything seems to be in order." He passed back the paper. "Go on ahead." He waved at the blank wall behind him.

"Sir?"

"Oh, I am *sorry*. I am so absentminded." He shook his head, then leaned across his desk and touched his nameplate.

The back wall vanished.

"Let me know if you need anything," Sir Humfrey whispered. "And remember: keep your voice low, *pianissimo*."

Now, *this* was more like what Mikal Kronos had described. The ceiling was rocky. Silent birds swooped above. Shelves many times taller than Petra flanked either side of the library. A woman approached a nearby shelf and pulled a lever. The stacks silently yawned open, revealing whatever hidden treasure she was seeking. A handful of readers studied at desks lit by the green glow of brassica-fueled lamps.

After consulting a map on the wall of how the books were arranged, Petra went to the natural history section. Using a railed ladder that had a silence spell on it, Petra climbed up to gather a few likely books on minerals and their uses.

Stay under my hair, she sternly ordered Astrophil. *Don't even think about gallivanting all over the library.*

You have become joyless in your time here at the castle. I prefer the old, fun-loving Petra.

She stepped down the ladder and was about to return to the entrance when she realized that someone was watching her.

He was a reader. His robes, like Sir Humfrey's, were black. His brown hair and beard were long, flowing down his back and chest. There was a buzz of energy about him, and he didn't stare at Petra the way humans normally do. A human looks away when he is caught secretly gazing at someone. His brown eyes watched her the way a fox watches anything, waiting to see what the thing moving across its territory will do first.

Petra turned her back on him, unnerved. She walked toward Sir Humfrey, trying to keep her pace steady. When she approached Sir Humfrey's desk, the blank wall appeared behind her, and her shoulders sank with relief.

The librarian noted down the books she was taking. "There you go." He handed the small pile to her.

"There was a man in there . . ." Petra described the reader who had stared at her. "Who is he?"

"Ah, that would be Master John Dee. He's the ambassador from England. A very learned man. He speaks many languages, even dead ones."

Despite her plan, Petra did not feel eager to return to the third floor, if the third floor held Master Dee.

BUT RETURN SHE DID. Luckily, she did not see John Dee again during her third-floor excursions. Unluckily, it did not seem that what she really wanted was on the third floor: bedrooms.

"Well, I could have told you that," Sadie said. "The private chambers of anyone of rank are on the fourth floor. That's where I work."

They were at dinner, talking quietly amid the uproar of hundreds of men, women, boys, and girls. Dana, one of Sadie's friends, had finally turned away from them to tell anyone else who would listen about her latest crush. Petra seized the opportunity to ask Sadie for a favor.

"Can you find out something for me?" Petra asked casually, reaching for the large bowl of stewed cabbage.

Sadie's face grew wary. She lowered her fork. "What?"

"Have you ever heard of something called a Worry Vial?"

When Sadie shook her head, Petra began to explain what the vial was, and what it looked like. "The darker it is, the better. Would you tell me if you see one that looks really purple, and whose room it's in?"

"Petra, you're going to get into so much trouble. Don't you understand that you could get really hurt? You should go back to your village."

"I'm not going to *take* anyone's Worry Vial. I swear." Petra crossed her heart in mock solemnity. "Anyway," she continued lightly, "the worst thing that could possibly happen is that someone will catch me cleaning a room where I don't really belong. Then I'd just say that I'm sick of working for Iris. That's believable. I could claim that I'm hoping to prove myself in a new position as a chambermaid. Maybe I'd get fired, but I won't get sent to prison. Hey, will you pass me the salt?"

Sadie shook her head. "Don't try to pretend that we're not talking about something truly dangerous, Petra. If the Worry Vial works the way you say it does, don't you think that if they catch you playing with some powerful lord's vial, they'll be a tiny bit suspicious?"

Petra shrugged. "As far as anyone knows, Worry Vials are foolproof. And the gentry don't expect people like me to even know that the vial is anything other than a decorative vase. If someone sees me handling a vial, I'll just say I'm dusting it."

"You're going to do it whether I help you or not, aren't you?"

"Yes. But it'd take me a lot longer. I'd have to search dozens of rooms. Of course, I'm more likely to get caught that way. But what else can I do?"

That worked.

A few days later, when they were tucked under their wool blankets in the darkness, Sadie whispered, "Try the captain of the guard's private chambers. Fourth floor, northwest corner. The doorknob is shaped like a boar's head. But it's usually locked. I don't know how you'll get in. And I won't help you do that."

"Is the vial dark purple?"

Sadie paused before replying. "It's black."

"THE POWDERED BERYL does absolutely nothing!" Iris pressed her forehead against her fist. "The dye is still yellow."

The gap of time between now and the birthday celebration was narrowing, and as they worked harder on the production of a new primary color, Iris grew ever more distressed.

"It's not *that* yellow," Petra tried to comfort her.

"I could fill my chamber pot with that dye!"

I think you are going about this in the wrong way, Astrophil commented. *You keep mixing things together in the hope that you are going to produce a color that* cannot *be made by blending other colors. Do you not think that you should look for* one *thing that can produce* one *color?*

Petra repeated Astrophil's suggestion to Iris as if it were her own.

Iris considered this, and murmured, "Rainbows."

"What?"

"A rainbow is one thing that shows us many colors."

"Yes, but we already know what those colors are. There's nothing new about them."

"But sometimes stones seem to have rainbows inside. Like diamonds. A diamond is clear, but if you look closely you can see flashes of rainbow light—red, orange, yellow, green, blue, purple. But what if there's a color that we haven't noticed, hidden among the rest?"

"You want to turn diamonds into dye?" Petra was skeptical.

"Don't be daft! Diamonds are too hard. You can't grind them or melt them down easily. Perhaps a moonstone."

Petra fetched a handful of the clear, translucent jewels and began to melt them down in a bowl held over a green flame fed by brassica oil. The moonstones puddled into a bluish gel.

Try an opal, Astrophil suggested. These milky white stones with sparkles of different colors had a reputation for bad luck. But Petra was not a superstitious sort of girl, so she put an opal to the test.

It flowed into a brown, glistening liquid.

Iris took one look at it and burst into tears. "Nothing ever works for me!" The old woman began to sink into the floor and holes appeared in her clothes, growing wider and wider.

Run, Petra! Astrophil ordered in a panicked voice.

But Petra had noticed that one of Iris's tears had fallen into the bowl. As the acid tear plopped into the melted opal, the color of the liquid in the bowl transformed. Petra had never seen anything like it. "Iris!" she shouted, her eyes flicking from the bowl to the floor, which was dipping into a cavity, causing Petra to slide toward the white and nearly naked woman. "Iris! Look in the bowl!"

To Petra's relief, the woman did. Her tears stopped. Her clothes hung in shreds. The floor beneath her feet was a shallow basin, but it had ceased sinking and spreading.

"There it is!" Iris breathed. "Rodolfinium."

You can imagine that Petra wasn't pleased by Iris's name for the new primary color. She tried to hide her disgust, but she needn't have worried. Iris wouldn't have noticed Petra's expression anyway. She was too enthralled by the new color in the bowl.

Colors tend to stir emotions in the heart. Blue seems peaceful but unreliable. Red makes you feel passionate. Yellow produces a feeling of energy and restlessness. The best way to describe rodolfinium is that when Petra gazed into the bowl, she felt lightheaded.

Iris was joyous, and told Petra to take the rest of the day off. "Go on, then! Scamper!"

Thinking to take advantage of Iris's good mood, Petra asked if she could take a bottle of India ink with her. "I want to write down everything that happened today in my journal."

"Of course you do! A fine idea! Yes, yes, take some ink. Just don't walk off with any opals!" Iris beamed.

But Petra took more than a bottle of ink. You might say that Iris had trained her too thoroughly. Petra's notion of what she needed was all too well informed. As Iris gazed into the bowl of rodolfinium, Petra took the following items in addition to India ink: powdered blue algae, sorrel vinegar, an empty bottle, iron tongs, and her third-floor pass.

19

The Captain's Secrets

THE PAIR OF FOURTH-FLOOR GUARDS stared at the paper. They stared at the tongs holding the paper. Finally, they stared at the girl holding the tongs.

"Huh?" One of them scratched his nose.

"It's my pass."

"Well, give it over, then."

"All right. But you probably should take the tongs, too."

The two men eyed each other. Who was this jumped-up cellar brat? Why was she gripping her pass with a pair of tongs as if it were poisonous? Was she a lunatic, a Thinkers' Wing experiment gone bad?

"What the blazes do we need tongs for?"

"My mistress is Countess Irenka December. She wrote the pass."

The first man scrunched up his face in confusion, but the second muttered something in his ear. The first man winced.

"Fine. Hand over them tongs."

But as the girl tried to pass the tongs, the folded note slipped to the ground.

"Blast!" growled one of the men. "Give 'em here." He snatched the tongs and bent over, trying (and failing miserably) to pick up the pass. His fellow guard smirked.

"There!" On his fourth or fifth try, the guard triumphantly held up the crumpled piece of paper, secure in the tongs' grip. The other guard clapped slowly, sarcastically.

The guard with the letter stopped smiling. "Uh, how do we open it?"

One guard held the letter with the tongs and the other tried to unfold it with his penknife, knocking it to the ground. Swearing loudly and long, neither of them noticed a dark shape slip by and dash down the hall to hide behind an enormous window curtain. The two guards continued to fumble with the pass, growing increasingly irritated.

"Give me them tongs!"

"Why? So you can drop the pass *again*? Give me my penknife back!"

"The girl gave them tongs to *me*, didn't she?"

"Right. And she's such an expert judge of character. Let's nominate her for the Lion's Paw."

In the end, one of them managed to unfold the note by placing an edge of it under his boot and slipping the tongs into the crease, flipping over the first fold. He gripped the pass and held it high, keeping it a good distance from his face. "Fourth Floor Clearance," it read, followed by a postscript saying that the assistant could check out library books. It was signed by Irenka December, Sixth Countess of Krumlov, and it bore a seal showing a white ermine. The guard heaved a long-suffering sigh and the paper wafted in the air. "Go on, then." He handed the tongs and the letter back to the girl, who solemnly accepted them. She walked down the hallway.

Petra was very pleased with herself. She had grown up in a village with busy adults and a long-winded schoolmaster, so she had had many opportunities to practice faking other people's handwriting. But working for Iris gave Petra a new edge in the art of forgery. Petra had learned that sorrel vinegar mixed with salt can make the strongest ink vanish. To produce the right kind of pass, all Petra had to do was apply the vinegary juice to the word "Third" and write the word "Fourth" in its place. The only problem was that sorrel vinegar lightens the color of paper as well as making the ink on it disappear, so a close look can easily reveal that a letter has been tampered with. Remembering Sir Humfrey Vitek's reluctance to touch paper handled by Iris, Petra cooked up a plan that would get her past the fourth-floor guards and provide enough distraction so that Neel could slip past them as well.

Petra walked down the corridor that would take her north. Her feet echoed on the gray, veined marble floor. She tried to stay focused, even though the splendor around her—ancient suits of armor, and round-bellied Chinese vases balanced on pretty tables—begged for her attention. It was also hard to ignore Neel as he followed her up the hallway, dashing from one set of window curtains to the next. They had decided to break into the captain's bedchamber during dinnertime, when he was likely to be away and there would be few people in the halls.

"What about your job?" Petra had asked Neel.

"*Pfft,*" had been Neel's dismissive response. "I give 'em the slip all the time. Easy as breathing."

A valet passed Petra in the hallway, giving her a doubtful look. Neel stayed behind his curtain. The valet shrugged and walked on. Otherwise, the halls stretched emptily before them as they then headed west.

When they reached the chambers at the northwest corner, they spotted a room whose doorknob was a snarling boar's head. Neel put one eye to the keyhole, screwing the other one shut. Then he took a small glass out of his pocket and pressed one end against the door, holding the other end to his ear. Nodding briskly, he moved his fingers over the door and they heard a click.

Checking the hallway to make sure no one was there, Petra slipped in after Neel. She held her breath, hoping that the captain of the guard was happily stuffing food in his mouth someplace far from here.

They shut the door softly. The captain's bedchamber was a suite. They had entered into an empty drawing room. A door to the bedroom was at the opposite end.

"Did Sadie say where he keeps it?" Neel whispered.

"It'll be right by his bed."

"That ain't a very safe spot to keep all your secrets."

"Nobody knows that you can suck the secrets out of Worry Vials. Everyone thinks they're reliable. And you'd better not tell anyone otherwise."

Neel unlocked the bedroom door. "Think of all the krona you could get from blackmailing . . ." His eyes were wide.

"Not now!" She pushed open the door. And there, right on the nightstand, was a fat, black bottle. Petra reached in her pocket for a flask of water. She uncorked the Worry Vial and poured the water in.

"How long do we have to wait?" Neel scooped up a pile of coins on the dressing table.

"*Neel*," she hissed. "Put that back."

"What for? I want to get something out of this, too."

"But the captain will notice that the money's missing."

"So? He'll think one of the servants took it."

"Exactly. One of the servants. Don't you care that one of the servants will get in trouble?"

"Nah. Not really."

"Even if the servant is *your sister*, who cleans this room?"

"Oh. Yeah. Right." He sighed and put the money back on the dresser. "Can't figure why she didn't take it herself."

"Just steal something that the captain won't notice is missing for a while, will you?"

Neel began inspecting the room, pulling open drawers and peeking inside of trunks. "Hate to repeat myself, but how long is this going to take?"

"I don't know." She placed her palm over the Worry Vial's opening and shook the bottle, hoping that agitating the water would make the process go faster.

"It's not like we got time for taking tea and biscuits."

"Agreed," Astrophil spoke up. "Petra, we should get out of here as soon as possible."

"See? The spider thinks so, too."

"All *right*." She poured the treated water back into the flask it came from. She was gratified to see that the water was very dark—not quite black, but it would have to do. The Worry Vial had a sort of grayish color to it now. From her pocket, Petra pulled the bottle of India ink, which she had mixed with the algae earlier that day to make the ink stick to glass. She tipped the black liquid into the vial. Not exactly wanting to walk around the castle with a black hand, she bent down and pulled up her petticoat. She held the beige cloth over the opening of the vial and shook it so that the ink coated the inside of the vial. Letting her stained petticoat fall, she poured the leftover ink back into its original container. She stoppered the Worry Vial. Now it looked almost exactly the way it had when they entered the room.

They hastily exited the captain's chambers. Neel locked the doors as they left. It was not until they were safe in the basement of the castle that Petra handed him the flask of dark water and asked, "So what did you steal?"

"A silver codpiece. He's got a zillion of them." He caught Petra's look. "I'm not going to *keep* it! I'm going sell it. They fetch a fair price on the market. They make a fellow look all manlylike."

Petra, however, had her doubts.

THEY DECIDED they would listen to the captain's worries on their next day off in the woods near the Lovari campsite. Petra had a hard time agreeing to this, eager as she was to hear the contents of the Worry Vial, which Neel had left out to dry in his family's wagon. "The garden seems safe enough," Petra argued. "Why don't we do it there?"

But Neel looked uncomfortable. He said he had been to the menagerie since they had visited it together, and felt that something was wrong. "The elephant was trumpeting away like there was no tomorrow. She was looking right at me, flapping her ears. So I started to back up. And then I swear she nodded at me, like she'd been saying 'Get out' and I finally caught on."

Petra teased him for taking the moods of an elephant so seriously, but Neel insisted that they should not return to the garden.

At the campsite, the small children ran up to Petra and tugged at her skirt for attention. Neel kissed his mother, slipping some money into her skirt pocket. Then he dashed into the family wagon to fetch the vial.

Ethelenda was there, and introduced Petra to an old woman named Drabardi, who looked surprisingly fit for her age. She said something to Petra, which Ethelenda translated. "She offers to tell you your fortune."

Petra felt uncomfortable. Not for the first time, she was glad that she seemed to have inherited her father's gift rather than her mother's. Mind-magic was her least favorite kind. Despite—or maybe because of—the fact that her mother had been able to read the future, the very thought of magic like the Second Sight, scrying, or mind reading made her feel as if something were weighing her down, like the time she got sick and Dita piled blankets on top of her until Petra couldn't move. She could only lie there, breathing and sweating. She tried to think of a polite way to say no to Drabardi. The woman might be a fraud, but even if she wasn't, Petra didn't want to hear what she had to say. As far as Petra could tell, knowing the future had never done anyone a bit of good.

Drabardi laughed and said something. Ethelenda translated in a puzzled voice, "She says you're probably right."

Petra was relieved when Neel emerged from the wagon and gestured for her to follow him. They walked among the pines and slender birch trees, which were shrugging off their pale leaves.

When they were a good distance from the campsite, Neel pulled out the bottle Petra had given him. No liquid remained in it, just dust. Petra tipped the dust into her palm and stirred it with her finger.

Like a ghost, a disembodied voice began to speak. The captain of the guard's voice was low and rasping. "*And we took them to dungeons and let them starve first . . . Then we . . .*"

The voice droned on, telling Petra and Neel of horrible things: torture, murder, large graves, and missing limbs. Petra wanted nothing more than to dash the black dust from her hand and scrub it clean. Nausea and a sense of despair welled up in the back of her throat. Her eyes stung with unshed tears and she wanted to make the voice stop. But she kept her hand still.

"*. . . until they stopped. Tomorrow night we will seize the clockmaker. Fiala Broshek will remove his eyes and put a spell on them. She says the prince wants them for his collection, to lock up in his Cabinet of Wonders . . .*"

Petra flung the dust to the ground. She began scraping earth over it. Neel watched her, his face inscrutable. Petra didn't try to guess his thoughts. She didn't want to. After she had made a small mound over the dust she rubbed her hands with dirt. She sat there, shaken.

Neel stood up first. He turned around, walked a few paces, and stopped. He spat. Then he kept walking.

Petra followed him, but at a distance. She let him disappear into the trees ahead of her. Without having said anything, they understood that they both wanted to be alone.

Petra . . .

She said nothing to the spider. She did not want to listen to any more voices.

You cannot change what happened, he said. *But now you know where Master Kronos's eyes are. And you can do something about that.*

Petra didn't know what she would have said to this, if indeed she would have replied at all. A rustle of leaves interrupted their one-sided conversation. She spun around.

"Well, well, *gadje*, what brings you back to our neck of the woods?"

It was Emil. He looked at ease, one arm slinging a brace of rabbits over his shoulder, the other loosely hanging by his side.

"You speak Czech," she said warily.

"I do. I understand it, too. And from what I understand, what you just planted there"—he nodded back into the trees, which hid the grave of the captain's secrets—"is a sickness. Even now, the ants in that bit of earth are tunneling far away from it. Not a blade of grass will ever grow there. And what I wonder is, who is this girl who brings her poison among my people and buries it in our earth?"

"This land does not belong to you," Petra said.

"I don't care if it doesn't."

Petra started to turn away when Emil trapped her wrist with his free hand. The rabbits still hung nonchalantly over his shoulder. If it weren't for the fact that Petra's hand was seized in a viselike grip, anyone watching this scene would have thought that Emil was completely relaxed. "What I *do* care about," he said, "is Neel. And his mother. And his sister. Now, I may be just an ignorant Gypsy"—he smiled, his teeth shining like a blade against the blackness of his beard—"but I think that you have invited Neel to play with your poison. You are involving him with something. I don't know what it is, but I don't like it."

She twisted in his grip and felt her wrist burn. "Neel's his own person."

"Neel is a child! *You* are a child!" He shook her. "The funny thing is, even children can get people hurt."

"I'm not going to hurt anybody!"

But her next action probably didn't make Emil believe very strongly in what she had just said. She kicked him hard in the shins. Gasping in pain, he loosened his hold on her and she pulled herself away. He started to stumble toward her. She scooped up dirt and flung it in his eyes. Petra ran, leaving him limping, cursing, and rubbing at his face.

She left the Lovari almost immediately after she reached the campsite. She said nothing of her encounter with Emil to Neel, but she didn't want to be around when the man returned. Since Neel would be spending the night with the Lovari and she would have to walk back to the castle alone, she said she wanted to leave before it got dark.

Neel nodded. "Turn up at the stables the morning of the party," he said. "We have to plan."

But as Petra walked up the hill, she decided she would not meet Neel on the day of the birthday celebration. She would search for the Cabinet of Wonders by herself. Not because Emil had frightened her, but because what he had said was right.

20
The Prince's Birthday

PETRA GREETED HALLOWEEN with a jumpy heart. She found it difficult that day to concentrate in the Dye Works, where she and Iris were mixing edible dyes for the kitchen to brighten up the desserts for the feast. Iris wasn't terribly pleased about doing anything that might make Mistress Hild's efforts look good. But overall she was cheerful, for she had personally given the prince his rodolfinium robes several days ago, and had received nothing but praise in return. So when Petra produced a dye that was a sick green instead of peony pink, Iris simply chuckled. "You're too excited, aren't you, poor lamb? You and half the castle! The festivities are already under way, even as we sit in my laboratory. And I should say that you've never seen fireworks, have you?"

"What *are* fireworks, Iris?"

"Oh, you shall see."

Not one of the servants would be set free from his duties until the evening. Throughout the day, Prince Rodolfo and his guests would be in the garden, basking in its artificial warmth and bright flowers. They were being entertained by theatrical performances, as well as acrobatics (Petra heard that a high wire had been rigged fifty feet off the ground) and musical arrangements. They would then sit down to an elaborate fourteen-course dinner. After dessert at midnight, the nobles would return to the garden to see the fireworks, whatever that was. The servants were allowed to watch the procession of the nobles and the fireworks from the castle yard. When the court returned to the castle for a masked ball that would last until dawn, the servants would treat themselves to a delicious meal of roasted pig, with several barrels of ale to share. It was during the masked ball and the servants' dinner that Petra hoped to find the prince's Cabinet of Wonders.

Iris preferred to work rather than attend the performances in the garden. But she would join the court later for dinner, the procession, and the dance.

"Aren't you worried that you'll have an acid attack?" asked Petra.

"I think I shall be too happy for that. Unless, of course"—her expression darkened—"I'm seated next to nincompoops at dinner. Which is highly likely, given that the court holds so many of them. And I'm sure no one will ask me to dance. I'll have to drink punch in a corner and hope that some young lord with pins for brains starts a fight. That would at least keep me from going stark-raving mad with boredom. But, well, there's no help for it." Her face cleared. "I've been ordered to be present," she said proudly. "Prince Rodolfo especially wishes me to see the reaction to his new robes."

Petra felt a twinge of guilt for not meeting Neel that morning, but she told herself that she would feel far worse if he became a secret for the captain of the guard to whisper into his Worry Vial one night. When it came time for the servants to crowd into the courtyard, Petra avoided Sadie, fearing that Neel might be present among the blue-gray sea of people, and that he would seek his sister and her. Petra instead stood next to Susana, who was so overwhelmed with excitement that she grew pale, her freckles standing out like brown stars. Petra let the two of them get shoved around by the older, taller servants, who blocked the girls' view but also hid them from the sight of others.

The courtyard was ablaze with torches. The procession began with the young children of the members of the prince's circle. Dressed like fairies with gossamer wings, they marched solemnly. Their quietness seemed unnatural to Petra. If you put the smallest villagers of Okno into fairy costumes and asked them to parade around town, they would be pure mischief. But these children, David's age and even younger, walked as if they were going to a funeral in inappropriate attire. They had probably been threatened with spankings if they dared embarrass their parents in front of the entire court.

"Ooh," Susana breathed. "Look!"

The courtiers stepped out of the castle and filed toward the garden, where they waited by the door. They shimmered in bright fabrics and jewels, their faces hidden behind masks. Many nobles were dressed like fairy tale characters. Petra spotted Iris disguised as the Snow Queen, and watched Rusalka, the water goblin's daughter, slip past. There was Finist the Falcon, a man-bird who captured a human girl's heart. There walked Koshei the Deathless: wicked, immortal, and a wild horse rider.

After the last of the courtiers had taken his place at the opposite end of the courtyard, trumpets sounded. Prince Rodolfo emerged.

Petra would have to give Neel a krona. The prince did not wear a mask. He was not dressed as anything but himself, but that was enough. His skin was smooth and pale, his face attractively sharp. His lips were unexpectedly full and soft-seeming, like the mouths of the stone angels Petra had seen in Mala Strana. He was slender, and walked loftily. His robes were made of simple silk, without a pleat, tuck, or frill. But their color sent a wave of awe through the servants.

Petra was prepared for the effect of rodolfinium. But there is a difference between seeing the color in a small bowl and seeing it spread over yards of rippling fabric. For the first time in her life, she felt like she might faint. She was not alone in this feeling. Several servants swooned, including Susana. Trying to support the girl and pat her cheek, Petra didn't see the prince's progression to the far end of the courtyard. She looked up again when Prince Rodolfo began to address the crowd.

"My people," he called. "I thank you for sharing the first day of a new year. I am sure that, with your love and support, my nineteenth year will be the happiest I have yet known."

The audience applauded. Prince Rodolfo's gaze swept across the nobles and his servants. As he turned toward Petra's corner, the girl was so startled that she nearly let go of Susana. The eyes that were just about to look into her face were silver. And they were not his own.

Look down! Astrophil commanded.

Petra hurriedly did so, hoping that the prince hadn't noticed her.

But he had. He stared briefly at the downcast face of the servant girl, whose features were a general blur. He was pleased by the way she stared so resolutely at the ground. He could hardly bear it when a servant returned his gaze. But soon he realized that his satisfaction came from another corner that he could not identify right away. Cocking his head as if listening to a distant tune, he grew to understand that the feeling that warmed him at the sight of the girl had something to do with the clockmaker's eyes. They were never wrong. Whenever he wore them, his judgment of what was fine and beautiful was as accurate as a perfectly shot arrow. There must be something extraordinary about this very ordinary girl, though he could not tell what or why.

But now was not the time to consider this. Now was the time to celebrate his fortune and his life.

Petra didn't look up until she heard the iron door clang shut behind the prince and his court. They alone were allowed to watch the fireworks from the blooming garden.

Susana revived and said, feebly, "That was lovely. But it was awful, too, wasn't it?"

Petra didn't have time to reply, because fire suddenly shot into the sky and exploded into a thousand red stars. The crowd collectively gasped and Astrophil trembled on her ear. Susana turned around and ran back to the castle in fear. Volleys of fire burst into the sky above the garden, and rained down over the walls like streaming jewels. Petra gazed into the sky with pleasure, the thunder of the explosions making her body thud with a second heartbeat. Some fireworks spilled their color down in a fiery rain, and others opened into sunflowers. The last one drew an orange salamander, which ran across the sky until it dissolved into glowing embers.

A stunned silence followed. Then whooping cheers filled the courtyard.

Petra was awestruck. She couldn't imagine how the fireworks had been made.

They must have been done with strong magic, Astrophil murmured, still shaking a little.

"Did you like it?" she heard a man ask.

Without looking to see who spoke she said, "Oh yes. It was amazing. It was . . . yes. It was."

"Ah, good. To have produced such an incoherent reaction is a compliment to my work indeed."

As if roused from a dream, Petra frowned. She turned around.

There, standing before her in a green velvet robe, without a mask, was the man from the library, Master John Dee.

"I designed the fireworks, you see."

"You're a magician," she warily guessed.

"I?" He laughed, but his eyes remained keen. "I am a scholar."

"So the fireworks were not made by magic."

"No. They were made from a not very simple mixture of gunpowder and certain minerals. I would tell you which minerals, but I fear that this would lead us to a topic of conversation about which you would have too much to say. And we have far more important matters to discuss. Don't we, Petra Kronos?"

21

The Magician Who Wasn't

MASTER DEE STOOD TO THE SIDE of the open door to his chambers, his hands hidden inside his robes. "Do come in, my dear."

His voice was polite, but Petra had been a servant long enough to recognize an order when she heard one.

She stepped into the room, lit by only one green brassica lamp. Astrophil was perfectly still and silent. She had the impression that he did not dare speak to her in the company of John Dee. She, too, felt uneasy that this foreigner knew her name, had plucked her out of hundreds of servants, and had steered her past the guards onto the fourth floor.

He moved in the shadows. He lit several candles by two velvet chairs. "Would you care to sit down?"

Petra sat. So did he. His robes blended into the chair. Petra couldn't tell where the chair stopped and the man began. He waited for her to speak.

She looked around the room. John Dee was a lover of games. There was a chessboard, an open box with a red felt interior and two sets of dice, and an odd board covered with black and white disks. The only game she could play decently was cards, and even then Tomik often beat her. Still, she decided to try bluffing. In a voice strong with all the confidence that she didn't feel, she said, "What do you want from me? I haven't done anything wrong."

She wasn't sure what effect she hoped for, but amusement wasn't it. As Dee laughed, Petra suspected that he had noticed her eyeing his games (maybe he had, in fact, left them out deliberately) and guessed her feeble attempt at strategy. It was even possible, she thought with dawning fear, that he was able to read her mind. She remembered Astrophil's silence, and realized that this had already occurred to the spider.

"My dear," Dee said, "the question you should be asking is this: 'Do we want the same thing?'"

Petra folded her arms. "Fine. Do we?"

"Look in the box on my writing table."

"Which box?" For there were several, of all sizes and made of different kinds of wood. The man was clearly fascinated by boxes—or, at least, he wanted people who entered his room to believe he was.

"The long, flat one made of mahogany," Dee said.

She paused.

"Mahogany is a red wood, harvested in a tropical land where everyone is born as a twin," he told her.

Petra gave Dee an odd look. Did he know that she had been a twin? She walked toward the escritoire, making sure not to turn her back on him. She selected the box and opened it. Inside was a small oil painting of a woman with red hair piled on her head in elaborate twists. She was wearing a full yellow dress studded with jewels. But as Petra looked more closely, she saw that they were not jewels but dozens of eyes and ears. She slammed the box shut.

"She is the queen of my country," said Dee. "I am Her Majesty's most valued eyes and ears. I suppose you could call me a 'spy,' though I think that word hardly suits my skills. Your prince may think I am here on a purely ambassadorial visit, to amuse him with fireworks and stories about places he has never seen. I hope, however, that he does not think this, for that would belie the intelligence I know he has."

"I don't see what I have to do with anything you're talking about. I'm just a servant girl."

"If you are a servant, then you will obey my commands. You will obey me when I suggest that you do not pretend to be ignorant. It wastes my time and yours."

She was silent.

"Let us play a quick game. It is a game of deduction. If I know who you are, then does it not stand to reason that I know a little more about you? What would Petra Kronos, daughter of Mikal Kronos, be doing miles away from her home in the sleepy village of Okno?"

"How do you know who I am?"

"I have my ways." Dee noted her frustrated expression with a small smile. "Being the daughter of an artisan, you won't blame me for keeping my trade secrets, I'm sure. If you would like to know what they are, why, then, you would have to come work for me."

Petra snorted. She forgot the nervousness she had felt when she first walked into the room. Strangely, the fact that this man knew her identity made her feel free. No matter what she said or did, her fate was now in John Dee's hands. There was only one thing left for her to do: despise him for it.

"I would like to share *some* information with you," Dee continued. "I would like to tell you that more things are at stake here than your little plot. England knows about the prince's weapon. I am speaking, of course, about the clock your father built. We know that the prince does not yet understand how to use it. But it is only a matter of time before he does, or finds someone who can. He would have done better to keep your father close at hand, locked up and easily accessible for information. But the prince is young and proud of his own skills. He also has a fatal weakness for beauty and those who produce it. No doubt he thought that by sending your father home, he was honoring both him and his own ability to eventually master the thing your father created. But what if the prince gives up trying to prove that he is just as talented as Mikal Kronos? It may not be long before the prince admits his mistake and sends your father an invitation to the castle. But will it be an invitation mounted on rich cloth and tied with a ribbon? Or will it perhaps be one accompanied by armor and swords and pikes?

"What? Silent, Petra? I would have thought that this was a topic close to your heart. But, well, if you do not feel it is important enough to discuss, we can move on.

"I wonder: have you ever considered why the symbol of Bohemian royalty is a salamander?"

She said nothing, but glared.

"A salamander loves fire. It lives in it, breathes in it, survives in spite of—because of—the heat that would kill you or me. The choice of symbols is never random. The princes of Bohemia have never been afraid of trouble. They have invited it. They have encouraged anger between the rich and poor to split the people into classes that despise each other. They have pushed their people to the brink of starvation. They have courted war. Prince Rodolfo is not afraid of, shall we say, a little heat. Because heat is what gives him power.

"It is one political view. It is not for me to say whether it is bad or good. It is a strategy, and certainly the princes of Bohemia have profited by it. We English, however, are rather cold fish. Ours is a chilly climate. It rains enough to make a person feel perpetually damp. Our patron saint is George the Dragon Slayer. The symbol we have chosen shows a battle against a fire-breathing beast. It shows the death of fire.

"Obviously international politics interests you very little. Those . . . *unusual* silver eyes of yours turn away as if you were listening to a boring school lesson. You do not see much beyond a horizon of yellow hills and your petty familial problems. But I assure you that Europe hangs in the balance. And I will make you care about it.

"The emperor is ill and old and has too many sons to whom he has given too much power. When he dies, will the Hapsburg princes be content with the small countries they already possess? Will they agree with Karl's choice of a new emperor? Or will they war among themselves and drag all of Europe into their struggle for the Hapsburg Empire? I think we both know the answers to these questions, and we know them because of what Prince Rodolfo commissioned your father to build. He clearly has higher ambitions than just being prince of Bohemia.

"England could choose to support one of the three princes now, before the coming war. Indeed, this is what Rodolfo hopes will come of my visit. But choosing the wrong side would be disastrous for England. Even choosing the right side would not make my country safe. Her Majesty prefers to keep England's neutrality. She prefers not to get involved at all in these central European problems. But inaction poses other problems, particularly when we consider the clock's powers. If he were able to make the clock work to control the weather, it would be easy for Rodolfo to defeat his brothers and seize control of the Empire. All he would have to do is dry up the lands of Hungary and Germany in a brutal drought. This would cause mass starvation in these countries.

"With the clock, it would be equally easy for him to cow other countries into agreeing to his every wish. Indeed, if he chose to, it would be child's play for him to conquer the rest of Europe. England, however, has no desire to be added to Rodolfo's collection. Which is why the clock's potential ability to control the weather must be destroyed. And which is why, dear Petra, I am very glad to have met you. You father has, so to speak, let a genie out of its bottle. It will be your job to put it back in."

"Me? Why don't you do it?" She sarcastically added, "You're obviously much more talented and intelligent than I am."

"True." He inclined his head. "But in order to play this game properly, I must do so invisibly. I must be like your father, and make pieces move without seeming to be responsible for their movements. If the prince were to suspect my intentions, there would be dire consequences for me. But"—for the first time he looked worried—"the consequences for my country would be far worse. And so I am ready to strike a deal with you, Petra."

"What kind of deal?"

"A very easy one. You only have to do a little favor for me. Then you might gain my help in your quest." He unfolded his arms and the dark velvet sleeves slipped back, revealing his hands for the first time. His nails were long, curved, and sharp, making his hands look like the claws of an animal. He reached into a pocket and drew forth a small glass bottle with green liquid inside. He uncorked it, dabbed a little on the tip of his forefinger like a lady might put on perfume, and then rubbed his left thumbnail with the oily finger, making the nail shine. "All you have to do is look carefully at this thumbnail and tell me what you see."

This did *not* seem like a good idea to Petra. Her father may not have cared to make sure she knew what kind of dress a twelve-year-old girl should wear, but he did see to it that certain parts of her education were not lacking, and that included knowing how to steer clear of dangerous magic. She knew perfectly well that the sort of thing Dee proposed, scrying, could break her mind. She liked her mind the way it was: sane. "I thought you said you weren't a magician."

"I hope you do not believe everything you are told, my dear."

"What if I don't want to look at your greasy old nail? What's to stop me from going directly to the prince and telling him all about your plans? You and your stupid queen wouldn't be so happy then."

"I would deny everything you told the prince. Whom would he believe, you or me? I would reveal *your* identity and *your* own plans. And then *there*"—he snapped his sharp fingers—"would go your hope to regain your father's sight. Oh, and I believe you would also lose your life."

She was trapped just as surely as if he had locked her inside one of his boxes.

"Come, Petra. It is a fair bargain. We are trading vision for a vision."

"So if I tell you what I see, you will help me get my father's eyes back?"

"I said that I *might* help you."

"That seems like a very bad deal to me."

"Sadly, it is the only one you will be offered."

"Then I refuse."

"Then I shall have to send for the prince."

She felt like kicking him.

Instead, she marched forward and glanced at his clawlike hands. "I don't see anything."

"How can you see if you do not look?" He held up his left hand and extended his thumb. "*Look.*"

The slick nail gleamed like a large green pearl. The lamplight flickered on its surface. As Petra gazed at it, she found that she could not look away. She grew dizzy, and the room darkened around her. But just as suddenly, her vision cleared and she lifted her head. "I didn't see anything," she said with relief.

Dee withdrew his hand. "That is a pity. Still, I think I shall keep up my end of the bargain. I shall help you first by giving you information. Surely you have some questions you would like answered?"

"How can the clock be destroyed?"

He gave a slight shrug. "I don't know."

"What is the prince's magical talent?"

"I'm not at liberty to say."

She gave him a look made of steel. "What good is it to ask you questions if *you don't have any answers*?"

"Try asking the right questions."

"What is the Cabinet of Wonders?"

"Ah!" Dee beamed. "So you know about that already. Good girl! The Cabinet of Wonders is the prince's private collection. He is a lover of objects that are beautiful, strange, and priceless. Naturally, your father's eyes fall into that category. Now, I have learned the source of the prince's difficulty in using the clock to control the weather. It appears that your father failed to assemble one last part before he was blinded. Wearing your father's eyes seems to give the prince some aid in putting together that part—because, I believe, they allow the prince to see the metal components as your father could. But the prince hasn't yet been entirely successful in his efforts.

"I suspect the prince keeps the part in his prized collection. It would be useful if you could gain access to the Cabinet of Wonders. I will suggest to the prince that he employ you as a maid to his chambers. Or, rather, I will make the suggestion to someone in a position to persuade the prince."

"And to take the blame if I succeed in getting my father's eyes back."

"I sense disapproval." He clucked. "Surely you are not suggesting that *I* should be the responsible party for your actions? Petra," Dee chided, "whether you wish to ignore the consequences of your actions is wholly beside the point that there will, indeed, be several unpleasant ones."

He paused, waiting to see if she would reply. When she did not, he continued, "The prince likes to have one person assigned to clean one room of the seven rooms in his suite. His collection is so important to him that he doesn't like to expose its existence to too many people. The problem is that he tends to grow suspicious of his pages and maids. He recently, hmm, fired one, a girl named Eliska."

A cold, creeping feeling stole over Petra. She recognized that name. It had been in the captain of the guard's Worry Vial.

"I think it should not be too hard to promote you to take her place. The Countess of Krumlov is pleased with your work. I observed you closely during the celebrations in the courtyard, and I noticed that the prince took an interest in you. You caught his eye. Or, I should say, you caught your father's eye. The prince is a man led by his curiosity. You have sparked his.

"And now I shall help you in one last way." Dee reached into a pocket, pulled out a small, brown bottle, and gave it to her. Petra did not like the way he kept presenting bottles out of his pockets. It made her realize that he had planned this conversation with her for a while.

"What is it?"

"It is belladonna. If you put one drop in each eye, it will make them look black. You look a great deal like your father. I would advise you to hide any family resemblance as much as possible. Use the belladonna when you go to the prince's chambers. Do not use it if you plan on seeing the Countess of Krumlov. She will notice the difference."

"Obviously. I have a brain, you know."

"I do know. I have confidence in your abilities. In fact, I know that when you retrieve your father's eyes, you will also bring about the destruction of the clock's special powers. Find that part, and break it. Or I shall see that you and your family pay the price for the clock's creation in the first place."

"That was not part of our deal!"

Dee smirked. "Ah, but it was an *implicit* part of our deal. You are an honorable young girl. Surely you will keep to the spirit of our pact, and not just the letter. And remember: there are more ways than one to skin a cat—or, in this case, to make certain that the prince is never able to use the clock. Let's say your father were to . . . disappear. This would eliminate the chance that the prince could send for him to solve his rather annoying problem of not knowing how to make the clock of Mikal Kronos work the way he wishes."

"But I don't know what the part looks like! And I certainly don't know how to destroy it!"

"Oh, it can't be that hard. It's easier to break something than to create it." He tapped a finger against his lips, considering. When he spoke, it was with the voice of someone who thought he was being very generous. "I'll tell you what, my dear. If I gather any new information on the clock I shall pass it along to you. When you receive my message, you shall do exactly as I say. Now, how does that sound?"

She struggled not to shout, but what she said still came out as a growl. "The day I come into my powers is the day you'd better be worried, Dee."

"But who knows if you will have any?" he replied airily. "You may be as talented as a block of wood. Perhaps your father has—*had*—skills to be wary of, but what about your mother? She was no one special."

Petra nearly told him that indeed she had been, but stopped the words before they reached her lips. He already had collected too much knowledge about her through unknown means. She shouldn't present him with details about her life as if they were little cakes on a platter. She certainly shouldn't mention her newfound ability to speak secretly with the tin spider hiding in her hair, or her accuracy with throwing daggers. "Are we done? I want to leave."

"Allow me to accompany you to the door." In a fluid movement of velvet, he stood up and walked with her. "Petra," he said as she stepped into the hallway, "let me give you a word of advice. It is not wise to make threats." He smiled. "Someone might take them seriously."

And then he shut the door.

22

Neel Talks Sense

NEEL WAS FURIOUS. "Where *were* you? I waited until dawn!"

He pounced out of the cellar shadows the evening after the celebrations, as servants milled into the dining hall, still red-eyed from too much drinking and too little sleep. Petra didn't even have a chance to ask how he had gotten inside the castle. He yanked open a door she had never noticed before, pulled her upstairs and outside onto the grounds, and dragged her behind an enormous woodpile.

"Well, I—" She tried to speak.

"I thought maybe something happened to you! Or did you get scared? You did, didn't you? That was *stupid*, Pet. We had a prime opportunity last night!"

"I wasn't scared! I—"

Neel's eyes burned with yellow-green fire. "Don't tell me," he said slowly, "that you went *alone*."

"Not exactly."

"So you did. I see. Just like a cat carrying a mouse to her own secret corner, aren't you? Didn't think I deserved a bite, did you?"

"That's not it. That's not it at all. I was trying to . . . Neel, it isn't safe for you."

Sudden understanding turned Neel's face into a wooden mask. Petra hurriedly explained what had happened in the forest after he had walked ahead to the Lovari camp. She told him about Emil and his fierce desire to protect Neel.

"And you listened to him?" Neel exploded. "Emil's the last person who's got *any* call to have *any* say over what I do! He ain't my brother or my father!"

"Emil's right, Neel. You heard what the captain of the guard said. You heard about those people. I shouldn't have gotten you involved."

He was too angry to speak.

Then a snowflake drifted past his face. Another one appeared out of the gray sky, landed on Neel's nose, and disappeared.

"Petra." Neel's voice didn't sound angry anymore, just tired. "You've got to do something for me."

"What?"

"You've got to take one minute—*one minute*—to stop being so . . ." He grew frustrated. "So *sunora*."

Petra wasn't used to being called names she didn't understand. She folded her arms across her chest and frowned. "What do you mean?"

"You're so *green*. I know you're not used to the ways of life around here, but you've got to *think*. If pinching the purse of some hill-bred nobody would get me sent to the gallows, what do you think is going to happen when the prince finds out that a bunch of Gypsies have been eating his deer, eating his conies, and living on his own hunting grounds? He won't think twice about turning us all into dust in the captain's vial. How long is it going to take before that happens?" He flung his hand into the sky and the snowflakes sifting down. "You got your reasons for wanting what's inside the Cabinet. I got mine. Leastways I know that if things don't go our way and I get caught, what'll happen to me will happen just to *me*."

Astrophil cleared his throat. "And Petra."

"Right. So no more second-guessing." Neel took a small knife from his pocket and cut his palm. "Swear." He passed her the knife and held up his left hand, where a thin line of blood shone.

Petra, you know the rules of a blood oath, Astrophil warned. *Maybe you should—*

"I do swear." She cut her palm. Ignoring the sting, she grasped Neel's bloody, dirty hand.

Astrophil sighed.

"Good." Neel shook her hand for good measure. "Now let's talk sense."

"Let me tell you what happened last night." Petra began to relate the conversation that had taken place between her and John Dee. She held back any details concerning the clock. As she spoke, the two of them leaned against the woodpile, shivering under the white sky.

"He made you scry?" Neel frowned.

"Yes."

"What did you see?"

"Nothing. At least, I don't think I saw anything."

"You might not've. That might not've been what he wanted."

Petra gave him a searching look. "What do you know about scrying?"

"Nothing. Well, nothing much. But the Roma are good at mind-magic—foretelling, scrying, and the like. As far as I know, asking someone to look at a shiny bit of something doesn't always mean you want to know the truth about the present or the past. There's other stuff a scryer can do."

"Like drive someone insane."

"There's that, too." He peered at her and smiled. "Looks like you got all your marbles, though."

She felt a pang of homesickness when he said this. She missed Tomik. She missed Okno. She missed her family.

Neel was pensive. "I've got to ask Drabardi about this. But tell me: how come this Dee knows stuff about you? Did he drop a word about me? Or Astro?"

"No," Astrophil said to Neel. "But he is a difficult man to read. He acted as if he was being honest. Even too honest. But listening to him speak is like seeing the curve of a tree root just above the ground. You can see only one piece, and you have no idea what the rest of the root looks like, how far down it goes, and how far it stretches out under the earth."

"Is he a friend of your da's?"

"*No*," Petra said, insulted. "He's a *spy*."

"No need to get all prickly. I was just asking. Because it's weird that some foreign gentleman is offering to help you. Give me that bottle of bella-whatsit." Neel took the brown bottle from her. He opened it, sniffed the liquid, and put a little on his tongue. Then, before Petra could stop him, he tipped back his head and let a drop fall into one eye.

"Neel!"

"That could be poisonous!" Astrophil cried, wringing four legs.

"Well, yeah. Why do you think I put it in only one eye?" He blinked, and belladonna ran down his face like a black tear.

Petra groaned. "If the poison's strong enough, that won't matter! You didn't have to do that! I was going to test it in the laboratory before I tried using it."

"You know how to tell if something's poisonous?"

"Not exactly, but if belladonna is made from a mineral, I—" She broke off, startled to see that John Dee's gift was working just like he said it would. The pupil in Neel's right eye swelled like a small black balloon. Soon Neel looked very odd indeed, with one black eye and one yellow. She couldn't help but chuckle.

"Laughing at me when I might drop dead? That's a fine thank-you." He continued to blink. "Well, I'm not dead. And I'm not blind. So I guess your potion's all right." He passed back the bottle.

As Petra took it, she considered the sight of his mismatched eyes. She ran her thumb along the shallow cut in her palm, which was already beginning to crust over. A blood oath is a promise to protect your friend's life as much as your own, and to keep no secrets between you. It's a way of making a friend family.

"Neel, why haven't you told anyone at the castle about us? Or about my father's notebook? You would probably get a reward. I know you've thought about it."

"Someone like me wouldn't exactly get a private meeting with the prince. So who would I tell? The captain of the guard? And a right pleasant fellow he is. First thing he'd do is chuck my Gypsy hide into the nearest jail cell and claim any reward for himself."

"So you *have* thought about it," she accused.

"I can't help thinking. But it ain't my style to betray the ladies. Or spiders." He nodded at Astrophil.

She scowled. "I can't believe you even *thought* about it. I trusted you."

"I know." He thrust his hands in his pockets and looked down. "I'm not used to that. The fact that you trust me . . . well, it makes me want to be someone you can trust."

They were silent.

I should tell him about the clock, Astro.

You promised your father you would tell nobody, he said.

I know.

This is unlike you, Petra. You never break your word.

I know. But I've taken a blood oath, and—

I tried to stop you, Astrophil interrupted. *If you make too many promises, one of them is bound to crash into another, and then one of them is bound to break.*

If Neel's going to risk his life, he needs to know everything about the situation. I have to think about what Father would say now, if he were right here. I think he would want Neel to know.

Astrophil shook his head. *Petra, if your father were here right now, he would want you and Neel to be as far away from Salamander Castle as your feet could take you.*

But Petra had made up her mind. "Neel, I know why Dee wants to help me." The snow was now falling in fat clusters. The flakes floated in the breeze like goose down as Petra told him about the clock and its powers. "So now Dee's ordering me to make sure the clock can never work to control the weather. Dee wants to impress his redheaded queen . . . and stop Prince Rodolfo from taking over Europe," she added, reluctant to acknowledge that there was good in Dee's plan.

Neel whistled. "Always knew there was something special about the Staro Clock. But what's Dee thinking? How does he figure you're going to break into the Cabinet of Wonders *and* bust the clock, when the Cabinet's in the castle and the clock's across the sopping river? It's not possible."

"There's a special part of the clock that will make it work to control the weather," Petra clarified. "Dee thinks it's in the Cabinet of Wonders. Right now the prince doesn't understand how to assemble the final piece. We have to find that piece, whatever it is, and destroy or steal it." She shook her head. "But that's impossible, too. We don't even know what it looks like."

"What about your da's notebook? Maybe something's in there. Some clue about this missing part Dee wants you to find."

"I don't know. I looked at it, but there were just those baffling equations, ordinary blueprints, and some drawings that didn't have anything to do with the clock. I don't think that a sketch of a ship without sails can help us. Still, you're right. We should look at the notebook again."

He nodded. "I got it safe in the *vurdon*. In our wagon, I mean. We can study it on our next day off."

"I don't think we can wait until then," Petra said darkly. "Father was so *sure* that the prince wouldn't be able to figure out how to make the clock work the way he wants it to. Father said that it would always be just a beautiful time-telling device and nothing more. But the way Dee was talking, you'd think that Prince Rodolfo is inches away from discovering my father's secret."

"Maybe you should believe your da."

"I *do* believe him," she spluttered. "Do you think I want to follow Dee's orders? I'd rather listen to my father. My father told me that the clock isn't my concern. And it isn't. It *shouldn't* be. I don't care what happens to it." But her last words sounded like a lie Petra was desperately trying to believe.

Neel cocked his head and gave her a half smile.

"Fine," she admitted. "Maybe I care."

"I bet the prince can't make the clock work the way he wants to anyway. There's a Lovari tale . . ."

"Neel, don't you think it's a little cold for fairy tales?" It had grown dark. Petra's teeth chattered, her stomach growled for dinner, and snow gathered at their feet.

"Oh, I do not know," Astrophil interjected. "I am not so cold."

"Of course you're not, you're made of metal!"

"It's a quick tale," Neel promised. "There once was a Lovari named Camlo, and he was a fiddler like no other. He carved himself a fine fiddle. It was smooth and curved and strung with twangy strings. It made a music that was wild and free, and folks from all over would come to listen. Well, one day he was fiddling in the forest and the devil came up. He was right pleased by the music, and he fell to thinking that if he had Camlo's fiddle, everyone on earth would want to hear him play. So the devil said, 'Give me that there fiddle, man.' And Camlo said, cool as anything, 'I'm not in the habit of giving my best things away.' So the devil said, 'I'll give you plenty of gold.' 'Well, how much?' said Camlo. 'As much as in all the Ganges,' said the devil."

"The Ganges?"

"It is a river in India," said Astrophil.

"So the devil showed him the Ganges and how the water sparkled with gold. It shimmered like a thousand little suns. And the devil pulled out that Ganges gold and stuffed Camlo's pockets. He filled a big wheelbarrow full of it. Camlo said, 'Mister Devil, you got yourself a deal.' He handed over the fiddle, though he loved it so, and walked off to enjoy being rich.

"The devil was keen to start impressing people with his music, so he tuned up and began to play. But imagine his surprise when no one paid him any mind! He played and played but folks just ignored him. So he hunted down Camlo. 'Your blasted fiddle doesn't work!' the devil cried. 'It works just fine,' said Camlo. 'I can't make it play the way you can! You've tricked me somehow!' raged the devil. 'Well, of course,' said Camlo. 'I sold you my fiddle, but I didn't sell you my soul with it.' "

Petra stood silent. The snow swirled. She said, "Tell that to John Dee."

23

The Lion and the Salamander

IMPOSSIBLE!" Iris hissed. She brought the parchment close to her spectacles, then held it at arm's length. "Absurd!" The paper began to smoke in her fingers.

A young boy dressed in the red and gold suit of a page shifted his feet nervously. He looked at Petra. He looked at the door. He gave a little cough.

"You!" Iris scowled at him. "What are you still doing here? Get out!"

The page jumped and made a beeline for the door.

The letter in Iris's hand disintegrated, but not before Petra saw the wax seal that had been stamped on it. It was a coat of arms showing a salamander, a lion rampant, and a sword. Petra had a good idea of what the letter said.

"And *you*." Iris turned to Petra. "Is your name Viera?"

"Yes."

"Well, why didn't you say so before? And don't tell me it's because you were too shy. I won't believe you. Well? Why?"

"You never asked me."

"Hmph." The corner of her mouth seemed to lift, but Petra immediately doubted what she had seen when Iris continued to speak. "It's suspicious, you see, when a servant works for me for several weeks and doesn't let slip so much as a word about herself—about where she's from, what her family's like, why she reads so well, and why she knows details about the most arcane kinds of metals and minerals."

"What's *arcane* mean?"

"It's too late to play the innocent with *me*, young lady!" Iris pounded the worktable.

"Arcane" means—

Later, Astro!

"I don't suppose you could tell me why Prince Rodolfo would send me a letter volunteering to take an assistant named Viera off my hands?"

"Is that what the letter said?" Petra pretended to be confused. "I can't imagine why the prince would be interested in me."

"Nor can I." Iris frowned. "You realize, of course, that Prince Rodolfo changes servants about as often as he changes his gloves. You'll have a short career working for him. He likes to hire and fire servants, not keep them."

He does more than fire them, Petra thought grimly. She wondered if Iris really had no idea about the true fate of the prince's chambermaids.

Iris no longer seemed irked, just puzzled. "Perhaps he is trying to punish me. But why? Rodolfinium was a success." She muttered to herself, ignoring Petra and pacing the room. "Could the Krumlovs have . . . ? No, that doesn't make any sense either. And I have about as much interest in political intrigues as I do in the spawning season of frogs. Perhaps it's those silver eyes of his . . ."

Petra was suddenly alert.

". . . he makes such odd decisions when he wears them, as if he's not wholly himself. I wonder where he got them to begin with . . . who made them . . . who—" Iris stared into Petra's eyes.

Oh, no, said Astrophil.

"Ah," said Iris.

Petra began to wipe her hands, but the brown juice from the henna paste she had been making wouldn't come off. "I don't suppose I have a choice, though, do I?" She tried to speak calmly.

"No, you don't."

Petra glanced around, instinctively looking for something to pack up and take with her, just like when she left her family at the Sign of the Compass, and when she left Lucie and Pavel at the inn. But there was nothing here that belonged to her. So she let her hands fall. "Goodbye, Iris," she said awkwardly. "I liked working for you. I really did."

Iris didn't say anything until Petra was opening the door. "I don't suppose you'd tell me what your last name is, hmm?"

Petra turned around.

"Oh, forget it. I don't particularly feel like making you tell a lie. It gives one such a sense of dissatisfaction."

PETRA SCREWED HER belladonna-black eyes shut in nervousness and opened them again. She took a deep breath, and stared at the double door that soared in the shape of two trees, one pine and one oak. At the base of the pine tree was a sitting lion with green glowing eyes, keeping guard. There was a hole in the trunk of the oak tree, one that blazed with a small, real fire. A green-eyed salamander was curled up in the flames. Petra wondered how the small blaze could burn in the wood without setting the entire door on fire. The last detail of this magnificent entrance to the prince's quarters was a silver line that split the pine from the oak, showing an upright sword whose hilt formed a handle for each door.

"Should I knock?" Petra whispered to herself.

The salamander blinked.

"State your purpose," growled the lion.

"I'm," Petra stammered, "I'm Prince Rodolfo's new servant."

"*His Highness's* new servant, we are sure you mean."

"Yes. Right. His Highness's."

"Very well. We assume you have some documentation to present."

"Documentation? Like . . . a letter? One was sent to my mistress, but it got burned up."

The lion sprung the claws of his left hand and peered at them, idly.

"My mistress is—*was*—Countess December. She has an acid problem. Sometimes she destroys things. Accidentally, of course."

The lion and the salamander exchanged a look. Some sort of communication seemed to pass between them.

"And what manner of servant are you?" asked the lion.

"What manner?"

"His Highness has many servants, who do many things. What are you to do?"

"Um, clean. I think."

"Name?"

"Viera."

The salamander disappeared from its nest of flames. After a brief moment, it reappeared. "Enter," it said.

The silver sword split down its center, and both doors swung open.

Petra faced a long, dark, windowless hallway. Green brassica lamps lined each side, glowing dimly as if under water. The carpet was red and so thick that it seemed to be made of fur. Petra's feet sank as the red plush came up to her ankles. Walking forward felt as if she were slogging through mud. She was wondering if the carpet was indeed made from some animal's pelt and, if so, what kind of animal it could be, when the hallway opened into a vast chamber.

Here the carpet bloomed into a network of elaborate hunting

scenes. With arrows, spears, and swords, men on horses were chasing down boars, foxes, quail, and even mythical beasts like unicorns and griffins. Seven doors flanked the chamber. Birch logs burned in the fireplace, the heart of the fire glowing blue amid shreds of orange flame. There was no furniture, save a large wooden throne in the center of the room. The throne was empty. Prince Rodolfo stood before an enormous, many-paned window, watching the sparse snow sift down.

Petra meant to be silent. She meant to wait for the prince to notice her. But then she happened to glance at the ceiling and gasped.

The heads of countless men and women were staring down at her.

At the sound of Petra's stifled cry, the prince turned around. He examined her. "Do not worry, they are made of wood."

He advanced. His velvet robes were dyed a color Petra quickly recognized as Tyrian purple. The color, made from a spiny snail shell, looked like clotted blood. The cuffs and hem of the robe were trimmed with the rough gray fur of a wolf.

You had better bow, Petra.

Though disliking herself for doing it, she obeyed the spider and sank into a deep curtsy.

"Rise."

She looked up, and her father's eyes flickered over her face. Prince Rodolfo sat, and pondered why he felt so kindly toward this young girl. "They are the heads of the former rulers of Bohemia," he explained. "Quite gruesome, are they not, even if they are made of wood? Someday I, too, will look down from the ceiling. Between you and me, I do not look forward to that day." He smiled.

Petra was taken aback. Was the prince trying to be friendly?

"Much here is not what it seems. That window, for instance, is not real."

"But isn't it actually snowing outside, Your Highness?"

"Indeed it is. But the window is really bewitched rock. Watch." He pulled a gold coin from a pocket and flung it at the window. There was no crack or shatter, but a mere thunk as the coin hit a windowpane and fell to the carpet. He let the coin rest there. "There can be no real windows in my chambers, for reasons of security. Which brings me to the subject of my presence and yours. I interview every one of my personal servants—my valets, my pages, and my chambermaids. I am forced to do this, because some servants have proven to be . . . disloyal." His face did not grow angry. It emptied itself of any expression.

Petra. Astrophil tapped her head.

"You don't have to worry about that with me, Your Highness." She took a deep breath and dragged out the next few words: "I am devoted to Your Highness."

He nodded, pleased. He sat in his throne. "Tell me about yourself."

Petra spun a story of country life. She was an orphan, she explained, from the hills.

"You are quite all alone, then?"

She nodded.

"No brothers or sisters?"

She nodded.

"You need not look so sad. I assure you that having siblings is overrated. And if you miss having a family, Salamander Castle offers you hundreds of mothers, fathers, sisters, and brothers."

Petra remained silent, unsure how to respond when he looked so earnest.

He studied her. He was perplexed. Why were the Kronos eyes

so interested in this girl? She possessed no special beauty. She seemed like every other servant girl in the castle—except, perhaps, less afraid. Nevertheless he had to admit there was something intriguing, and also . . . *familiar*, about her, as if he had encountered her face many times before. But where? Perhaps she reminded him of a work of art . . . No. Prince Rodolfo dismissed that idea. The girl's face was too common to remind him of anything in his collection.

"These seven doors"—he gestured at the sides of the room—"lead to seven different rooms. There is only one door you will be allowed to open, and only one room that you may enter. That room is my study, which you will clean. Can you read?"

She hesitated, then gave him the answer he seemed to expect: "No."

"Can you guess which door leads to my office? I will give you a treat if you can."

Petra was not sure she wanted whatever "treat" Prince Rodolfo would give her. But as she looked around the room, it became utterly clear to her which door led to his office, even though every door was identical and plain. She simply *knew* what the right answer was. She pointed to that door with a confidence that might not have been wise.

Prince Rodolfo was startled, though he did his best to hide it. "Why, well spotted!" The silver eyes glinted. "There is one door that leads to a room I value most of all. Can you guess which door that is?"

Again, a feeling of certainty stole over Petra. She started to raise her hand when Astrophil commanded with alarm: *Point to whichever one you think he values* least, *Petra!*

She did.

The prince noticeably relaxed. "Our conversation is nearly concluded. I am to attend a meeting in a few minutes. I need to . . . change. You will wait here. When I have left my chamber you will remain, and clean my study."

She nodded.

The prince rose from his throne and walked slowly to the very door that Petra would have marked as the one most important to him. He withdrew a large key with complicated swirls and squiggles of metal, unlocked the door, and stepped inside.

When he emerged a few moments later, the gaze he directed toward Petra was no longer silver, but an ordinary dark brown.

She couldn't help herself. "Your Highness . . . your eyes . . ."

"Yes. As I said, much here is not what it seems. I am attending a meeting of the Tribunal of the Lion's Paw, and my other eyes are distracting."

Her father's eyes were a plaything to Prince Rodolfo, Petra realized. They were something to change his vision of the world, to amuse him.

"I promised you a reward." He held out something spherical. It was an orange. Oranges were the prince's favorite fruit. He always peeled them himself, and took some pleasure in tearing the bright skin away to expose the soft wedges within. He liked the spray of tiny citrus beads, he liked the tangy taste, and above all he liked that an orange is a fruit to be eaten piece by piece. If he came across a pebble-sized seed, he would swallow it rather than spit it out, even if he was alone.

This orange, however, was not meant to be eaten. It was studded all over with cloves that were stuck into the fruit like nails.

Petra accepted the orange. She forced herself to curtsy again. "Thank you, Your Highness."

He peered at her. To his own eyes, the girl looked like nothing, nothing at all. "You are quite a mystery."

She was silent.

"Luckily for you, I enjoy mysteries." He smiled, like the young man he was, like someone entertained.

As Petra walked away from the prince's chambers, an unfinished thought swam at the back of her mind, wriggling away like a slippery minnow. Petra grasped at it. Even if stealing and wearing her father's eyes seemed to be just a game to the prince, he must have wanted them very badly. Petra wondered why she was so certain of this. Then she realized something so obvious, yet so unthinkable that she had never before considered it: the prince must have undergone the same painful operation he ordered to be performed on her father. The prince had done it willingly. He had had his own eyes gouged out and enspelled so that he could trade them for another's.

Petra was stunned. What kind of person would do that?

24

Bad News

PETRA SAT AT THE EDGE of the wooden bench, gripping the towel around her and watching the young women climb out of the large bath. She listened to their laughter and the slap of wet feet on stone. None of the other girls waiting for their turn in the bath sat next to her. They crowded together at the other end of the bench like pigeons. Petra peered around the bathing room one more time for Susana. She was nowhere to be seen. Even Astrophil had abandoned her, asking to be left in a corner of the dormitory. *Spiders do not need baths,* he had said.

"Hey, Poxy!" Dana called. Sadie followed closely behind her. Their faces glowed from the bath. Dana gently tugged Petra's ponytail. "Your hair has grown."

"Poxy?" Petra was confused, and then remembered how she had explained away her unconventional short hair during her first week at Salamander Castle. She claimed to have had the pox. It seemed so long ago that she had told that lie. "Listen, Dana," she began, choosing her words carefully. Dana was Sadie's friend, and she was friendly to Petra. But that did not mean she was *Petra's* friend. "I know that I'm overwhelmingly popular here, and that nothing can make a dent in the long line of people who want to be my friend, but could you maybe not call me names like 'Poxy'? Because somehow it's not appealing to have a nickname that's a disease."

Dana giggled. "I'm sorry. But your hair *has* grown, and gotten darker, glossy. I was trying to pay you a compliment."

"In her own illogical way," Sadie added. She looked at the empty bench. While they were speaking, the other girls had plunged into the bath. "Where's Susana?"

"I haven't seen her all day," Petra grumbled.

Dana had a stricken look on her face.

"What's wrong, Dana?" Sadie asked.

"Don't you know?"

"Know what?"

"Susana's village, Morado, was burned to the ground. I heard that . . . that there was a freak lightning storm. It was a nice day. Cold, windy, but nice. Then suddenly several buildings were struck by bolts of lightning. They caught fire, the fire spread, and . . . Morado's small and, well, kind of poor. Everything was built with old wood and thatch. Everything burned. Susana's family died in the fire."

"All of them?" Petra was horrified.

"Her parents. Her brothers and sisters. Susana has a cousin, though, that lives in a village not too far from Morado. She sent for Susana. Master Listek said she packed up her things and left in the night. She was too upset to say goodbye to anybody."

"I can't believe it." Sadie shook her head. "Who expects a lightning storm this late in the year? It's such bad luck."

No, Petra thought. *It is worse.*

"No! No, *no*, *NO!*" the prince howled, sweeping pieces of metal to the floor. They glittered in the dark, torch-lit clock tower. The prince pressed his gloved hands to his head and listened to machinery spinning around him, to the cogs of the Staro Clock fitting and turning together like something inevitable. He listened to the clanking, he saw the pendulums swinging, and he thought his head would explode from frustration.

The guards who flanked the entrance to the inner chamber of the clock tower gazed straight ahead. They kept their faces as blank as if their lives depended on it. And their lives did.

The woman at the prince's side exchanged a glance with the wispy-haired, pointy-chinned man standing at the other end of the worktable.

"Your Highness," the man began hesitantly. "I have a small gift for metal. If I might try—"

"I want to do it *myself*," the prince snarled.

"Yes—of—I—course—"

The gloved hands dropped from the prince's face. The fury of his expression smoothed away. His silken black fingers reached for a small scrap of metal that still rocked on the table. He approached the pointy-chinned man, who backed away, skirting the table's corner. "Your Highness, I apolo—apologize . . ."

"Stop."

The man stopped. He gazed into the marble features of the prince's face and trembled.

"Open your mouth," the prince said, his voice soft. "You will like this." He offered the glittering metal. "It is sweet."

"No!" the man cried. "Please! I'm so sorry! I'm so—"

"Your Highness." The willowy woman approached. "It would be a shame to let Karel go to waste. May I have him? As it pleases Your Highness, of course. But I am working on an experiment for which he might be apt."

"Ah, Fiala." The prince gazed at her. "I always admire your flair for invention. Take him, then, if he is useful to you. Karel, you will go with Mistress Broshek to the Thinkers' Wing."

The man nodded, but was still shaking. He looked at Fiala. "An experiment? What kind of—?"

"Oh, don't be such a baby, Karel," she snapped. "Of course, if you prefer your other option"—she tilted her blond head toward the metal scrap in the prince's hand—"just say so."

Karel shook his head and backed away until he bumped into one of the guards.

The prince let the glittering fragment fall to the table. "I cannot assemble it properly," he muttered to himself. "Nothing is working the way I wish. I cannot control the clock's power if I cannot piece together the heart."

"You will," Fiala Broshek consoled. She pulled on an extra pair of silk gloves and gathered up the metal pieces, placing them in a silken bag that she slung over her shoulder.

They exited the inner chamber of the clock tower, the guards forming an armored shell around them. They didn't notice that one of the guards had an unfamiliar face. Nor did Prince Rodolfo and Fiala Broshek notice, after they had mounted a carriage, crossed Karlov Bridge, and reached the castle, that the unknown guard did not follow the other soldiers to the barracks, but slipped away to meet his true master, the English ambassador.

THE ORANGE AND CLOVE SCENT drifted from Petra's pocket, making her feel drowsy. Nobles often carried such oranges in their pockets as perfume, but Petra began to hate the smell. One evening, when she finally dragged herself into the sleeping hall, she barely murmured a greeting to Sadie before she tumbled down onto her pallet and fell asleep.

At first, she slept soundly. But in the middle of the night she began to twitch and turn.

She dreamed of John Dee. He was dressed in robes the color of the night sky. Stars glimmered. *You must not waste any time*, he said.

She turned onto her side and tried to dream of something else.

The snow is falling. The snow will hamper your escape—if, indeed, you hope to escape.

Go away, Petra thought.

The day after tomorrow, he insisted, *would be the perfect time to strike. Do it during the prince's dinnertime. He will be dining with several European ambassadors, including myself.*

She tried to wake herself up. When Dee continued to hover before her in his night-colored robes, she frowned in her sleep. *You just want the perfect alibi, don't you?*

Naturally. But breaking into the Cabinet of Wonders then will also suit you. I doubt the prince will wear your father's eyes to a meeting where he must concentrate carefully, when he must try to persuade all of us to lend Bohemia our support, without admitting that he plans to defy his brothers if his father chooses one of them to become the next emperor. The meeting will also take place when it is just dark enough outside for you to try to escape after breaking the clock's heart. You must destroy or steal it.

What do you mean, the clock's heart?

But his face faded, and if he replied, Petra didn't hear it. She was waking up. She caught his last words: *Don't fail me, Petra Kronos.*

She opened her eyes.

PETRA FLUNG THE ORANGE into the woodpile. It sat there, prickly, squat, and reproachful.

"Good throw," Neel commented. The belladonna had worn off, and today he looked more like himself and less like some odd offspring of a bumblebee.

She told him what had occurred over the past several days, of the prince's letter, his private chambers, and the door that she was sure led to the Cabinet of Wonders.

"Tell me about that door again."

"Well, it's plain—"

"No, the one with the lion and the lizard."

She described it, and Neel's face grew grim. "And the window ain't a window?"

Petra nodded.

"Then there's no way I can help you. Danior's Fingers won't trick a lion and a lizard like that. There's no keyhole?"

She had to admit that there was not.

Neel shook his head. "Even if there was, I guess the lion would just roar like anything while we tried to bust in. It won't work."

"I already thought of that," she said excitedly, and produced a sheet of paper stamped with the prince's coat of arms. "It's your documentation." She explained her plan.

"All right. When are we going to do this, then?"

His question raised a subject that she was reluctant to discuss, but did anyway: her troubling dream the night before. "Dee said we should do it the day after tomorrow. That is, tomorrow."

"You dreamed this?"

"Look, I'm not the type to go around believing in dreams either, but—"

"*That's* what he did!" Neel slammed his fist into his palm. "It was no dream, Petali!"

"Come on," Petra scoffed. "What else would it be? I don't have the Second Sight or anything." But she was uneasy.

"You don't need to have the Second Sight! It was the scrying that did it!"

"What do you mean?"

"When you met with Dee, he asked you to scry. You didn't see anything, right? That's because what he wanted was to make a link between your mind and his."

Disgust oozed all over her flesh. "He can read my mind?"

Neel shook his head. "I don't think so. But I've heard of this sort of thing before. It's been used in war, to make it easy for generals to send messages. The Roma use it sometimes for tricksy things. The Company of Rogues, they do it, too, if they can lay their hands on someone able to do the scrying. But it's risky. It can wreck the mind of the magician and whoever's doing the scrying. It can scramble your brain like an egg."

"But . . . but what does this mean? Am I going to dream of"—she shuddered—"Dee all my life?"

"It means that he can talk to you when he feels like it. It'll be easier for Dee when you're sleeping, because your mind will be relaxed. It means you weren't dreaming, and we should listen to him."

"We should *not*! It could be a trap!"

"Just find out if the prince really is eating with those foreigners. If so, Dee's idea is probably right on the money. Plus"—he grimaced—"I got my own reasons for wanting to move fast."

"The snow?"

"There's that, too. But I was thinking about Sadie. You see, she spotted me lurking in the castle cellar today. Tabor's kept quiet about my working here, like I asked, but I guess it was only a matter of time before she saw me. She's no fool. If she catches hold of me, she won't let go until she shakes the story out of me."

Petra looked at him with scorn. "Just don't *tell* her, Neel."

He spread his hands. "I can swear up and down and on the grave that I won't tell her a word, but the fact of the matter is that she's been waiting for this ever since you talked to her and Ma in the *vurdon*. She was always worrying that I'd want a piece of your scheme. If she corners me, I can lie my head off, but she won't believe a word I say. If I say nothing, she'll know I'm stirring up trouble. Either way, she'll figure out that what she *thinks* is going on *is* going on."

"So what're you going to do?"

"Avoid her. You should, too, 'cause I don't suppose she's thinking of you as one of her best pals now."

Petra winced. She wanted to explain everything to Sadie, but the plan was moving much too quickly now, like one of her father's music boxes when the wind-up key was cranked too tightly. Would she have time to ask Sadie to forgive her, to make her understand her feelings, and Neel's? She pushed aside these thoughts, for they reminded her of something she and Neel had to discuss: time.

"When we get past the lion and the salamander—"

"*If.*"

"Trust me, we will! Now, when we get into the Cabinet of Wonders, we'll have to move fast."

"Tell me something I don't know," he said coolly.

"The Cabinet of Wonders is a collection. The prince is rich. He probably has mountains of things in there."

"I'm still waiting to hear something I don't know."

"We have to move quickly to find the eyes."

"And stuff to steal," he reminded.

"And stuff to steal. So the question is: how are we going to be able to get in and out with what we need in a short amount of time? We can't count on the prince being occupied by his dinner forever."

Astrophil cleared his throat. "I believe I can help," he said proudly.

As Petra neared Iris's laboratory, she heard a great crash of glass against the door, which flung open. A wild-eyed boy darted out. As some sort of lumpy blue slime trickled down the door, the boy stared at Petra. "Run!" he shouted. Taking his own advice, he sprinted down the hall.

Petra stepped into the room warily, but Iris looked normal. That is to say, she looked highly vexed, but at least her clothes were still on and she wasn't making the floor melt beneath her.

"What did he do?" asked Petra, relieved to see that Iris wasn't in the middle of a full-blown emotional disaster.

"Do? *Do*? He *existed*, that's what he did! And you"—she narrowed her eyes—"what are you doing here, Viera, Sweeper of the Prince's Study? Don't you have some royal feet to kiss?"

"Um, actually, I wondered if I might sleep on the floor of the Dye Works?"

"What's the matter with the servants' sleeping hall?"

Aside from the fact that it houses someone who would like my head on a platter, nothing at all, Petra thought. But she said out loud (and somewhat truthfully), "The girls there don't like me."

Iris put her hands on her hips, considering. Then she said, "What have you done with your eyes?"

Oh, no. Petra wanted to bury her face in her hands. How could she have forgotten about the belladonna? "Well, you see," she stammered, "it's, um, really popular to have dark eyes and I wanted to impress the other girls and I heard that belladonna could—"

Iris raised her hand. "I'm not even going to ask *how* you managed to get hold of belladonna. I'm just going to tell you that *no*, you may *not* sleep on the floor of my laboratory, because you no longer work here."

Petra's heart sank. Where would she go? She was already starving from having skipped yet another dinner to talk with Neel. Over the past weeks, she had found herself fantasizing about Dita's cooking. Astrophil had said she was getting thin in the face. Now, on top of her hunger, she was dead tired. But she had no idea what Sadie would do if she saw Petra. Would she announce Petra's plan to the whole sleeping hall? Would she march Petra before Master Listek and demand that she be fired? No, Petra couldn't risk seeing Neel's sister. She would have to find some corner of the castle where she could spend the night. Maybe there was a cupboard somewhere, or she could enter the library and sit at a desk and sleep with her head on her arms . . .

Iris interrupted Petra's train of thought. "Follow me," she commanded, and led Petra past the black curtain. Iris lit a candle and opened the door that Petra had noticed a long time ago. "These are my private chambers," she said, ushering Petra into the room. "I don't care to keep company with those fourth-floor flibbertigibbets. Here I'm closer to my work."

It was a very simple room, bare of any furniture except a wooden table with chairs, a wardrobe, a large bed, and a small bed made in a boxy shape. There was a tiny window and a closet door.

"It's not a luxury suite, but fancy furniture is hardly practical when you can burn them down to cinders once a month. Well. You can sleep there, if you like." She pointed at the boxy bed.

"Really? Iris, that's so—"

"First things first. Sit." She waved Petra toward the table and then left the room.

She returned bearing a tray with bread and butter and a cup of warm milk. "Young girls like their bedtime snacks, if I remember correctly." She set the tray down in front of Petra. Iris ordered her to eat, and Petra was glad to obey. As Petra chewed large mouthfuls of buttered bread rinsed down by gulps of frothy milk, Iris pulled bed linen out of the wardrobe. "My niece Zora used to sleep here sometimes." She waved her hand as if dismissing the memory. "But that was a long time ago."

When Petra had curled under a feather blanket and Iris was settled in her own bed, Petra felt such grateful fondness for Iris that it took her a few moments to speak. Then she said softly, "Iris, thank you so much. This is perfect. I—"

"Oh, don't get too comfy! I snore."

MEANWHILE, several floors above Petra, something small and sparkling crept along the ceiling. The spider sauntered over the heads of the fourth-floor guards (who, it is shameful to say, were sleeping). Astrophil ducked into the corner where the ceiling met the wall, and carefully inched toward the pine and oak door. The lion and the salamander stared into the hallway, but they didn't see the spider as he made his way toward the entrance to the prince's suite. When Astrophil reached the wall in which the double doors were set, he walked carefully down the side of the door frame until he reached the floor. The lion and the salamander continued to gaze calmly ahead. Astrophil slipped under the door.

He began to creep over the red, furry carpet of the hallway, but this was as difficult for him as it would be for you to push your way past vegetation in an Amazonian rain forest. So he shot a spiderweb to one of the walls and walked along there under the glow of the brassica lamps.

When he reached the chamber with seven doors, he crawled toward the door that Petra thought led to the Cabinet of Wonders. To his frustration, however, the crack between the door and the floor was extremely narrow. He tried to flatten himself out and push his way under the door, but the most he managed to do was wiggle a few legs into the crack. He pulled back. If he was the swearing type of spider, he might have cursed. But he just grimaced, and tried to think quickly.

Now, thinking quickly is what Astrophil did best, so he soon had an idea. He twinkled toward another door, avoiding the one he knew to be the prince's study. He managed to slip under the second door, but frowned when this new room turned out to be an armory. He tried a third door, but walked into a bathing room with a tub the size of a small swimming pool.

The fourth door, however, led him exactly to where he wanted to go: the prince's bedchamber. The sumptuous room was almost entirely taken up by an enormous four-poster bed. Normally this type of bed has curtains hanging on every side to help keep the sleeper warm during a cold Bohemian night, but in the prince's room flames crackled in two fireplaces. Probably for security reasons, the bed was bare of any curtains, and the prince slumbered under thick blankets. His pale face seemed to be the same color and made of the same fabric as the white silk pillows.

Astrophil's gaze was drawn to the nightstand. He shuddered. There, in a room filled with soft and polished things, was a fierce plant that someone in Astrophil's position likes least out of all the plants in the world. It was a Venus flytrap. A large bell jar covered this botanic beast. Instead of flowers, it had wide mouths trimmed with jagged teeth. They were wide open, waiting for some insect to step inside. Astrophil had read about these plants, which don't survive on only sun and water. The insides of their mouths are sweet and sappy. Many bugs, not just flies, are attracted by the smell. As soon as they step inside a mouth, it slams shut.

Astrophil tried not to think about the Venus flytrap. Instead, he jumped up onto a small table on which sat a cup, a saucer, and a spoon. Walking along the table, Astrophil deliberately bumped into the spoon, sending it over the edge with a clatter. The spider leaped to the floor.

He couldn't move any farther. A domed glass object plunged down from the sky and covered him. It was the bell jar that up until a moment ago had been covering the Venus flytrap. Astrophil quivered in fear, but sternly told himself to remain calm. He froze as the prince bent down to stare at him. From Astrophil's point of view, the curve of his glass prison distorted the prince's face. It was deformed, and bent in odd directions as the prince tilted his head. When the prince spoke, his words vibrated through the glass. "My," he said. "How *curious*."

25

Coins and Cogs

I LOOK LIKE A PARROT." Neel fidgeted with the red and gold jacket as he and Petra walked down the hall.

"What are you complaining about? Half the Lovari wear clothes in those colors."

"Yeah, but the *cut* . . ."

Stuffed somewhere into one of the dark corners of the stables was a page who would dearly love to look like a parrot. But instead he was dressed in Neel's clothes, and bound and gagged. Petra had lured Damek into the stables by telling him that there were bushels of apples stored there for the nobles' favorite horses. When Neel pounced on poor Damek, Petra explained to the page that she was sorry, but there were no apples for him to steal and he wasn't likely to get his uniform back anytime soon. Petra supposed that her deeds tonight wouldn't improve Prince Rodolfo's opinion of shifty chambermaids. But when Iris confirmed that, yes, she had heard that the prince was dining with several ambassadors that night, Petra swung the plan into action. Damek actually cried when Neel put on his uniform, but Petra hardened her heart and told the page that his outfit looked ridiculous anyway, and he should be glad to be rid of it.

Petra and Neel had managed to get past the series of human

guards without any trouble. They knew Petra by now and waved her past without looking at her papers. Neel drew some doubtful looks, but Petra had made good use of the prince's study during her first day of work as one of his chambermaids. She had examined several of the prince's letters. She supposed that she would have been in serious trouble if she had been caught, even though none of the letters said anything interesting. They were about raising the price of grain, awarding knighthoods, and setting aside more money for Bohemian ships to sail from Italy. Doing a very decent job of imitating the prince's handwriting, she introduced Branko (that is, Neel). He was a new page, replacing Damek, who had proved himself to be unworthy to work for the prince. Branko had already been interviewed by Prince Rodolfo. Petra stamped the note with the prince's seal and hoped fervently that this letter would do the trick.

The lion and the salamander gazed at the letter in Neel's outstretched hand. Silent communication passed between the two of them for quite some time. Finally, the lion said, "Viera, you may pass."

"What about me?" Neel said.

"You have never entered these doors before, therefore we doubt that you have been interviewed. We regret to inform you that His Highness is not here. You will have to return at another time for your interview."

"But it's already taken place!" Petra argued. "The letter says so."

"It would be highly unusual for His Highness to conduct an interview outside his chambers."

"But His Highness *himself* wrote that he *has* done so. Are you telling me that you doubt His Highness's word?"

The salamander shifted. The lion said, "Certainly we do not doubt it."

"Damek was taken away by the captain of the guard. Everything happened so fast. The interview was conducted in Master Listek's office. His Highness has important matters for Branko to attend to. His Highness will be very upset if he returns from his meeting and finds that Branko's duties haven't been taken care of."

The lion and the salamander looked at each other.

"Would you like to examine the letter again? These"—Petra waved the paper—"are His Highness's orders."

The lion sighed. "You may pass, Branko."

They waited until the double doors had shut behind them to share a triumphant grin.

They rushed down the hallway. Just before they reached the main chamber, Petra took Astrophil's drinking spoon from her pocket and dipped it into one of the brassica lamps, collecting a dollop of oil. She carried the full spoon above her left palm, trying not to spill any green liquid. They walked into the chamber with its empty throne and false window. Petra nodded at the door in the middle, to the right. Neel dropped to his knees before it and began to go to work.

He grimaced. "This one's tricky."

Petra's heart was pounding. But she and Neel exchanged elated glances when they heard a *click*.

Neel pushed open the door. He let out a groan.

There was a second door.

This one was made of glass. There was not one but three keyholes.

"Should we break the glass?" Petra whispered worriedly.

"*No*. Don't get so jumpy. Give me a minute, will you?"

As Neel moved his hands over the first keyhole, Petra peered into the Cabinet of Wonders, trying to calm herself. It was a room that seemed to stretch on forever. Several large statues were set on the floor, and shelves lined the walls, heavy with countless objects.

Petra strained to see what they were, but she didn't have a good view. *Astrophil?* she called, searching for the spidery twitching in the back of her mind. She noticed shards of broken glass on the floor several feet ahead. Her anxiety increased. *Astro? Tell me you're in there!*

A silvery web jetted from one of the shelves to the floor. Astrophil speedily lowered himself and ran to the glass door. *Petra! Petra!* He jumped up and down. *I am so glad you are here! I was worried that you would never come! And I am so hungry!*

We'll get this door open soon. Did you find Father's eyes?

Yes, but you cannot imagine what I had to do to get in here! There was a Venus flytrap, and the prince caught me, and I truly meant for him to do that, but I did not know I would get trapped under a bell jar, and then the prince put me inside the Cabinet, like I planned, but he kept me under the bell jar on a shelf, the fiend! Then he left, and I had to push against the glass jar with all my strength until it fell to the ground and took me with it. There was broken glass, and I fell, there was broken glass, and I fell, and . . . He was babbling, a rare thing for Astrophil to do. But then, he had been under a fair amount of stress.

Calm down! What are you talking about?

Astrophil took a deep breath and explained how he hadn't been able to slip under the door as planned, and so tricked the prince into locking him up in the Cabinet of Wonders.

He said that I was lucky he was too busy today to arrange for tests *to be done on me. He said it as if he knew I could understand!*

"Got it," Neel said. He pushed open the door.

Petra kneeled and held out the spoon. Astrophil eagerly sucked at the green oil.

"Better?" Petra asked.

"Much!"

"You were very brave, Astro."

"Oh"—he tried to speak with nonchalance—"I did what any self-respecting spider would do."

Petra smiled. "Now, where are they?"

She followed Astrophil deeper into the Cabinet of Wonders. Odd and beautiful objects lined their path, such as a small potted tree whose leaves were curled-up paper scrolls. Petra glanced at a paper leaf that had unfurled and saw a three-line poem written in sappy ink. Some things in the Cabinet were magnificent without being unusual, such as a blue and green life-sized statue of a peacock. Others were bizarre and unsettling, like a six-foot-tall skeleton of a mermaid strung from a pole and hanger.

Neel pulled down a box, looked inside, and made a face. Petra glanced at the box's label. "It says 'Dragon's Teeth.' "

"What am I going to do with dragon's teeth?"

"If you plant them in the earth, they sprout soldiers," Astrophil said. "Or so I have read."

"Well, maybe they'll come in handy," Neel said doubtfully. He pulled his purse from his waist and poured in the teeth.

"Try this." Petra opened a box labeled "Phoenician Coins."

Neel's eyes lit up when he saw the heap of gold. But then he noticed the designs marking the coins. His face fell. "Those aren't Bohemian. Or Spanish. Or anything. I can't use those."

"You can if you melt them down."

"Oh. Yeah. Right." He began stuffing his purse.

Meanwhile, Astrophil had scrambled on top of a small box. Burned into its wood was one word: "Kronos."

With trembling fingers, Petra opened the lid. There were her father's eyes, silver and familiar.

She hesitated to touch them. When she finally picked them up, she was surprised to find that they were smooth and hard like round pebbles. She carefully put them in her pocket.

She heard Neel make a delighted noise. She turned around. He had discovered a hoard of jewels carved into the shapes of various animals. There was a ruby pelican, an emerald turtle, a sapphire wolf, and a diamond dove. "Shame I'll have to bust these into pieces." He put them in his purse. "But I can live with that."

Petra made a quick tour of the Cabinet, looking for something, anything, that might help her fulfill her promise to John Dee. She found powdered unicorn horn, yes. She saw a cocoon the size of her arm. But she came across nothing that resembled a piece of an enormous clock. Or a heart.

She decided that she would have to let Dee solve his own problems. He could make whatever threats he wanted. Her family would deal with him when they had to. Her father might know somebody who could sever the connection Dee had made with her mind, or perhaps Drabardi could do it. In any event, she knew that she, Neel, and Astrophil couldn't linger in the Cabinet much longer. She had what she had come for: the only thing that really mattered. "I'm ready to go," she told Neel. "Are you?"

He patted his purse. "Yeah."

Petra strode toward the door but then halted. She thought of Susana. She remembered her father's words: "The clock is no longer our concern." But it did concern other people. Her shoulders sagged, as if in defeat, as if weighed down, and she said reluctantly, "Neel. Let's look one more time for the clock's heart."

They paced up and down, inspecting the stacks of objects. Precious time slipped by and Petra grew nervous in the silence. She was about to give up yet again when Neel stopped and raised a hand. "Wait." He stared over Petra's shoulder. "That thing . . ."

Petra looked behind her. "*What* thing? There are *thousands* of things."

Neel pushed past her and pointed at a small table holding several scraps of metal. "*That.* It looks like something from your da's book. I studied it a bit after you told me what the clock could do. Of course, I couldn't read any of it, but I looked at the pictures. And those metal pieces remind me of something."

Petra stared at the table. At first it seemed as if the curved metal pieces were carelessly arranged. But as she looked more closely, she realized the pieces that were roughly of the same size and shape lay next to one another. It looked like the pieces of a jigsaw puzzle someone couldn't quite put together. Petra tried to imagine what the bronze-colored metal scraps would make if they fit together. Then she suddenly understood. "It's the clock's heart," she whispered. She remembered the sketch in her father's notebook of something that looked like a human heart cut into fragments.

Neel reached out to touch a piece of the heart, but Petra grabbed his hand. She had seen a red glitter in the bronze-colored metal. "The pieces are made of banium," she warned. "Human skin can't touch it. It will kill you. It will send shock waves into your body. You'll die slowly, and very painfully. Banium pulses . . . like a heartbeat . . ."

Neel shook off Petra's grip and picked up a piece of banium with his ghostly fingers. "So this one's supposed to fit with another? But it's not easy to tell which goes with which."

"Try that one." She pointed.

A second curve of banium lifted in the air. Neel clinked the two pieces against each other. He tried a few different combinations of fitting them together, but they did not match up.

"Neel, you're doing it wrong."

"What d'you mean?"

"Can't you *see*? Look at the jagged teeth along the edges of each piece. Each piece is a cog, and if you fit them together, the cogs will turn." She tried to imagine the sort of energy the clock's heart would produce when fully assembled, how each cog of the heart would turn, how the banium would make the heart pulse.

"What're you talking about? There are no teeth."

Petra shot him a frustrated look. The uneven edges of each cog were as clear as day, and they obviously were meant to match up with other cogs. "You really don't see it?"

"Yeah, Pet, of *course* I do," he replied sarcastically. "And I'm just saying otherwise 'cause I like to waste time when my life's at stake."

Then Petra realized that the prince could see the cogs clearly with the stolen eyes. And *she* could see them because of who she was.

"Turn your wrist like *that*," she said, and tilted Neel's right hand. "Now push them together."

He did, and the two cogs united.

"Have you both lost your minds?" Astrophil cried. "Do not *assemble* the heart! You are supposed to do the very opposite!"

Neel and Petra looked at the spider guiltily.

"Silk neutralizes banium. Find some, split the cogs between you, and wrap each one in silk so they do not shock you. Then we will get rid of them once we are outside the castle. And I highly recommend that you move quickly! How long could it possibly take for the prince to eat dinner?"

Petra found a silk kimono embroidered with cranes. She borrowed Neel's knife and began hacking the kimono into pieces. Then she paused, thinking. She spoke: "But what are we going to do with the cogs, toss them in the river? That's not going to be enough. The prince would just fish them out. If we bury the pieces, he'll find them and dig them up. Your idea won't work, Astro."

"Can we not fight?" Neel pleaded. "Because picking apart each other's plans at the moment we're supposed to be getting our sweet selves out of here seems to me like a *bad plan*. Let's just break the blasted heart."

"It is already broken." Astrophil gestured at the metal pieces.

"No, it isn't," Petra stated. As she looked at the banium, the entire pattern of the puzzle suddenly made perfect sense. "Not really. Not yet." Wrapping her hands with the silk rags, she told Neel to cut the kimono belt. "Use each half of the belt to tie the rags over my hands," she instructed. "Just like mittens. Knot the belt halves over my wrists. Good."

With her silk-covered hands, she picked up another cog and fitted it to the ones she and Neel had already connected.

"Petra!" Astrophil was shocked.

"I know what I'm doing, Astrophil." Petra rapidly began to attach the cogs. "Listen, I have some magic over metal. Some. But I'm not sure how much and I haven't exactly been trying to find out. I've been too busy." *Or too lazy?* she asked herself. *Too afraid?* "If I can smash those little teeth along the edges of the cogs, they won't fit together anymore. But I don't think I have that kind of power. Luckily, the banium does. Once the heart is assembled I can use its own energy to help me."

Astrophil dragged his gaze from Petra's quick hands. He looked at her. "It might work," he said grudgingly.

"Is this an idea you got from your da?" Neel asked Petra. He reached out his ghostly fingers to help her balance the growing ball of metal. It was now thrumming with energy.

"No," she admitted. "But will you trust me?" she begged, even though she didn't totally trust herself.

He lifted the last cog. "Let's see what happens."

Petra took the last piece. It almost pulled itself into place. The heart began to beat loudly.

"Somebody might hear that," Astrophil said in a tiny voice.

"Be quick, Pet!" Neel urged.

Petra stared at the thumping heart in her silken hands. She tried to focus on the banium, to invite it inside her mind the same way she did Astrophil and the Lovari dagger. Then she paused, afraid. If the touch of banium could kill a person, what would this magic do to her? *If my father built the heart and survived,* she told herself, *I can break it and do the same.* Tomik would have recognized this attitude in Petra, because it was the same steely stubbornness that had brought her to Prague in the first place.

The banium heartbeat began to thud inside Petra's mind. Quietly, at first. Then it swelled and pressed against her skull. A whimper escaped her.

"What's wrong?" Neel cried.

Astrophil jumped up and clung to her shoulder. "Petra?"

She ignored them, trying to cope with the throbbing in her brain. It was worse than any headache. It was beyond painful. Just when she thought her head would split apart from the force of the magical connection between her and the banium, Petra focused on the seams in the clock's heart, the places where the cogs met. *Split THERE*, she willed.

There was a sound like ice cracking. As the throbbing in her head drained away, Petra watched the teeth of the cogs shatter along the lines that held them together. The heart still held its shape somehow, like the fractured shell of a hard-boiled egg. But the teeth were gone.

"Have you done it?" Astrophil asked. "Is it finished? Petra, are you all right?"

"Yes," she whispered. Then she let her hands fall away from the heart. She leaned over and vomited.

Surprised, Neel fumbled with the heart. It dropped to the ground and broke open with an earsplitting *BOOM*.

The three of them looked at one another.

"Now, I *know*," Astrophil said shakily, "that someone heard *that*."

26

A Gift Horse

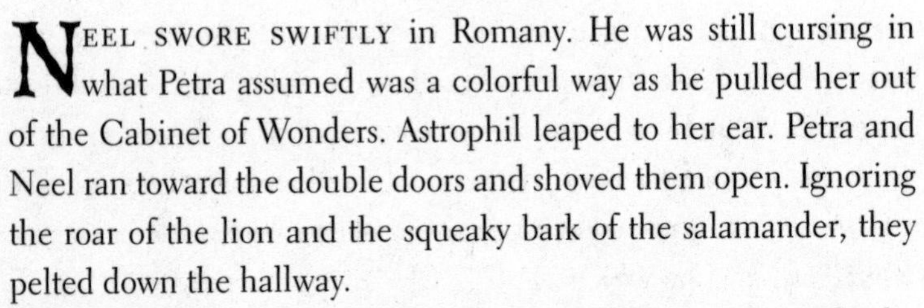

NEEL SWORE SWIFTLY in Romany. He was still cursing in what Petra assumed was a colorful way as he pulled her out of the Cabinet of Wonders. Astrophil leaped to her ear. Petra and Neel ran toward the double doors and shoved them open. Ignoring the roar of the lion and the squeaky bark of the salamander, they pelted down the hallway.

There was a sour taste in Petra's mouth. But the sick mind-ache of the banium was gone, and relief from the pain made her feel a little giddy. She almost forgot she was in danger. Blood sang in her ears, and she was running too quickly to be really afraid.

Then, just before Petra and Neel were going to do their best to race past the guards blocking the stairs to the third floor, she saw a small group of soldiers bearing down on them from another hallway. Following right behind them, his face rigid with fury, was Prince Rodolfo. A quaking fear seized Petra. She skidded to a halt and froze.

"Pet!" Neel had spun around, staring at her. "*Petra!*"

His voice shook her out of her panicky trance. She tore off the silk mittens and flung them to the ground. She reached for the hem of her skirt and ripped at an uneven set of stitches. Then she squeezed Tomik's Marvels into her left hand. "Close your eyes!"

she called to Neel and the spider. She snatched the Marvel she had named Firefly. The lightning in the sphere flickered. Aiming for the space on the floor just ahead of the advancing soldiers' feet, Petra threw the marble and screwed her eyes shut.

BANG! Red light flared behind her closed eyelids. When she opened them, a scene of destruction spread before her. The stone floor was blackened, broken, and heaved up in angular chunks. Some of the men sprawled on the ground. Those who were on their feet staggered, covering their faces with their hands and moaning. A scorched piece of the ceiling fell down with a large thud on a man's foot. He screamed. Thunder rumbled down the hall.

"Come *on*!" Neel cried. They ran past the fallen guards and tore down the passageways of the third floor.

But over the pounding of their feet, Neel and Petra could hear another, terrible noise: the thudding, regular rhythm of many soldiers filing from every corner of the castle to capture them.

Petra glanced in her palm at the two marbles. The wasp buzzed. The water sloshed.

"Not the wasp, Petra!" Astrophil shouted in her ear. "The Hive could attack you, too!"

She tucked the Hive in her pocket and dearly hoped that the Bubble would do something useful. Petra threw the water-filled marble, smashing it against the wall behind them.

A tidal wave instantly engulfed the third floor. Petra was submerged under water and pulled by a fierce current. Something smacked against her leg. She felt a sharp pinch of Astrophil on her right ear, and her chest burned from lack of oxygen as she tumbled in the water.

When she finally broke the surface, gasping for air, she saw Neel floating rapidly past her. He clung to a wooden table. "What're you *doing*?" he yelled. "Quit throwing those *things*!"

She struggled to splash toward him. She wasn't able to make any headway, but as the current pushed them down a flight of stairs and several corridors, the flow of water began to lose its strength, and soon they were able to wade in water that rose only to their thighs, then only to their calves. They were on the second floor, in the Thinkers' Wing.

They had just begun to think that they might actually be able to escape when they heard the thump of soldiers' feet coming from up ahead. Neel and Petra exchanged a look of dread.

That was when a door with two handles, one iron and one red, opened.

Iris stepped into the hallway. She glanced down with a little cry to find herself standing in a foot of water, then looked up at Neel and Petra, astonished at their waterlogged clothes, soaked hair plastered to their heads, and dripping faces. "What in the name of the seven planets is going on here?"

"Iris." Petra waded toward her. "Did you know Mikal Kronos?"

Petra. Astrophil spat out water. *This is unwise.*

"Why, yes, he used to work down the hall. I—" Iris broke off. Her mouth pursed as she looked at Petra's face with the expression of someone whose suspicions have been proven true. "And I suppose you know him, too. Rather well, I would guess."

"I'm his daughter, Petra. My father worked here for six months. But one day, when the clock was almost completed, the prince blinded him. He stole his eyes. I came to this castle to get them back."

Iris gazed at Petra, uncertain. The thud of soldiers grew closer.

"Where do you think the prince got those silver eyes he wears for fun?"

Iris said nothing.

"We have to get out of here! Which way should we go? Please help us. If the castle guards catch us, our lives are worth nothing!"

Desperate, Petra searched for some way to convince Iris that she was telling the truth. "Fiala Broshek removed his eyes, on the prince's command!"

"Fiala!" The name burst from Iris's lips. Then she pushed open her door. "Get in here, both of you."

She slammed the door shut behind them. "Fiala Broshek! Unscrupulous woman! Kristof's work is nothing compared to the abominations she creates! And the operations she performs! 'Surgeon,' she calls herself! Why doesn't she try seeing what *her* insides look like for a change!" She led them into her bedchamber. Neel gave Petra a quizzical look. Iris opened the closet door. "Go in there," she said.

"Um," Neel objected, "I don't think hiding's going to work. They're going to search the castle when they don't find us."

"There's a stairway in there, you dolt! It leads directly to the castle courtyard."

Petra looked at Iris in surprise.

"I am a countess, am I not? I deserve to be able to come and go as I please without dealing with the hassles of guards. Well"—she pushed her spectacles up her nose—"I don't suppose we'll be seeing each other again, Petra Kronos."

There was only one thing Petra could do when Iris said that. She gave the old woman a soaking-wet hug.

To someone very unused to being touched, let alone embraced, this came as a shock. She stood still for a moment, then patted Petra awkwardly on the back. "Now, now. Enough of that. You're going to incriminate me, girl!" They broke apart, and Iris stared down at her newly wet clothes. "The soldiers are going to come around asking if I've seen a soggy-wet criminal and here I'll be, marked with water from hugging the enemy! A fine kettle of fish that will be!" But her smile was warm, gentle, and pleased. "Now, get on with you! Get out of my laboratory!"

Neel plummeted down the stairs. With a glance behind her, Petra followed. They heard the door close behind them.

They soon found themselves in an empty courtyard. Any soldiers who might have been there had, it seemed, entered the castle to find them.

Neel and Petra dashed into the stables. They hid behind a stack of hay, watching as a couple of stable boys cleaned out some stalls, apparently oblivious to the commotion going on inside the castle. Then a third stable boy ran into the building, yelling that they should come out and see the action. He shouted that an army of bandits had broken into the prince's private chambers, and that a fierce battle complete with explosions was going on inside the castle. The other two boys dropped their rakes and raced out of the stables with him.

Neel and Petra couldn't believe their luck.

"This one." Neel led a huge chestnut stallion out of its stall. "Ain't he a beauty? He can carry both of us. Let's take him."

"I wouldn't do that if I was you," said a deep voice.

They turned around. There was Jarek, leaning against a stall, with narrowed eyes and long jowls.

Neel swung up onto the horse. He beckoned to Petra. "Come on. I know this man. He can take care of the prince's horses all right, but he can't ride better or faster than *me*."

But Petra knew that all Jarek had to do was run from the stables, shout for the soldiers, and point them after their galloping horse. The entire castle army would come crashing down on them as they tried to race down the hill, in plain sight. And, Petra realized, as she watched the man chew idly on a stick of straw, Jarek knew this, too.

"So you're responsible for the jumble and noise in the castle," he said. "I guess that's what you two were plotting in the prince's garden. I suppose you also trussed up that lad I found among the tack. You kids are in a lot of trouble. The kind that ends with a death sentence."

Petra and Neel had done so much, planned so well, had the luck to escape so many bad situations, only to be caught by a man who had treated Petra's father as if he were a bundle of sticks tossed in the back of his cart. *Unfair! Unfair!* cried every fiber of Petra's being. "Why?" she demanded, her voice thick with emotion. "Why does it have to be *you* who ruins everything for me?"

"But it's not *over*," Neel yelled. "Enough talking, Pet! Let's go!"

"Yes, enough talking." Jarek stood up straight. "I didn't hurt your da. I just took him home for a bit of money. Now, that isn't the worst thing in the world a man can do. But I'm not exactly proud of it either. I know you fancy Carlsbad, but that horse isn't reliable. He's skittish. He might throw you if a squirrel runs across his path. You should take Boshena." He opened a stall and led out an aging mare. "She's the best horse in the stables, even if she doesn't look it. She's the smartest, the most trustworthy. You could say that she and I are friends. She's not fast, but she's steady. And she knows where you"—he nodded at Petra—"are going. That's more than you can say for yourself, am I right? Do you know how to get back to Okno?"

Petra glared.

"Thought so. Promise to take good care of her, and she'll take you home. I don't suppose you can return her." He patted the horse's head. "But I've seen your family. I think I'm leaving her in good hands."

Neel sighed and sprang down from Carlsbad. "You got funny friends, Pet."

"He's not my friend," Petra hissed through gritted teeth as Neel mounted Boshena.

"Come now," Jarek said to Petra with a touch of humor. "Didn't your da ever teach you not to look a gift horse in the mouth?"

Then, in a swift movement, he picked her up and set her behind Neel.

Boshena's velvet lips brushed over Jarek's hand, her large brown eyes reproachful. Then her ears pricked. She heard it before the humans did: the sound of approaching hooves.

I won't have the deaths of two children on my conscience, Jarek silently told the horse. *Help them.* He patted Boshena gently on the rump and she burst from the stables in a canter.

27

The Fox on the Snow

NEEL LOOSENED THE REINS, letting the horse stride into a gallop. They had almost reached the forest when they heard the thudding of many horse hooves behind them. A dragoon of about twenty castle soldiers on horseback were in pursuit, sweeping down the snow-covered hill.

"I'm surprised there ain't more," Neel said, as if nothing could stop them.

"Well, *I* think there's plenty!" Petra pulled the Hive out of her pocket.

Neel swiveled around. "Oh, no." He looked into her palm. "Not another one of those things. First, you nearly blast us all into bits of bits. Then, you try to drown us. I don't like the looks of that one."

"Neither do I," she admitted. But what choice did they have? She waited until the castle soldiers were just close enough for her throw to reach them, and far enough away to put some distance between their horse and whatever disaster the Hive unleashed. She threw, and they nudged Boshena to go even faster.

Cries rose up behind them and horses screamed in panic as a loud buzz filled the air. Petra couldn't help looking back. A cloud of insects was attacking the men. Wasps wriggled under helmets.

They stung every bare inch of human skin they could find. They stung the horses, which threw their masters and ran wild, stomping the ground and bucking in the air.

Petra and Neel disappeared into the trees. Though guiding Boshena at a slow pace, Neel expertly led them deeper into the forest, picking out the ground where little snow had fallen because it had been trapped in the pine trees above. "The bare earth is frozen hard," he explained. "The horse hooves won't mark it up an awful lot, and we'll stay off the snow. This way, we won't leave any tracks."

After about half an hour, they stopped and dismounted. This was where Neel would go ahead by foot to the Lovari camp, and Petra would make her way back to Okno. It was almost full night. Soon it would be pitch-black, and she would have to ride on alone. She shivered.

Do not worry, Petra, Astrophil said. *You will not be alone. I will be with you.*

She felt comforted.

"Will you ask Sadie to forgive me?" she said to Neel.

"Oh, I think she will, once she sees what I've brought home. We'll be riding new horses into Spain in no time. It's my best theft yet." He grinned. "I can't wait to see Emil's face."

Somewhat awkwardly, they shook hands. "Well, I guess that's it, then," Petra said. It was hard for her to believe that she would probably never see Neel again. It was even harder to find that she didn't know how to say goodbye.

Neel was digging in his pockets. "You know, I was sure we'd be warming a prison floor tonight. But I thought that maybe, just maybe, things would work out all right. And if they did, I would give you this."

It was a circle of leather string. Dangling from it was a miniature iron horseshoe.

Petra took it. She turned the horseshoe over. There was an engraved sentence written in words she didn't understand. There, in the middle of it, was her name, or something close enough to it: *Petali Kronos.*

"Do you like it? Course, I couldn't write it myself. Had to ask someone else. But it means that you're a friend of my clan. Actually . . ." Neel paused. He seemed to make up his mind about something. "It means more than that. There's something you don't know about me. Sadie isn't really my sis." He began to tell Petra about how he had been adopted as a baby. Petra pretended as if she were hearing this for the first time. "So here's what I think." Neel came to the end of his story. "Family is what you make of it. And that horseshoe makes you part of mine. If you need help, or you need to find me, you just show that to a Roma."

"Why," she began and then stopped. She found it difficult to speak. "Why a horseshoe?" *The horseshoe makes its own luck,* she thought.

"Because that's *you,* you see?"

Petra did not see.

"*Petali* means 'horseshoe.'"

"But . . . but you told me it meant 'lucky.'"

"Same thing. One word, two meanings. We use *petali* to talk about a horseshoe *and* to talk about good luck. Don't you *gadje* think horseshoes are lucky?"

"We do." Petra didn't know how to react. She didn't know what to think about her mother's prediction and how it had, in a way, come true. She put on the necklace. "It's the best present I've ever been given."

"Excuse me?" Astrophil objected.

"Well, except Astro, of course." Petra laughed. "Thanks, Neel. I couldn't have done any of this without you."

"I know." He smiled. "But I guess I'd have to say the same thing about you, too. Anyway, I hate goodbyes. I don't believe in 'em. So I'll just say, 'See you later, Petali.' "

"See you later, Neel."

PETRA LEANED HER HEAD against Boshena's bristly neck and shivered. She was miserable. After the excitement of escaping from the castle had worn off, she realized that she had no food or water. Her empty stomach was a dead thing inside her. She had no idea where she was going. Her wet clothes had frozen stiffly against her skin. She sneezed. She had tried guiding Boshena to walk on the bare ground, to avoid patches of snow, like Neel had done. But after a couple hours of this she was too tired, too cold, and too hungry to bother. She just let Boshena walk ahead as she liked, hoping that Jarek was right when he had said the horse knew the way to Okno.

She grew thirsty. When Astrophil suggested that she eat snow, Petra just shuddered. But a few hours later, she was scooping up snow in the dark and forcing herself to swallow some.

Finally, during the coldest hour of the night, when whatever warmth from the day before had been sucked out of the earth, Petra fell asleep, her head on Boshena's mane. The horse plodded along.

Then Petra heard something, a skittering on the snow. She raised her head. They had reached a clearing. A ray of moonlight filtered through the bare trees, and Petra saw the slinky brown body of a fox picking its way across the snow. As she watched, the fox turned its head and looked back. Its brown eyes fixed upon hers, and grew larger. The fox stood on its hind paws and stretched into a tall human with a long beard. It was John Dee.

I'm dreaming, Petra stated.

You are, Dee agreed. *I have come to wish you a happy birthday.*

Petra stared. *What?*

This is the hour you were born, on a November night thirteen years ago. Am I not correct?

Petra thought about it, and realized that it *was* her birthday. She hadn't remembered it at all. It had been the furthest thing from her mind these past months. She shivered against her hard clothes and laughed. Some birthday she was having.

You and your accomplice did very well. Admirably well. I confess that I am impressed by your skills, my dear.

She didn't look at him. Maybe if she ignored him he would go away.

The Staro Clock still possesses power, Dee continued. *The power of beauty, and of time. But it cannot harm anyone now. The prince will surely seek some other means to increase his political strength. But your father's clock can no longer become his tool, Petra, thanks to you.*

His words were flattering, oily. This angered Petra.

Thanks to me! she cried. *You talk as if I had a choice! You threatened my family! You* made *me do this! And, and*, she stuttered, wondering how she had ended up here (wherever "here" was), alone on a stolen horse and trapped in a nightmare that was real. Her voice rose: *And I'm only twelve years old!*

Thirteen, he reminded.

She fumed.

Petra, do you think that I would have really harmed you, or your family? I am not a monster. You simply lacked the proper motivation. A good threat goes a long way. Think of what the clock's secret power could have done. Is not the world better off without it?

Petra thought of Susana. She couldn't say no. But she refused to say yes.

Since you kept our bargain, Dee continued, *and since it is your birthday, I thought I would offer you a present. You may ask something of me: a favor.*

How about this: I want you to get out of my head.

Oh, now, really. Dee chuckled. *You do not want that. That would not do. Believe me when I say that I refuse your request out of my earnest wish to protect your best interests.*

Funny, I never had the impression that you cared about my best interests.

I will not, as you put it, "get out of your head." But if it is any consolation to you, I will be leaving your country. My purpose in Bohemia was to eliminate the threat of the clock. Now I can go home. Like you.

You are not *like me.*

Let us agree on this, Petra: you shall think about whatever favor you would like most *to ask of me. I shall give it to you whenever you ask.*

Petra heaved a disgusted sigh. It seemed as if she would be stuck with Dee for a while. She looked into the clear night sky. The stars glimmered. *Tell me something.*

Is this the present you will request?

No. I'm going to save that for later.

Wise girl.

This is just a question. You can answer it or not. I don't care. I've been wondering about something my father said.

Ah?

Petra could tell that she had piqued his curiosity. *Is it really true that the earth goes around the sun, and not the other way around, as we learn in school?*

Is that all? Yes, Petra Kronos, the earth goes around the sun. He pointed to the sky, and traced his finger along the white stream of stars that was the Milky Way, curving above them in a bending line. *And the sun and the earth are just specks among many, many other things like them, spinning on some part of the galaxy, which is shaped like a spiral. We are standing on a point in that spiral, you and I. The Milky Way that bends above us is a spiral that, to our eyes, has been flattened into a line.*

Petra said nothing.

Let us be allies, if not quite friends, Petra.

I'll think about it, she said.

28

The Most Beautiful Thing

AT DAWN, Josef stepped outside the Sign of the Compass. He blinked.

Slouched over a horse was a sleeping girl. Her dress was water-stained and dirty. Her face was hidden against the horse's mane, but it was her hair—shorter than he remembered, less snarled than he had thought—that convinced him who the girl was, for her hair was the same color as his wife's. He had barely dared to hope when he first saw the girl, but now he was sure: it was Petra.

He picked her up as if she weighed no more than air. She mumbled. He strode into the house, calling, "Dita! Mikal!"

But it was David who ran down first. "What is it? What is it?" he cried excitedly. Then he saw what his father carried. "Petra!"

"Get your mother," Josef ordered.

"I'm always being told to fetch people," David complained.

Josef frowned.

David turned and ran up the stairs.

By now, Petra had woken up, though she felt groggy. Her throat was on fire and it was hard for her to swallow. *Astro?* she thought confusedly. *Am I really home?*

Yes, but I think you are ill.

"Josef," she croaked.

He smiled at her. He carried her up the stairs and into her bedroom, where he sat her on the bed. He told her to lie down, but she refused. "I'm all right," she insisted.

Dita entered the room and paused in the doorway, staring at Petra unbelievingly. Petra braced herself, for she knew Dita's fury would be fierce. She waited for her cousin's silence to break. She waited for Dita to berate her.

But, to her surprise, Dita did no such thing. She just walked across the room, pressed Petra's hair back from her face, gazed at her, and then held her tight. "We thought you were dead," she said. Her voice shook.

"Is it true?" Mikal Kronos stood in the doorway. David was leading him by the hand. "She's not really here? Safe?"

"I am, Father!" said Petra. "And I've brought back your eyes!"

"You . . . what?" He let go of David and felt along the wall for a chair, then sank into one. Astrophil darted across the room and climbed onto his knee. Dita, Josef, and David stared at Petra.

"You did not," David scoffed.

"I did!" Forgetting her sickness, she launched with excited energy into the entire story, from the moment Neel tried to steal her purse to her dream last night. Josef listened, his face impassive. Petra couldn't see Dita's reactions, for the woman stayed beside Petra, sitting on the edge of the bed, with her arm around her. David was riveted. He looked tense during the moments that had scared Petra, laughed at the funny parts, and wrinkled his brow when she explained a dilemma that she'd had to solve. But when Petra finished speaking and a silence stole over the room, David just said, "That's a great story, Petra. But I don't believe any of it."

"Maybe you'll believe this." She reached into her pocket and pulled out her father's eyes. They rested on her palm.

"Those are the ones Master Stakan made," David said.

"That's what *you* think. Father will know the difference." She marched to where Mikal Kronos sat, and put the eyes in his hand.

Petra stood before him, waiting for him to speak. He just sat there, holding his eyes with one hand and his bandaged head with the other.

He closed his hand into a fist, opened his mouth, and then shut it into a thin line. "What have you done?"

"What—what do you mean? I've brought you your eyes."

"You've brought danger on this house!" He flung his silver eyes across the room and they rolled on the floor.

"But—"

"You told Iris December who you were! That man recognized you!"

"But they won't tell. I trust Iris. And they helped me. They can't tell anyone about me without getting themselves into trouble, too."

He gave a hollow laugh. "It's when they *are* in trouble that they will reveal every detail they can about you."

Petra felt suddenly angry. "For someone who was stupid enough to be tricked by the prince, to think he was so friendly and nice and smart, you seem to pretend to know an awful lot about what people really think, and how they act, and how they feel!"

"Petra," Josef said warningly.

"And for someone who's done the last thing in the world I would have ever wanted, you seem to pretend you know what's best for me!" Mikal Kronos shouted back. "How long do you think it will take before the prince realizes that a theft from the Cabinet of Wonders by two children has something to do with me? It'll take about two seconds, Petra. It will take two seconds for the prince to realize that the clock's heart is destroyed."

"Lots of people could have wanted to break that heart! I told you what John Dee said. If he knew about it, plenty of other people must have known, too. The prince will think that one of his brothers found out about it, and hired somebody to destroy it."

"And my eyes? Do you think that he won't notice that they're missing?"

Petra was at a loss for words. "Well . . . so what?"

"So what? A few months ago, I was blind but we were all safe. Now, we are not."

"You—you think we would have been safe here? The prince couldn't figure out how to put the heart together, but he wouldn't have waited around forever. He would have sent for you. He would have made you do it."

"And that would have involved only *me*. Petra, don't you see? I made my decisions. I made my plans. I didn't ask you to become part of them."

"But I already *was*! I know you wanted to send me to the Academy. Oh, yes, I know!"

Mikal Kronos waved his hand. "Well, that will never happen now."

"Good! I'm glad! Because I never would have gone! You—" Her voice broke. She felt as if something were wringing her insides, as if she were a rag. "What do you want from me? What do you want me to say? I did this for you."

"Did you really?" He raised his hands and then let them fall to the arms of the chair. Petra stood before him. He shook his head again. "This is the worst thing you could have done."

This was not what Petra had imagined. This was not what she had imagined at all. And so she said something she could never have imagined she would ever say. "I hate you," she whispered. Then she ran out of the room.

SHE SPED across the wet snow, which was already melting in the rising sun. She ran until she choked on her own breath. She pushed her way into the woods, sat in the cold mud, and cried. Unless you count several hours of chopping onions, Petra hadn't shed a tear since her father had been brought home to Okno, even though there were many times when she had wanted badly to do so. Now Petra didn't think she would ever stop crying.

When she did, she felt like a dried-up riverbed. Like packed, cracked dirt with no chance of ever being anything else. She stared blankly ahead, and wondered if she should run away again, if she should try to find the Lovari. She fingered the horseshoe around her neck. Maybe it wasn't too late . . .

But then something silvery crept across her foot.

"Go away, Astro," she said in a dull voice, without looking down.

"I'm not Astrophil. I'm Roshina."

It was a tin mouse with a long tail and tiny paws. Petra saw Josef pushing aside bare tree branches. He walked steadily toward her. She didn't move. He hunkered down beside her. "Petra, you've done a brave thing."

She didn't look at him. She rubbed at her tears.

"When your da's less scared he's going to realize that, too."

"Scared?"

"When Lucie and Pavel returned from Prague and said they'd left you there with some make-believe aunt, we were very worried. Prague isn't a place for a twelve-year-old girl on her own."

"I'm thirteen," she said sullenly.

"Thirteen." He nodded. "Everyone rounded on Tomik. I don't think he's been let out of his room all this time you've been gone. He kept claiming that the only thing he knew was that you wanted to go to Prague."

Petra had known she could trust Tomik not to reveal her plan.

"So I went to the city to look for you," Josef said.

"You did?"

"Of course. Do you think we would have waited around until you came home, *if* you came home? What would you've done in our shoes?

"I asked the beggar children about you. I saw homeless, crippled, and mad children your own age. And I had to go home empty-handed, thinking the worst things. Don't you understand that when your da's upset the way he is, it's because he's still seeing all the things that we thought must've happened to you? Even though you're here and alive and safe? He blames himself that you left in the first place."

As Petra listened, she imagined how everything could have gone wrong. She had never let herself think about it before, because then she might not have had the courage to go through with her plan. But she understood now what it would have been like if she had been caught, thrown into prison, or hanged. She realized that this would have given her father misery on top of his blindness. She imagined what it would have been like if she had returned home, as triumphant as she had felt only an hour ago, and discovered that her father was dying from a sickness, or from worry, or from anything. Then everything she had done would have been for nothing.

"Let's go back," Josef said, and held out his hand.

She took it.

WHEN SHE WALKED into the Sign of the Compass, she could hear Dita and her father arguing. They stopped when they heard the door creak. Her father turned around. He wore no bandages, and his face was whole and cured. His silver eyes gleamed. "Petra." He walked toward her and put his hand on her cheek. He looked into her face. "Now, that—" he started to say. He tried again: "That is the most beautiful thing I have ever seen."

Epilogue

PETRA HAD TO LIE IN BED for two weeks while she recovered from her fever. She wasn't unhappy, however, for she had visitors.

Tomik, freed by his father, was at first thrilled to see Petra. The tin dog thumped her tail with fierce delight as she and Tomik stood by Petra's bedside. Atalanta had grown into a hulking, bristling, sweet-tempered beast. The dog's shoulders were powerful, but her slender flanks suggested that she might fill out even further. Oil dripped from her fangs as she wriggled her broad head under Petra's arm. She drooled all over Petra's pillow until it was splotched with grass-green stains.

Tomik proudly said that he had always known Petra would be able to accomplish what she had set out to do. He told her about his new inventions. Tomik had created an antidote to the Worry Vial's flaw: a gel that coated the inside of the jar, just like Petra had suggested. Tomas Stakan's gratitude had made Tomik's virtual imprisonment at the Sign of Fire after Petra had disappeared a little more bearable. A little.

Tomik was impressed when Petra described how she had used his Marvels. "That much water?" he said. "I'll have to fix that." As he mused about how to do that, he looked at his friend's tired face. A sudden awareness of how much danger Petra had faced without him rose in his heart, and awoke the seeds of unpleasant questions: Should he have gone to Prague with Petra? Would their friendship change because he hadn't?

"Maybe you should leave it as it is," Petra suggested. "Make the next Bubble just like the first. It was pretty useful." She didn't notice the shadow that changed Tomik's expression. Astrophil did, but he remained silent.

David made her tell the story over and over again. Neel was his new hero, and he kept pestering his mother to make a red and gold page's jacket for him.

Dita scolded Petra for talking too much, reading too much, staying up too late, and overall doing just about everything she could do to avoid getting better. Petra found herself breaking rules deliberately, just so Dita would complain that she'd have to check in on Petra every hour, since the girl clearly didn't have the wits to take care of herself. The cousins played this game with each other, and Petra realized, perhaps for the first time, that they played it with love.

After his rare burst of eloquence, Josef went quiet again. He nodded at Petra if he passed by her room. He said very little, as if he were embarrassed for having said so much. But then, he was busy, for he had a lot of work to do as a laborer. During the winter months, there wasn't much work related to farming, so Josef hired himself out. He did odd jobs, repaired houses, and took care of horses. He rode Boshena. She obeyed him willingly, and he didn't ask too much of her, for they recognized that some affinity rested between them.

Petra's father came by her bedroom several times a day. Although he was no longer blind, the family had decided that this should remain a secret from everyone but their closest friends, the Stakans. This meant that Mikal Kronos rarely left the house, and if he did, he had to wrap bandages over his face and pretend the need to lean on someone's arm. He didn't like to fake blindness. But he knew that word of his miraculous recovery could so easily reach the prince.

Petra and her father shared ideas as they had almost a year ago, before Mikal Kronos left for Prague to build a clock for Prince Rodolfo. But things were different. You could see this in the slightly stiff way that they talked together, as if they each wanted to ask for the other's forgiveness.

One morning, Petra woke up at dawn. This was another way in which things had changed. Ever since she had worked as a servant, she had gotten used to rising early, and found that she liked it. Today she felt strong and well.

She slipped from her bed and went to her father's library. Astrophil rode on her shoulder.

Petra shut the library door behind her, and then opened the secret compartment in the floor. She pulled out the bag of invisible tools. This action marked another change. For, you see, she now knew why her father had hidden that bag away. It was because the tools could be used as weapons.

She carefully sorted through the bag, trying not to prick her fingers on any sharp edges or points. Feeling along the invisible shapes, she found one that was not really a tool. It was not a screwdriver, or a hammer, or a wrench. It was a thin sword. She hefted it in her hand. It felt light. It felt as if it had been made for her. Indeed, it probably had been.

The greatest change of all for her family had been shouted by her father: they were no longer safe. He hadn't meant to be so angry. He hadn't meant to accuse her. Petra knew this. But she also knew that some of the things he had said were true. It might not be long before the prince came looking for them.

She stared at the blade, even though she saw nothing.

What are you going to do with it?

She replied to Astrophil as if the answer were obvious: "I'm going to practice."

Author's Note

WHEN I VISITED PRAGUE for the first time, my cousin David walked with me to see the astronomical clock that stands in the center of Old Town Square. He said that legend has it that the clockmaker, upon completion of his project, was blinded so that he could never build anything like it again.

David said nothing more on the subject, and I have never investigated this legend.

I don't get to see my Czech cousins very often, but this past summer I found myself in Prague, sitting in an outdoor restaurant with him, his sister (Petra), his mother (Jana), and his grandmother (Mila). I told them about *The Cabinet of Wonders*, and reminded David of the conversation we had had about ten years ago by the clocktower.

He paused. Then, in that careful, generous way he has when speaking my language, he said, "But I think this legend is not true."

It never mattered to me whether the story was true or not. Most of *The Cabinet of Wonders* is pure invention, brewed in my own personal Thinkers' Wing laboratory. I took what I wanted from history. What I took, I changed.

The Cabinet of Wonders is set during the European Renaissance, at the very end of the sixteenth century, but my Renaissance has magic and all sorts of events that are different from what actually happened. Mikal Kronos's clock is similar to the one David showed me, but it is not the same.

Prince Rodolfo is loosely based on Rudolf II, who was part of the Hapsburg family and inherited the title of Holy Roman Emperor after the death of his father, Maximilian II. Rudolf was already emperor and more than thirty years old when he moved his court from Vienna to Prague. Rodolfo, on the other hand, is very young and doesn't have nearly as much power. But Rudolf and Rodolfo have something in common: they both owned a cabinet of wonders.

Originally, a cabinet of wonders was a piece of furniture meant to display odd, beautiful objects. Wealthy people built their collections over time, and a cabinet could house things like narwhal tusks (which some people thought were unicorn horns), oil paintings, and ostrich eggs. Sometimes a collection grew until the cabinet overflowed, and its contents filled an entire room. Then the collection filled many rooms. Eventually, it became what today we call a museum.

Rudolf II's cabinet of wonders was one of the most impressive in Europe. The king was attracted to bizarre items, machinery, and new inventions. Magic fascinated him, and he welcomed people who claimed they could practice it.

One such person was John Dee. He was a real man, and a fascinating one at that. He was a well-known magician, mathematician, astrologer, adviser to Queen Elizabeth, a visitor to Bohemia, and (probably) a spy.

Dee and many other people in the Renaissance believed in the power of scrying. It was thought that only children could scry, and that they needed to stare at a crystal, mirror, or oil-covered surface in order to do it. Dee tried to teach his eight-year-old son, Arthur, how to scry, though the boy saw nothing special in the crystal. Before you think that the real John Dee was just as unpleasant as mine, I should say that there are no historical documents about children losing their minds as a result of scrying. I made that part up.

Neel is fictional, but the Roma certainly are real. Though their origins are uncertain, the Roma likely came from India and then traveled throughout the Middle East, Europe, and other parts of the world, facing suspicion and even persecution. For five hundred years, they suffered enslavement in Romania until this was abolished in the nineteenth century. In more recent history, hundreds of thousands of Roma were killed during the Holocaust.

Although the Roma in *The Cabinet of Wonders* share some things in common with real Roma, Neel's culture is highly fictionalized. The story of Danior has no origin in anything other than my imagination (and my love of elephants), but the one Neel tells Petra about the fiddler is based on a Hungarian Romany tale recorded by Vladislav Kornel in *A Book of Gypsy Folk-Tales*. I have changed this oral legend in several ways.

Now it's time for me to confess something. I'm a little worried that someone, somewhere is going to object to the way I've manhandled history. I can already hear a disapproving sniff, followed by the words, "History is not a toy for you to play with, Marie."

So I asked Astrophil what he thought.

He pondered. "But—correct me if I am wrong—you are not a historian."

No, I replied. I write fiction.

"Did you make any promises to anyone to be historically accurate?" the spider asked.

Not that I recall.

"Well, then." Astrophil settled into his favorite resting position. "I do not think you need to worry."

Oh, good.

"I am also relieved," he admitted. "After all, *I* am not historically accurate. But I exist."

Which, I thought, was as good a perspective as I am likely to get.

December 2007
New York City

Acknowledgments

I owe my first thanks to my grandmother, Jennie Hlavac (born Zděnka Pavliček) for always keeping me aware of my Bohemian heritage. I am also grateful to our relatives Mila Kostová and Viktor, Jana, David, and Petra Valouch.

Many friends read drafts of *The Cabinet of Wonders*, offered me a beautiful place in which to write it, discussed ideas with me, or gave encouragement: Manuel Amador, Eric Bennett, Esther Duflo, Dave Elfving, Caroline Ellison, Francesco Franco (whose Genovese is acclaimed in several countries), Erik Gray, Dominic Leggett, Jonathan Murphy, Becky Rosenthal, and Holger Syme. My greatest debt is to two amazing friends: Neel Mukherjee and Bret Anthony Johnston. This book would not exist without you.

I'm grateful to Charlotte Sheedy, Meredith Kaffel, Violaine Huisman, and Marcy Posner for their faith in *Cabinet*. Finally, many thanks to Janine O'Malley, who helped make this book the best it could be. I'm lucky to have such a wise and delightful editor.

GOFISH

QUESTIONS FOR THE AUTHOR

MARIE RUTKOSKI

© Stephen Scott Gross

What did you want to be when you grew up?

In kindergarten, I wanted to be an ice skater, a nurse, or a writer when I grew up. I didn't know how to skate, but it looked like a lot of fun. As for being a nurse, that's what all the other girls were writing down on their sheets of construction paper, so I figured I'd better do the same thing (looking back, I'm astonished by how easily I was influenced by peer pressure and what was expected of girls versus boys). Being a writer, though was the one choice that felt truly right, truly mine.

When did you realize you wanted to be a writer?

I don't remember. It seems like the desire was always there, just like I always had ten fingers and ten toes.

The first time that I received some sign that maybe I could be a good writer was when I won a Young Authors competition in first grade for an illustrated story called "Midnight Cat," about a black cat that always goes outside at midnight. One night, however, she stays indoors. Midnight Cat's worried owner rushes her to the vet, certain that something is desperately wrong. It turns out, though, that she's just pregnant, and gives birth to three kittens. The "joyful" owner names them Fuzzy, Corduroy, and Unicorn. "From that day on," I wrote, "everyone was happy!"

What's your first childhood memory?
The clearest, earliest memory I have is of me running into the backyard, which was heaped high with snow. My mother yelled for me to come back inside, saying, "You're going to catch pneumonia!" I remember turning the world "pneumonia" over in my mind, thinking that it sounded funny, and wondering what it meant. I do not remember if I went back inside.

What's your most embarrassing childhood memory?
When I was in second grade, I had a huge crush on a boy named Todd. I wondered how I could make him like me, and it crossed my mind that I needed to find something we had in common. Then, eureka! I remembered that he wore a retainer, which I thought was really cute. Although I didn't have a retainer or braces, at the time I really wanted one or the other. So I made one out of an unbent paper clip and wore it to school. I marched up to Todd, pointed to my mouth, and said, sigh, that my parents had made me get a retainer. Wasn't life tough and didn't he feel my pain? He did, and we became friends. But after a while I began to feel guilty—here I was, living a lie, showing up to school each day with a paper clip in my mouth. One afternoon, I confessed the truth. Todd, feeling betrayed, said he was never going to speak to me again. And he never did.

What's your favorite childhood memory?
Night fishing with my father. My mother reading me bedtime stories.

What was your worst subject in school?
Math! (or Handwriting).

What was your best subject in school?
English!

What was your first job?
When I was sixteen, I worked in a record store with my best friend, Becky, and several twentysomething hipsters who were too cool for school. I worshipped every single one of them (but tried not to show it). They introduced me to bootleg recordings, obscure EPs, and random punk bands that sang about sushi. More importantly, they taught me that there was life outside of high school.

I've stayed in close touch with Becky, and recently have reconnected with some of my other coworkers. One of them is a defense lawyer, another a schoolteacher, and another a furniture designer who lives in New York City. Just last weekend, we met up and chatted while our kids played in the park. It was awesome.

How did you celebrate publishing your first book?
I think I had a fancy dinner with my husband. I'm not sure. It was such a giddy moment for me that my memory's a blur.

Where do you write your books?
Wherever I can. All I ask is either a room with a door that shuts, or to be lost in a crowd of reasonably quiet people.

Which of your characters is most like you?
Astrophil. He's the part of me that gets really excited whenever I go to a rare books room. Once, when I was in Dublin, I went to Marsh's Library to do some research. It had been closed for renovation for several months, and the dear, elderly ladies who ran the place greeted me with such joy. I was their very first "reader" since the library had been reopened. All afternoon, I sat with sixteenth-century books spread out in front of

me, and the librarians would offer me tea and shush the tourists who came in to look around (Marsh's Library is very pretty). "You must be quiet," they told the visitors. "We have a *reader*."

Astrophil would have understood how much I loved those librarians, and how that afternoon is one of my very favorite memories.

When you finish a book, who reads it first?

When I lived in Boston, my housemate Esther did. Usually she's insanely busy saving the world through economics projects in developing countries, but she made time for my books, which I appreciate.

Now that I live in New York, I swap drafts with many children's and YA writers, but my first reader is always Donna Freitas, author of *The Possibilities of Sainthood*. We get bossy and opinionated with each other when we discuss our books, but it's tough love.

Are you a morning person or a night owl?

Now that my baby is sleeping through the night, I am (thank God) a 6:30 A.M. person (though I don't write until I have caffeine in my system).

What's your idea of the best meal ever?

My wedding dinner.

What do you value most in your friends?

What I admire most in my parents: their good hearts.

What makes you laugh out loud?

My son, Eliot, who, as I write this, is almost one year old. He'll laugh at something, I'll laugh because his laugh is so cute, and then he'll laugh because I'm laughing . . . this can go on for a long time.

He made a grab for my pasta the other night, so I pulled a string of spaghetti off my fork and handed it to him. He wiggled it and stretched it and nibbled on it and finally stared, dumbfounded, at the noodle in his hands. WOW, his expression seemed to say, SPAGHETTI. And I had to laugh. A baby is such a special creature, and it's a delight to watch mine explore the world. How often do you get to see a string of spaghetti blow someone's mind?

What's your favorite song?

"Time" by Tom Waits, "A Case of You" by Joni Mitchell, "Pale Green Things" by the Mountain Goats, "Hyperballad" by Bjork, and "I Still Haven't Found What I'm Looking For" by U2.

Who is your favorite fictional character?

I am very fond of Charlotte A. Cavatica (from E.B. White's *Charlotte's Web*). I cry every time I read the last lines of that book: "It's not often someone comes along who is a true friend and a good writer. Charlotte was both."

What are you most afraid of?

Many, many things, most of them perfectly rational. But I do have one fear that has no explanation, and I've had it since I was little. If I'm outside in the dark, I can see the moon overhead, it's cold, there's a wind, and I'm only ten feet or so from my house, I feel something clutch my heart. And I have to run inside. It's a little silly, but there it is.

What time of the year do you like best?

A Manhattan spring, a French summer, a New England fall, or a Midwestern winter.

What is your favorite TV show?

The Wire is the best thing television has produced, as far as I'm concerned. Every episode is excellent. But when I want to curl up on the sofa with a bowl of ice cream and do some comfort TV watching, I'll reach for my *Buffy the Vampire Slayer* DVDs. Or *Battlestar Galactica*.

If you were stranded on a desert island, who would you want for company?

Why, my family, of course.

If you could travel in time, where would you go?

I'd like to have a chat with Shakespeare. I have a lot of questions, and I want answers!

But I don't want to *live* in Renaissance England. I just want to go, hang out for a day, and come right back. People didn't live for very long in the sixteenth century, and the food was bad. If I stayed there for more than a day I'd probably catch a cold and die.

What's the best advice you have ever received about writing?

In *Bird by Bird*, Anne Lamott quotes Thurber: "You might as well fall flat on your face as lean over too far backwards." I make mistakes as a writer, but I'd rather make them by trying too hard than by being too afraid to make a fool out of myself.

What would you do if you ever stopped writing?

I have no idea. If I ever stop writing, I will have changed so drastically from who I am now that I wouldn't recognize myself, and therefore there is no way to predict anything this Not-Me Me would do.

What do you like best about yourself?

I like that I am never bored. Pretty interesting things go on inside my head, so I'm happy to just sit around and think. Sometimes this means that I'm not paying attention to the world around me, though.

What's your worst habit?

I never get straight to the point. Except, of course, with this answer.

What do you wish you could do better?

Um, everything.

What would your readers be most surprised to learn about you?

I once rappelled 1,000 feet down into a gorge and then climbed back up. I will never, ever do anything like that again.

Author Marie Rutkoski Interviews Astrophil, the Tin Spider

Marie: Don't be nervous.

Astrophil: I am not.

Marie: Your legs are trembling. All eight of them.

Astrophil: Oh.

Marie: This is just a brief interview. I'd like to ask you a few questions. That's all.

Astrophil: Well, perhaps I *am* a tad nervous, but only for your sake.

Marie: Mine?

Astrophil: Oh, yes. I am a very brave spider, you see, and I have endured many dangerous adventures. If I tell you about them, you might faint.

Marie: I'll try not to.

Astrophil: Very good.

Marie: The last time we met, you and your friend Petra had just escaped from Prince Rodolfo's palace with a strange treasure: the eyes of Petra's father. The prince had stolen them, and enspelled them so that he could wear them whenever he liked. So you and Petra stole them back.

Astrophil: Yes, with the help of Neel, a very talented thief. If you look at his hands, they appear to be the normal hands of any grubby boy who should bathe more often. His fingers, however, can grow very long and invisible. But you know all of this. You wrote a book about our adventures.

Marie: Yes: *The Cabinet of Wonders*. Have you read it?

Astrophil: Of course.

Marie: Did you like it?

Astrophil: Yes, but it was far too short. There should have been more pages about me.

Marie: I'm writing a new book called *The Celestial Globe*. You're in it.

Astrophil: Really?

Marie: It's about what happened to you and Petra after you returned home with her father's eyes. Um . . . Astrophil? Your legs are trembling again.

Astrophil: Well, you see, soon after we returned home, the prince sent monsters to attack us.

Marie: Monsters?

Astrophil: Terrible creatures. They are called the Gray Men. Petra and I were whisked away to London. In fact, I am supposed to be there right now. I stole a few minutes to speak with you, but I cannot leave Petra alone for very long. I must return to her.

Marie: Wait! What's happening in London?

Astrophil: For one thing, Petra is finally receiving a decent education. She is being trained in magic, and there is a dashing young fencing master named Kit who teaches her how to use a sword. She is very good. However, we want to return home as soon as possible. I cannot bear to think about what might be happening to Petra's father at this very moment.

Marie: How frightening! How will you get back to Bohemia?

Astrophil: Petra made a bargain. One of the Queen of England's counselors has been murdered. If Petra discovers who did this dastardly crime, we will be sent home.

Marie: I hope you solve it.

Astrophil: Don't worry. I shall help her.

Marie: I've heard a rumor. . . .

Astrophil: You shouldn't gossip.

Marie: It's about Neel and Tomik, Petra's childhood friend.

Astrophil: Tell me everything!

Marie: I've heard that they're looking for you and Petra. You disappeared from Bohemia, and now nobody knows where you went. So Neel and Tomik are sailing the high seas in search of you.

Astrophil: But . . . but the open sea is so perilous! There are pirates, storms. . . . But no. It is not possible. Tomik and Neel cannot be sailing together. They do not even know each other.

Marie: They do now.

Astrophil: Indeed? So they're friends?

Marie: Mmm . . . I wouldn't say that. Actually, I think they kind of hate each other.

Astrophil: Oh my.

Marie: But they're still working together. They have to, if they're going to find Petra—and the location of a magical object called the Celestial Globe.

Astrophil: Oh, I've read all about the Celestial Globe. It is extremely powerful. But then . . . that must mean that the prince of Bohemia will want it, too.

Marie: Yes, he does.

Astrophil: This is troubling news. I must tell Petra at once.

Marie: I'm not so sure you should. It will only worry her.

Astrophil: Perhaps you are right.

Marie: I think I am.

Astrophil: Very well. It will be our secret.

Petra Kronos may have escaped from Salamander Castle, but that doesn't mean Prince Rodolfo won't come looking for her. . . .

Keep reading for an excerpt from

THE CELESTIAL GLOBE

by Marie Rutkoski.

1

The Gray Men

SOME DAYS are just born bad. You know the type. The kind you want to sweep into your palm like spilled salt and toss over your left shoulder, hoping that if you don't look back nothing worse will happen.

Petra Kronos snapped awake. Her heart thudded. The bedsheets were damp with sweat.

She turned her head to the left and looked out the window: it was foggy, wintry, dreary.

She turned her head to the right, and there was Astrophil. The tin spider was curled into a tiny, spiky ball. With a squeak, he bunched his shiny legs together, sprang them into the air one by one, and wriggled onto the tips of his legs. "Petra, is something wrong?"

"I had a bad dream." Her pulse was still racing.

"Ah. Was it . . . relevant to the events at Salamander Castle?"

"No." Petra didn't want to think about what had happened more than a month ago. "Anyway, dreams don't mean anything. They're just empty pictures."

"Was it," said the spider gingerly, "related to John Dee?"

"No." Petra huffed with annoyance and got out of bed. Astrophil had the frustrating habit of pointing out exceptions to her rules. She would claim something (dreams did not mean anything) and he would immediately provide a counterexample (John Dee).

"If you dreamed of him," Astrophil persisted, "it might have been real. He could have been sending you a message. Your minds are connected."

"Don't remind me." She shivered as she dressed.

"Do you remember what you dreamed?"

"No," she lied. She pulled a necklace out from under her shirt. A small horseshoe swung from the thin leather cord. She flipped the horseshoe over and looked at the engraving. It was written in a language she didn't understand, but she saw her name, and a friend's. "Where do you think Neel is now? Do you think he's still in Spain?"

There was a reproachful pause. Astrophil wasn't fooled by her attempt to distract him. "I do not know."

"Let's go out to the forest. Before Father wakes up."

"If you wish."

She got down on her hands and knees, and rummaged under the bed. When she stood up, she held nothing. But her hands, though empty, moved oddly. Petra seemed to buckle an invisible object at her waist. She looked like an actor playing a pantomime.

Astrophil crept up her arm, and she smiled at him cheerfully.

But that was an act, too. Petra was troubled. She remembered her dream well enough. She had been angry—more than angry. She had been filled with a rage that was almost panic, almost despair. She had been pounding at a door. The room that trapped her was luxurious, with carved furniture and brocade fabrics. But that didn't change the fact that she was in some sort of prison.

JAREK WAS FLUNG into the corner of his cell. His cheek grazed against the stone wall as he fell to the floor, and the door shrieked shut.

The session had been mercifully short. After all, he had given them the information they wanted.

There was a window in his cell, Jarek reminded himself. Not a window, really, just a square hole. It was big enough for one hand.

Jarek struggled to his feet. As he reached up, pain shot through his arm. He shoved his hand through the hole. Cold rain tingled over his bloody fingers.

Then something besides the rain tickled his palm. A small body nestled into Jarek's cupped hand. He felt warm feathers and a quick heartbeat. *My poor friend*, the sparrow murmured in Jarek's mind.

Jarek imagined what the bird could see: his own wrist growing out of the dungeon wall like a twisted root, the sky blurry with rain, and the red rooftops of Prague.

The idea of the sparrow leaving him alone was perhaps the worst torture of all. Still, he said to the bird, *I need you to bear a message for me.*

THE HOUSE at the Sign of the Compass was filled with echoes. Most of the furniture had been sold, or loaded into the cart Josef and Dita had driven with their son, David, into southern Bohemia. Dita was Petra's older cousin, but she was more than that. Dita and her husband, Josef, were like a second set of parents to Petra, and David was like her little brother.

When Petra's father had first proposed that the entire family leave the village of Okno, everybody began arguing. Petra protested. Josef disagreed by refusing to respond at all. Dita said flatly, "It's a foolish idea, Uncle Mikal."

Mikal Kronos talked about his plan every morning, and every morning a fresh battle erupted over breakfast until one day David dropped his spoon into his porridge, covered his ears, and yelled, "*Shut up!* Shut *up*, all of you!" He burst into tears. His tin raven swooped anxiously overhead. His parents exchanged a glance.

"Think of the children's safety," Mikal Kronos urged Dita and Josef. "When the prince discovers who is responsible for ransacking his Cabinet of Wonders, he won't be merciful to anyone in this family. The four of you need to move as quickly as possible. I don't want to leave behind anything that he could use, so I'll need some time to dismantle the workshop. I promise I won't be far behind."

Slowly, Dita nodded.

"I won't go," Petra told her father. "You can't make me."

There was a long pause. "No," he finally said, "I don't suppose I can. You will leave with me, Petra, as soon as we're able to join the others."

Petra had won something. But it didn't feel that way now.

"Ahem," Astrophil coughed, startling Petra out of her memory. "Do you plan to stare into space all day, or will we actually do something important and worthy, like, say, attend to the business of breakfast?"

"Sorry, Astro."

Petra opened her nightstand drawer, which clattered with unwashed silver spoons. She fed the spider his daily meal, a spoonful of green brassica oil. When he had drained it, Petra ran a finger over the greasy metal and rubbed the leftover oil on her chapped lips.

She opened the wardrobe, pulled out a leather cloak lined with rabbit fur, and then began searching for the woolen cap Dita had made for her. It itched like mad, but Petra loved it. She rescued it from under a pile of worn books and dirty socks.

"What are *books* doing there?" Astrophil was horrified.

Petra ignored him, tucking the hat and cloak under her arm. She walked downstairs to the kitchen with Astrophil perched on her shoulder, muttering about Petra's shameful treatment of the books.

She took a wizened apple from the kitchen fruit bin and sawed some bread from a stale loaf. She would have liked a mug of warm milk, but starting a fire in the stove would take far too much effort. Petra arranged a slice of cow cheese on the tough bread and bit into it.

"In some societies," Astrophil informed her, "it would never cross anyone's mind to eat cheese. To them it would be nothing but spoiled milk."

"Too bad for them," Petra replied, chewing. The bread tasted like tree bark, but at least the cheese was fresh.

When she finished eating, she tiptoed down the stairs and through the shop.

Petra held the bell on the door frame so that it wouldn't ring as she slipped outside. The cold air hit her. She pulled the hat down over her ears, breathed deeply, and her head seemed to clear. Maybe she would be able to shake off her bad mood. Maybe the day was salvageable after all.

Her boots had crunched over just a few yards of snow when it began to rain. Astrophil ducked under her hair. Petra looked up at the falling drops. "Oh, *perfect*." She thought about going back into the house but then changed her mind. Petra drew the cloak tightly about her and trudged on.

"YOUR HIGHNESS, the prisoner has broken."

"And?" replied the young prince. "What have you learned?"

"He still claims that he doesn't know the name of the Gypsy who participated in the theft in November."

"No matter." Prince Rodolfo tried to control his irritation. "We will find out the boy's name the hard way. Sweep my country clear of this Gypsy trash."

"We've already begun to do this, Your Highness. As you recall, you ordered us last month to begin arresting Prague's Gypsies for questioning."

"I am not forgetful." The prince's voice was even but dangerous, like thin ice covering a deep pond. "I want you to have *all* of Bohemia searched for Gypsies. You know their ways. They travel everywhere, and quickly, like a disease. Watch our borders. Do not let them leave, and do not block the borders from those who wish to enter. Imprison them as well.

"Now, as for Jarek: I hope you have gleaned *some* useful information from him?"

"Yes, Your Highness. He has confirmed your suspicions. The girl who stole from the Cabinet of Wonders was not working for your brothers. It was Petra Kronos, the clockmaker's daughter."

The prince remembered the girl: a tall, unlovely thing who had scarcely pretended to be afraid of him.

Well, she would learn.

"I want there to be no mistakes," the prince said. "Send the Gristleki."

The guard flinched.

"Did you hear me?" the prince hissed. "Send the Gray Men."

The guard jerked his head in a nod. "Yes, Your Highness. What should I do with the prisoner?"

"Let them start with him. They are hungry."

2

The Sparrow

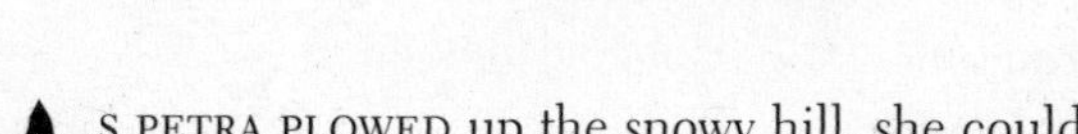

As PETRA PLOWED up the snowy hill, she couldn't have known what was speeding across the countryside toward her. Nothing could have prepared her to imagine the Gray Men, who loped like wolves under the trees, their clawed feet running almost as quickly as a bird flies.

When Petra and Astrophil had reached the forest, the spider said, "Perhaps you could try talking to him."

"Try talking to who?"

"The link John Dee made between your mind and his should be accessible by both of you. Neel said that such links are used between generals and soldiers, and between criminal allies. Surely forging a connection like that is valuable only if each person can mentally reach the other. Instead of waiting for Dee to contact you, you could try contacting him."

"I could try eating rotten goat intestines, but I'm not going to," Petra scoffed. "And let's get one thing straight: I'm not *waiting* for that man to pay a visit to my mind as if it were his summer cottage. My thoughts are my own. Not his."

"A mental link does not allow him to read your mind," Astrophil said. "When you and I speak using our thoughts, I hear only what you say to me, not your inner secrets. A mental link is simply a form of communication. You know this already. Neel explained it to us in Prague. You are just being difficult."

Petra pushed through the pine trees, and green bristles showered her with freezing water. She yelped.

"Petra, we are all worried about what the prince knows of you, and how he will react. It is not as if you lost one of his papers while cleaning his study. You broke into his prized collection of magnificent and magical objects, took your father's eyes—"

"They didn't belong to the prince! Now they are back where they belong, and Father can see."

"You also stole a small fortune of gold and jewels—"

"*Neel* did that. Not me."

"—and managed to destroy a hidden part of the Staro Clock that Master Kronos built, a part that would have allowed the prince to use the clock to control the weather, thereby wielding an enormous amount of power over all of Europe."

"That's right. You'd think someone would thank me for it."

They reached a clearing. The ground was rocky and uneven, and the space wasn't as large as the one she preferred to use, but that spot of woods was a mile ahead. She squinted at the rain. She would stay here. "All right, Astro: tree or ear?"

He clung to her earlobe tightly. "I am quite fine where I am, thank you. I believe it may be useful for me to learn how to be part of a skirmish. I could be an extra set of eyes. I could warn you if an enemy approaches. Plus . . . it is raining."

"Tin doesn't rust, Astro."

"Even so, the brim of your hat makes a nice umbrella."

Petra pulled at something by her left hip. There was a scraping sound, and her closed fist arced in the air. Raindrops plinked and halted in a horizontal line in front of her. Petra's fingers grasped the hilt of something long, thin, and wickedly sharp. It was a sword, and an invisible one at that.

Astrophil cleared his throat. "To return to my point—"

"I wish you wouldn't."

"—the prince is not likely to reward you with sugar plums for your actions. Once he learns who you are and, thus, *where* you are—"

"I *know*, Astrophil. Why do you think Josef, Dita, and David are halfway to Sumava by now?"

"John Dee is a trusted adviser to the queen of England."

"I think his official title is Arrogant Spy," Petra retorted.

"He is also a former ambassador to the prince of Bohemia. I am merely trying to suggest that John Dee may have useful information to share with you. Can you afford to make no effort to gain it? Dee promised to help you one day, if you ask for it. You should try contacting him to learn what the prince knows about you, and what he might do with that knowledge."

"Even if—*if*—I agreed with you, I have no idea how to tap into Dee's head. What am I supposed to do, go to the top of a hill and shout, 'Hey, Dee! Speak to me, you annoying, smirking—'?"

"It is a pity we cannot consult Neel. If his people know as much about mind-magic as he claims, he might be able to ask one of them about this situation."

"Neel is someplace warm and sunny. Not here." Petra tried not to care. Why should you miss someone you will never see again? It wasn't fair. Feelings like guilt and anxiety and missing people should have a certain life span. Like fruit flies.

"But perhaps—" Astrophil continued.

"Astrophil? You know what's so great about books?"

"Why, many things. I am so glad you asked. They possess many wonderful properties. They awaken the imagination, inform one about history—"

"And they *close*. Like this subject. I don't want to talk about John Dee. He threatened my father and me, and made *me* destroy the clock's magical power, all for the sake of his precious English queen."

"You would have done that anyway, once you knew the havoc the clock could wreak."

"Maybe, but John Dee got to sit snug in his little velvet chair, doing nothing to risk his neck while you, Neel, and I could have gotten caught and killed. Dee's always looking out for his best interests, and any help from him would come with so many strings attached I'd be tied up like a trussed pig. I don't want anything more to do with Dee, or to even think about him."

Astrophil's green eyes glowed with frustration. But he knew Petra. It would be easier to coax a stone to grow into a flower than it would be to make her listen to an idea she hated. "Very well. Shall we begin by running through a series of positions? I have consulted several books on sword-fighting. This took me some time because most of them were written in Italian, but I have translated several passages."

"Let's just do what we've been doing for weeks."

"Would that be: I watch while you slash at the air until you are tired?"

"Yes."

Astrophil sighed. "You could at least comment on how well my knowledge of Italian is progressing."

"Bravo," Petra said, and crouched. She felt ridiculous, shuffling back and forth over the snow and swinging the invisible sword. But she did it anyway.

"You can grip that hilt with both hands," said a voice behind her.

Petra spun around.

Mikal Kronos stepped forward. "You're letting your left hand dangle at your side. That's a waste. This sword is thin and light, like a rapier, but not as long as one. I thought a true rapier would be too long to keep unnoticed when sheathed. Of course, even an invisible sword isn't easy to hide. But if you're going to forge one, you obviously have some interest in secrecy, so why not do what you can to maximize that?

"Now, what did I want to tell you? Ah, yes, the left hand. Since the blade is on the short side, your ability to thrust it at your opponent is limited. Your *reach* is limited. So that means that you need to compensate by learning how to use your left hand, too. With that hand you can hold a dagger, and use it to block blows and swipe at your opponent. What happens if your dagger is knocked away? There's room enough for your left hand as well as your right on this hilt. That will give your blows more force. Do you feel the swirls of steel arcing over the hilt? That's to protect your fingers, in case someone tries to make you drop the sword by hacking at them. Remember that a master of fencing should be able to wield a sword just as well with the left hand as with the right. If you let your left arm stick out uselessly like a tree branch, it will get lopped off like one."

Petra stared. She had often wondered what would happen if her father ever caught her with the sword he had made and hidden away. Usually, she imagined a lot of yelling. Not this.

Mikal Kronos noticed her surprise. "I thought carefully about how to craft a sword that would work best for you."

"You really made it for *me*?"

He nodded. "You're a tall girl, Petra, and quick. But slender. The sword had to be light enough for you to wield easily. That"—he tapped the invisible sword and it rang like a bell—"is made with crucible steel. It has a hard spine yet also enough spring to absorb shocks. It won't break. This blade is double-edged, which gives you the freedom to cut from many directions as well as thrust at your opponent with the sword's point. This sword is meant to do damage, Petra, and I mean for you to do damage against anyone who tries to hurt you. *Anyone.*"

These words were so unlike Petra's gentle father, who always shook a log free of beetles before placing it on a fire. "How do you know so much about swords?"

"Now, really, Petra," said Astrophil. "Where do you think I found books on fencing? Where else but Master Kronos's library?"

"But, Father, you never told me you know how to fence."

"I don't. I only know the principles. You have to know the basics of fencing in order to forge a sword." He hesitated, and then said exactly what Petra hoped he wouldn't: "If you were able to go to the Academy, you would be taught how to use a sword properly."

Petra gritted her teeth. This argument wasn't old, but it felt that way. "Well, I can't go to the Academy. And I don't want to. You never even asked me if I wanted to." The Academy was a school for magic that admitted only children of high society, not lowly villagers like her. Petra's father had hoped, however, that an exception would be made in her case, and that is why he had agreed to build the prince's clock.

"Petra, you should have the opportunities I didn't. You've been gifted with a magical ability. If you learned how to use it, you could be better than I am—"

"No, I couldn't!" she burst out. "I can't do anything!"

That is not true, Astrophil spoke silently in her mind.

"Talking with Astro the way you do doesn't count, Father. I don't have your talent. I can't make metal move just by thinking about it. You *know* that. We've been practicing for *weeks*."

"You are still young. It may take some time."

"I'm not *that* young. I'm thirteen. Tomik made his first Marvel when he was my age." Petra pressed her point, even though she hoped to be proven wrong. "In Prague, I thought that maybe . . .

that maybe I was more talented than I am. Astrophil and I could talk without opening our mouths. When I picked up a knife, I thought I could *feel* it inside my mind. But that was my imagination."

"You broke the clock's heart."

"That was dumb luck."

"You *can* communicate with Astrophil."

"But that's all. If I inherited anything from you, it was just some watered-down version of your magic. Nothing to get excited about. Nothing worth sending someone to the Academy for. I probably wouldn't pass the entrance test, even if I were allowed to take it." Saying this somehow stole all of Petra's anger. Now she felt only cold and wet.

"Come here," her father said, and hugged her. "You're shivering. Let's go home, Petra. We'll start a fire and warm some milk over it. You'd like that, wouldn't you?"

WHEN PETRA and her father reached the Sign of the Compass, it had stopped raining and they were laughing at Astrophil as he tried to imitate a human sneeze.

They didn't see the sparrow leap from the roof. Astrophil spotted the bird before the others did and hid in Petra's hair.

The bird dived at them, stopping right in front of Petra's face. It hovered, screeching.

Astrophil, boomed a voice in the spider's head.

Master Kronos? Astrophil jumped in surprise.

Keep still. Don't let Petra know we're having this conversation.

But why?

Do you remember what we discussed?

Astrophil paused. *Yes.*

Good. Then go along with whatever I tell Petra to do. See that she does it.

Surely there is no cause for alarm.

Yes, there is, insisted Mikal Kronos. *The sparrow.*

Nonsense. If the bird poses a threat to anyone, it is to me. It wants to eat me!

No, Astrophil. Something is wrong. It is trying to warn us.

The spider had a sinking feeling in his tin stomach. *You are making far too much of the bizarre flight pattern of one bird.*

Maybe so. But I can't take the risk.

If this is a warning of some kind—and I do not agree that it is—will you not be in danger as well?

Astrophil, you gave me your word. Keep it.

"What's wrong with that sparrow?" Petra stared at the bird as it darted back and forth.

"Nothing," said Astrophil. "Or, hmm, well, I expect it has mad dog disease."

"Mad dog disease affects *dogs*, Astro."

"Petra," her father interrupted, "I need you to deliver something to Tomas Stakan. There's a tin sheet leaning against the wall in the shop. Bring it to the Sign of Fire."

"Sure. I'll just change my clothes first. I'm soaking wet."

"No. Take it to Tomas now."

Petra was puzzled by her father's stern expression. "Can't it wait until later?"

"Can't you just do as I ask?" he snapped. "For once in your life, do as I tell you!"

Petra felt as if she had been slapped. "Fine!" she shouted. She stalked into the shop.

The bird flew after her, but the shop door slammed shut, the bell jangling. The bird flapped outside the closed door, which soon burst open again. Petra gripped the tin sheet under her arm.

"Goodbye, Petra," Mikal Kronos said in a softened voice. Although the sword he had forged was invisible, he could tell that it was still buckled around Petra's waist. He tried not to show his relief. He tried not to show anything that would keep Petra at the Sign of the Compass.

Petra's lips thinned into a line. She whipped around and strode toward the village. Astrophil rode on her shoulder, gazing back at Master Kronos.

The bird landed on the melting snow and watched Petra storm off. Then it hopped toward Mikal. It cocked its head, scrutinizing the man. It couldn't be sure, but it thought that its message had been received, even if the man was behaving very strangely. But then, the bird never understood humans, who saved food rather than eating it right away, and whose nests were closed to the sky.

Mikal Kronos went inside the house, returning with a slice of old bread and a dish filled with water. He set the bowl on the ground, crumbled the bread onto the snow, and then walked around to the back of the house. He took a stool from the smithy. He brought it back to where the bird perched at the edge of the bowl, drinking deeply and flipping back its wings. Master Kronos placed the stool beneath the wooden sign with its many-pointed compass, hoping that if the prince seized him, he might not try to find Petra. Mikal sat down to wait.